Keith Dixon has worked as a college lectur_
copywriter and a management consultant.

He has written and published short stories and a long time ago
wrote an award-winning play about Isaac Newton. This is his first
published novel.

KEITH DIXON

ALTERED LIFE

A Sam Dyke Investigation

Semiologic

ISBN 9781475106008

For information, contact: kdixon7244@aol.com

Semiologic Ltd, 133 Sandbach Road, Rode Heath,
Cheshire, England ST7 3RZ

Set in Palatino Linotype

To Liz

ALTERED LIFE

"Assure me that I yet may change these shadows you have shown me, by an altered life!"
Dickens, *A Christmas Carol.*

1

I WISH I COULD say that the first time I met Rory Brand I knew he was a dead man walking.

But I can't.

At that moment he was just another client eager to get me on his side.

'Dyke, thanks for coming,' he said, pumping my arm vigorously. I didn't want to be outdone, so I matched the strength of his grip and watched him react with a swift competitive grin.

'Nice grip,' he said.

'Call me Sam,' I said.

He was a stocky man a head shorter than me with cropped dark hair peppered with grey. His actions were purposeful and confident, his body language practised at being in charge. He had vitality and life, like most entrepreneurs I'd met. He closed the door behind me with a casual swipe of his arm, then directed me into the room, a small airless office with two large windows and chairs either side of a wooden table. I had the sense that he was used to people doing what he wanted. Well that wasn't going to work with me—not without a good retainer anyway. 'I hope we can get one thing straight right now,' he said. 'Rumour's a bastard in this business so nobody else is to find out we talked, is that clear?'

'I agreed to that yesterday,' I said.

'So call me paranoid. I don't care. You obviously have more faith in people than I do.'

His manner suggested that my opinions of humankind were in fact of no interest to someone as important as he was. So I said nothing. I looked out of the window at the blue rooftops of Waverley, wondering what it must be like to live in a place where your only concern was which colour carpet to lay in the loft.

'Did Carol offer you a drink?' Brand asked.

'I've drunk enough coffee to float a yacht, Mr Brand,' I said. 'Before I sit down, I should tell you how it works. I ask for four hundred a day, plus expenses, with a non-returnable advance of two thousand. I have a standard contract we can work to, but I'll understand if you don't want to put anything in writing. I can give you a full receipt at the end of the assignment.'

He laughed, an open-mouthed and full-chested affair, his eyes turning up slightly at the corners as if astonished by his own response.

'Four hundred a day?' he said. 'You're joking. I'm a management consultant. I wouldn't get out of bed for that. Here's some consultancy for free—put up your rates or people will think you're crap.'

'They've had nothing to complain about so far,' I said.

He looked interested. 'I asked around but nobody knew how to get hold of a private investigator. I had to find you in the phone book. Struck me we could help you with some marketing. That box in the Yellow Pages can't get you much business.'

'It got you,' I said stiffly.

'Christ on a bike,' he said. 'Where's your ambition? I'd never have built up this business with that attitude. You've got to think big just to stand still in my line of work.'

Irritated by his willingness to tell me exactly where I was going wrong with my life, I took out my notebook and headed a fresh page. I don't know whether it's their own guilt or a belief that in some way they're morally superior, but some clients try to pull rank. I gave a mental sigh and hoped that Rory Brand wasn't going to be one of those difficult customers who wanted me to do something he didn't have the guts to do himself, then give me a hard time for not doing it properly.

I said, 'I'm flattered by your interest in my career prospects, but that's not why I'm here, is it? You wouldn't tell me what you wanted on the phone. So how about we get down to it now?'

'All right,' he said. 'Fair enough. This company is mine. Named after me. You know what it's like – you have to call your company something, don't you?'

'It helps people find you in the Yellow Pages.'

'Good point, well made. I set it up with my first wife, Gill, seven years ago. We started in north Manchester then moved here shortly afterwards. Hey – is this what I'm supposed to do?'

'What?'

'Spill my guts while you write it down.'

'It's traditional.'

'OK. So what else can I tell you? We're in management consultancy. Rather like your line of business—helping people who can't deal with things by themselves. As you can tell, I'm quite passionate about my business. Can you understand that, Sam?'

'You don't have to sell to me, Mr Brand.'

'Oh that's right. You need to keep a professional distance, don't you? Well the end of that particular story is that out of the blue, Gill left me for Australia and the sunshine of Bondi Beach and I haven't seen her since. I can't tell you what a blow that was. She'd been shoulder to shoulder with me and I just didn't understand what went wrong. Still don't.'

'Divorced yet? Or just long-distance lawyering?'

'The whole hog. Divorce with a bullet. A year after she left I married Tara. Lovely girl. Could sell teeth to crocodiles. Works with me in the business as sales director. I know what you're going to say—there was only a year between Gill leaving me and Tara coming on board, but I don't like living alone. I'm a gregarious person, Sam. I don't like going home to an empty house. You don't have to write that bit down.'

First rule they teach you in private eye school: Clients always want to give you context. Usually more than you need at the first stage. And I'd met enough of Brand's type to guess what was coming—something about a pre-nup, or perhaps he wanted me to talk to some woman who was giving him grief, perhaps an old flame who was on the verge of self-combusting and ruining his new marriage with tiresome revelations about his sexual proclivities. To some people in my line of work, rich businessmen were a never-ending source of funds based on marital distress. Personally, and despite the potential increase in my cash flow, I couldn't take the work, but for the moment I was here and, almost despite myself, listening.

'So you've got a good business,' I said. 'You're making loads of money and don't get out of bed for less than four hundred a day. What do you need me for? I told you on the phone that I don't bodyguard the rich and famous.'

He leaned over the table and stared at me with eyes that were as still as a hawk's, and about as friendly. 'Consultancy's a dog-eat-dog business, Sam, with everyone scrabbling for money from the same pot. The competition fries your eyeballs after a while. Gotta win, just to pay the rent and the photocopying bills.'

'I only had to look around here to see your life was tough.'

'Don't get me wrong, I love it. Gets my juices going when we win a bid. Nearly better than sex.' He stood up, as if he couldn't bear to be imprisoned by gravity. Then he turned and leaned over the desk again and his eyes darkened. 'But we're developing a secret weapon,' he said. 'And there are some people who can't stand that. They're coming after me and my business. They're trying to steal it—with both hands.'

2

I GRIMACED INWARDLY at this new information but kept my features neutral. So it was intellectual property, or copyright theft, or industrial espionage. What you might call the conceptual side of private investigation—not my strength. Though to be fair, two years in business and I was still trying to work out what my strength was. When I found out I was going to brag about it in my cheap advert in the Yellow Pages.

'Who are "they"?' I said.

'I'm getting there. You know, I'm enjoying this. Talking it over. Seeing it through your eyes, so to speak. It's good for me.'

'It's an additional benefit of the service I offer.'

He looked at me sideways, then carried on. 'So anyway, a year ago we had just twenty-three people working here. Twelve consultants, a couple of people looking after the accounts, some sales and marketing whiz-kids and admin. We were growing the company. Making a reputation.'

'Hasn't really worked, has it? I'd never heard of you before yesterday.'

'One-man businesses aren't exactly our target market,' he said, rather tetchily. 'Anyway, I suddenly hit the motherlode. I had an idea for a new direction for the company. That's what I do – come up with ideas. When you get to know me better you'll see me doing that all the time. Can't help myself. So now I needed money for investment, which meant I had to go cap in hand to the people who had it. Long boring meetings, ton of paperwork.' His eyes closed slowly at the memory—then snapped open. 'They call it venture capital—nothing adventurous about it. Dot the i's and cross the t's till your hands bleed. But eventually we got it.'

'So you became rich all of a sudden,' I said. 'Life is good.'

He ignored this. I wasn't sure whether he didn't get sarcasm or that it was just beneath him to acknowledge it. 'Let me tell you something, Sam. Our target market is largely the people in human resources. Ask them what they do and they'll tell you they're "people people". Unfortunately they know everything about people, but nothing about computers—and they want to know less. But all around them the world's been changing. Manufacturing, service industries, call centres—everything depends on computers and the web. That's the new battlefield.'

For some reason, this talk of battlefields made me think of my dad bent double to scrape coal from the Thurnscoe seam. He used to talk about fighting and winning against the Coal Board, and there was always talk of campaigns and tactics and wars. It was a language that pervaded our household. A battlefield to him was a serious place and meant more than a few electrons whizzing across a VDU display. I looked at Brand again, hoping that my disdain wasn't leaking out.

'So what's in it for you?' I said. 'If the people you want to sell to don't understand what you're selling, why bother?'

'Three million quid,' he replied coolly. 'That's the capital I got for developing the software.'

I needed him to slow down now. He'd gone a step ahead of me. 'What software?'

'That's what I'm telling you. Our new technology. I bought in expertise from this geek I met, and when we got the venture capital we set about expanding the company. We call the software Compsoft. Because it measures competency.'

'I guess that's consultant speak,' I said.

'I saw a gap in the market. There was a need for software that measured people's abilities at work, then compared them to a national database. I tell you, Sam, the night I came up with this idea was bloody exciting. When you have a brainwave like that it literally takes your breath away. I had to sit down or I would have burst.'

I suddenly saw where this was going. 'So this software means that companies could tell where their folk stood in relation to the competition.'

He smiled slowly, like a father seeing his child take those first unsteady steps.

'That's right,' he said. 'You find out where the skill gaps are in your own company. And then Compsoft lets you see where you are against other companies nationally.'

'You can track what your competitors are doing by looking at the skills of the people they're hiring.'

'There's a bit of educated guesswork, but you can make sure you're never lagging behind. It's called competitive advantage.'

He was too pleased with himself for my liking.

'So three million quid does what,' I said, 'apart from giving your bank manager orgasms?'

He lifted his arm sideways rather grandly, gathering in this office and the people outside. 'Ramped up the workforce. Recruited a couple of dozen programmers and researchers. Designers. Testers. Improved our image.'

'I can see that. Your backsides get to sit on nice comfy chairs. So how's it going—what have you sold?'

His eyes slid away. 'Well, nothing yet. The program's not finished. There's a demo of Compsoft on our website. It just needs a couple of months' more work.'

I stopped writing and put my notebook away. I'd heard

enough. Brand watched me, his cologne filling the air with musk as he breathed in and out.

'What's the matter?' he said. 'The dogged detective run out of questions? Don't just sit there looking superior.'

There wasn't an easy way to say it, so I just said it. 'I can't help you, Mr Brand.'

'Why the hell not?' he said, though he looked like he was expecting it, expecting disappointment.

'From what you've said, I'm guessing that you're worried someone's trying to buy out the share of your company held by the venture capitalists.' He nodded warily. 'I can understand that,' I went on. 'After all, you've persuaded them to lock three million quid into it and it might be a quick way for them to get their money back. But what you're telling me is pure speculation. Until something concrete happens, I can't help.'

'I've got to wait until I'm shafted before you're willing to do anything?'

'All you've got at the moment is the suspicion that you might be sold out. But in this game suspicion's not enough.' I spread out my hands. 'People tell me I'm a pretty good detective. But I can't invent a case where there isn't one.'

'Even though I know there is?'

'You go for outside investment, you run the risk they'll sell on their share. Have you talked to them?'

'I don't want to frighten them if I'm wrong. I told you, this conversation is between you and me.'

'Then I'm sorry, there's nothing I can do right now. If a chair or a person or a bit of your software goes missing, I'm your man. I'll chase it up hill and down dale. Until that happens, to be honest, I'd be wasting your money. And while I'm not against that in principle, the least I can do is tell you upfront.' Sam Dyke, the honourable detective.

He scowled. Like many entrepreneurs, he allowed a full range of emotions to show in his face as an attempt to manipulate the other person: this is important to me, so it should be to you. They acted as though a display of naked feeling was enough to create a commitment to buy what they sold. But I wasn't buying today.

'What if I had more information?' he said. 'Something that would make it easier?'

'It's not a question of easy or hard. It's a question of what I can do. I won't take your money and then sit staring into space waiting for someone to make you an offer you can't refuse. I don't work like that.'

'Right, a code of ethics,' he said mockingly.

'Plain Yorkshire common sense.'

He turned his head and looked through the windows at a ripple of grey cloud that had been slowly advancing towards us, making the room grow darker by the minute. As the weather sometimes does, it seemed to reflect his mood. At last he said quietly, 'I've got a suspect.'

'What?'

'Got your attention, didn't it, Mr Confident? Let's say I know that certain people have been in talks with certain other people, who in turn are interested in having my scalp.'

His phrasing was way up there on the theatrical delivery scale, but nonetheless I felt the question being dragged out of me. 'Who are you talking about?'

He sat back heavily in his chair and folded his arms. It struck me that he was actually quite frightened but I hadn't seen it before. He'd developed a good act to cover it up.

'I don't know who the bastard is who wants to buy the company,' he said. 'But I know who set the ball rolling. Who put out the feelers to see if anyone was interested. Who inserted the knife between my shoulder blades and hammered it home with the end of her expensive Italian shoe.'

'Who?' I asked.

His eyes turned towards me and he blinked slowly, once.

'My lovely new wife, Tara.'

3

BEFORE I COULD say anything, the door opened and Carol the receptionist put her head in. She was a woman in her early forties with an over-elaborate dress sense topped by a swirl of dark hair that became lighter as it spiralled further from her head, like cream dropped into coffee. I stared at her in fascination.

'Can I interest anyone in a drink yet?' she asked.

Brand looked up at her. 'Shut the door, Carol. Don't interrupt again unless I ask for you.'

She retreated quickly and closed the door. I waited but Brand said nothing.

'You're sure?' I said.

'It was her,' he replied bitterly, lowering his head to stare at the table. His attitude had changed. When I'd arrived he'd been confidently in control; now he gave off a quiet despair, like a man who'd lost something he knew he'd never get back. I found myself beginning to feel sorry for him. 'No one else apart from me knows the things that she knows,' he said. 'No one else could have set it up. You ever been married?'

'Long time ago. It didn't take.'

'She run off?'

'I don't remember. Look, are you saying that Tara is trying to steal your business?'

He looked at me severely. 'Damn right I am. Do you get it now?'

'Why would she do it?'

He raised his hands and let them drop on the table like dead weights. 'Call me old-fashioned, but I thought it was your job to find out that kind of thing.'

I sat back in my chair and looked at the people in the large room outside. They were mostly in their twenties and casually dressed in denim and tee-shirts. Hopelessly trendy. Behind them, filling each wall, racks of computer modules stood with their lights flashing, like Cubist Christmas trees. Cardboard boxes containing more hardware were stacked in one corner. 'Is she here?' I said.

'No—she's in London, with a client.' He seemed to make up his mind about something. 'Look, if it weren't for the fact that it's Tara I'd be dealing with this myself. But this is too difficult for me. So what I want from you is confirmation, one way or the other. Find out what she's been up to, who else is involved, what the plan is.'

I looked at him for fully fifteen seconds without saying anything. He took the scrutiny. Then he stood up abruptly and said, 'There's someone I want you to meet.'

'It won't help,' I said. I was beginning to feel exasperated. Clients who don't listen are more common than I'd like, but this one was beginning to irritate me with his unwillingness to take heed of what was fairly expensive advice. I added, 'Did I mention, I don't get involved in family disputes?'

'You're on the clock right now. It won't do any harm. Don't argue with a client, Sam, you'll never win.'

Without waiting for my reply he opened the office door and was striding away. I followed reluctantly. I glanced around at the staff. They took no notice of our re-entry into their world. Carol the receptionist showed me a sample from her repertoire of frosty glances as we passed in front of her to cross into the other half of the office, which was almost empty. I gave her a warm smile, just to worry her. 'This is the consultancy division,' Brand said briskly. 'Ah, here's one of the people I wanted you to meet.'

A slim woman with hair the colour of sun-dried straw was sitting on the corner of a desk. Her head was bent down as she read from a sheaf of papers. She looked up when she sensed us watching her. Her appearance was a neat blend of geometric shapes: her eyes were astonishingly round and almost transparently blue, set in a face that was mostly oval but with two straight and prominent cheekbones that lent her a serious, hard-edged look. Her skin was smooth and appeared to have been recently tanned. She wore a sharp grey suit that fitted her at every place that it touched her body, which was lean and athletic and radiated energy. She held herself at a slight angle and moved her gaze from one of us to the other, calmly expectant. Her large eyes made me feel inspected, measured and noted. What the judgement was, I couldn't tell.

Brand stepped forward. 'Laura—I'd like you to meet Sam Dyke. He's helping with that business I told you about.'

The woman held out her hand and I shook it. Her fingers were so slender it was like grasping a bunch of pencils. 'Laura Marshall,' she said. She looked around and said quietly, in an amused voice, 'Do you buy this idea of Rory's?'

'I don't know enough one way or the other.'

She turned to Brand. 'Rory, Mr Dyke's being diplomatic.'

'That's the first I've seen of it,' Brand said, and took my arm to lead me further into the open space. I shrugged at Laura Marshall as we passed.

Two women in their thirties sat side by side at a long desk looking down into purple Sony laptops and saying nothing. Their fingers moving silently over the keyboards. An older man with thinning hair leaned back in his chair, engaged in a long telephone conversation that was evidently boring him. I guessed these were consultants.

Brand led me to a desk where a large man in a suit the colour of slate was towering over a seated woman with a stiff helmet of white hair. They were talking quietly to each other. Brand walked into the woman's eyeline and the man immediately stood upright and grinned at him with a mouth full of white teeth.

'Well well,' he said jovially. 'Rory Brand comes to visit the little people.'

'Shut up, Eddie,' Brand said. 'Betty, this is Sam Dyke. He might be doing some work for us.'

The woman glanced up as though whatever I did was of no interest to her, so long as it didn't interfere with the smooth running of her own life. She had a face as thin and pale as Eddie's was full and florid. She also had a spiky manner that seemed to match her appearance. 'We've got those newsletters to get out tonight,' she said. 'You have to go over them before we put them in the mail.'

'I know,' Brand said, 'I haven't forgotten. How could I, with you on my back every half hour?'

Eddie took this as an opportunity for a bout of laughter. 'Got your number, Betty!' he crowed. As he turned, I saw a pack of muscle move in his shoulders. He was big, I thought, but he wasn't fat. He looked at Brand, grinning. 'Don't be such a tosspot, Rory. Betty's only looking after business, aren't you, love?'

Brand turned to me, including me in the conversation. 'Betty's worked here longer than anyone else. She's the keeper of the flame.'

'Loyalty's a rare virtue,' I said, looking at her.

She wore large round glasses that slipped down her nose as she found some paperwork on her desk to sort through. She seemed flustered to be suddenly the centre of attention.

'Someone's got to get the work done here,' she said.

'What's this then?' Eddie said, nodding familiarly at me. 'New blood?'

Brand said, 'A special project. Sam, this is Eddie Hampshire, one of our longest-serving consultants. Don't worry, Eddie, Sam's not here to steal any work from you.'

Eddie threw his head back and laughed again, showing the dark insides of his molars. 'Take it!' he said to me. 'Take it all! See if you last as long as I have.'

'You don't look that old,' I said mildly.

'What's that?'

'I said you're bearing up. Being a consultant seems to have treated you well.'

Hampshire looked at me closely. 'Are you saying I'm fat?' There was a sudden tension in the air. Betty turned away; Laura Marshall had come up beside us and looked on with amusement.

I'd seen Eddie's kind of bully before—the type that sets the emotional temperature for everyone else through sheer force of personality. He's happy, everyone else is happy; he's down, everyone else has to watch their step. I didn't like them. And I didn't mind letting them know.

'You're pleased to be here,' I said. 'Why don't we leave it at that?'

He stared at me bluntly for a moment, then allowed the smallest of smiles to lift the corners of his lips. 'The life I've lived, Sam, I'm pleased to be anywhere.' His mouth opened and the laughter came rumbling out again, though there was no sign of it in his eyes.

We turned to go, and I noticed that behind us Eddie stopped laughing at once, as though a tap had been turned off. I felt his gaze following us as we walked away and I wondered whether he always found life so amusing.

Brand said, 'Do you get it now?'

'What?'

'These are real people, Sam. With livelihoods. Betty's been with us seven years. The longest of anyone here. She'd be devastated if anything happened to the company so that it had to be sold.'

'And Eddie?'

'Ah, Eddie. One of our peak performers. Gives delegates a good time on courses. Always out in the hills somewhere, either going up or sliding down a rope. The delegates love him.'

'You're less keen.'

'Let's just say there's only so much bonhomie you can take, isn't there?'

I'd thought he was tiresome after a couple of minutes. I wouldn't have liked to work with him day in and day out.

Brand walked me to the door.

'I can't persuade you, can I?' he said.

'I'm sorry. There's nothing here for me. At this point I'd be wasting your money.'

'I wish I was as sure as you are,' he said. He drew a long breath and stared past me, a look of deep pain haunting his eyes. 'Something's going on and I don't like it, but I can't twist your arm.'

No he couldn't. But he should have tried harder.

The next morning, my telephone rang as I was having breakfast.

'Mr Dyke?'

'In business hours, yes.'

'Sorry to be so early.'

She identified herself as Laura Marshall, the blonde woman from Rory Brand's office. Her voice was cold and dispassionate but held an odd tremor.

'What can I do for you?' I asked.

'They killed him,' she said. 'They got to him and killed him.'

'Killed who?' I said.

'Rory, you fool. They killed Rory. He was found dead in his office this morning. They'd broken his neck. I want you to find out who did it. I want you to find out who did it and kill him. Do you understand?'

4

I FINISHED dressing and shaved without being conscious of any
of it. My mind was working overtime, trying to fix Rory Brand
in my memory. He was a bully of a kind—a perfectionist and a
quick thinker, an egotist who thought he could charm but was
probably as feared as he was admired.

I turned over in my head the thought that he knew there was
trouble. He'd sensed something rumbling and churning in the
background, but perhaps he'd misunderstood what he felt. He
thought it was about the business, but maybe it was about him. He
thought it was a commercial challenge, but perhaps it was a
personal threat. He was right to be paranoid, but he'd been
paranoid about the wrong thing.

And I'd turned him away. I'd got on a high horse that was just
passing, saddled up and rode off, declaring that I couldn't help. I
thought I was being reasonable and professional, but perhaps I
was just arrogant. There was nothing I could do, I said. Perhaps
there was nothing I wanted to do. It was the kind of investigation
that I'd done too many of in the past, in Customs & Excise, and
had tried to get out of because they bored me. Working the paper
trail wasn't something that I'd ever volunteered for. God knows,

there were plenty in C & E who just loved it – tracking the bad guys through their VISA payments and air tickets. Never getting their boots muddy out in the field. But I'd always chafed at the bit when put in that kind of harness. In this instance I'd given up before I'd even got started. Lazy, I told myself, just lazy.

I avoided the motorway and drove the back roads into Waverley, through Holmes Chapel and Great Warford, through the flat Cheshire plain that stretches towards Liverpool and from a distance is distinguished only by the gleaming white saucer of Jodrell Bank's radio telescope. The A50 was still swarming with commuters heading into Knutsford and south Manchester, so I had time to appreciate the frosted fields and picturesque farmhouses that we passed.

Perhaps appreciate is the wrong word.

There are parts of Cheshire that represent exactly what rural England should be, except that the driveways of the renovated cottages overflow with silver late-model Mercedes and BMWs, and the roads outside the schools groan with Range Rovers and people-carriers driven by blonde second wives with a jewellery fixation. I'd read somewhere that Waverley had the highest percentage of Porsche owners in the country, and I saw most of them that morning. Coming from one of the more deprived areas of Yorkshire, where Thatcherite economics had slapped the community's face like a vicious bully, I found it hard to stomach the casual acceptance of such extravagance. But that was my problem. It was always my problem. According to my friends, I had an attitude towards money and the moneyed that got me into trouble. In the two years since I'd opened for business, half of my clients had come from this part of the county, the other half being Government work. You would have thought that private clients would be grateful and pay up on time – but they didn't get to be wealthy and live in Cheshire by giving their money away to private detectives who didn't account properly for expenses or know how to draw up a VAT receipt. No sum was too small to be haggled over. No invoice so precise that it couldn't be returned unpaid. No wonder my attitude towards people with cash seemed sour.

So I hadn't trusted Rory Brand and I didn't trust Laura Marshall and I didn't trust any of the other inhabitants of that cold commercial world. Not all the shoplifters in Harvey Nicholls were doing it to feed a drug habit—I'd met the middle-class, upper-income, jewel-encrusted housewives who'd done it for kicks, so I had no illusions about who inhabited the moral high-ground in this landscape. It certainly wasn't white-collar workers with a bit of an education and a nose for a deal.

Waverley is the poshest of Manchester's southern satellite towns, once given a sort of industrial grandeur by the self-made textile millionaires who built the mills on which its wealth was based, now made popular again by footballers with money to burn and with wives or girlfriends who had a simple yen to boast a Cheshire address. When you approach Waverley from the south you pass through a suburban wet-dream—broad avenues of detached houses, each individually styled, with pavements sheltered by tall trees through which a dappled sun falls. Pleasant children in clean uniforms run excitedly towards school, and polite builders with letters after their names pull into driveways in white Mercedes vans, ready to extend the kitchen or convert the garage into a games room. It was probably only twenty miles from Crewe, but it was a different planet. Waverley was pashminas; Crewe was scarves.

When I got there it was almost ten o'clock. I parked in the leisure centre and walked to Brands' offices. From across the road I watched the police work their routine. Several Cheshire police Volvos were already angled in front of the main entrance, their blue and yellow check paintjobs vibrant in the morning air. When the Scene of Crime Officers had processed the building as best they could, they'd set up an incident room back at regional headquarters. Until then, they'd cordoned off the site, blocked the main entrance with cones and begun turning away delivery vans and other tradesmen. An officer stood to one side taking the names of everyone who was allowed in, even other officers. The crime scene manager would be doing his damnedest to protect the integrity of the crime scene for the sake of DNA gathering. The workers already in the building when the police arrived would be questioned, fingerprinted and released to go home one by one. There was nothing I could do or see, so I walked up into Waverley and waited.

*

'When I find out who murdered Rory,' I said, 'you know I can't kill him.'

'Some friend you are,' Laura Marshall said.

'I'm a hired hand. I'm not Fred MacMurray and you're not Barbara Stanwyck.'

'Who?'

'Never mind. A movie reference.'

'Good day to make jokes. Tasteful.'

'I'm sorry. You've had a rough day.'

She looked at me guardedly. I knew that look. It was the look clients gave you when they began to wonder what you were getting from the situation you were both involved in. They knew it wasn't money, though you might try to convince yourself that it was. As yet Laura couldn't tell what I was thinking, which was just as well. It wasn't good for clients to know that you were working on their case because you felt guilty—guilty that you hadn't acted more quickly or decisively.

She'd met me looking red-eyed and weary. She'd said she didn't want to sit inside a noisy café, so we sat on a bench in Waverley's paved pedestrian centre. I guessed it was her way of punishing herself. I could understand that because I felt the same way. She'd pushed her hair into a blue beret and wore a full-length coat made from what appeared to be Labrador hide. Now

she probably regretted the jaunty look she'd taken on for today –
how were you supposed to know it was going to be a terrible day?
How were you supposed to know what to wear when something
like this could happen?

'Tell me what you remember,' I said.

She looked down as if organising her thoughts. 'I was driving
in to work when I got a call from the office,' she said. 'It was Betty.
You met her yesterday.'

I nodded.

'She and Carol and one of the consultants, Mal O'Donovan,
got in about eight o'clock. Those three are usually the first in.
Carol and Betty because they have to be, Mal because he likes to
brown-nose and show the boss how hard he's working.
Apparently the lights were on but there was no one about. Carol
said Betty had a fit because the lights seemed to have been left on
overnight.'

'Carol's the dragon you use to frighten away unwanted
visitors.'

'Carol's the receptionist.'

'That's what I said.'

She gave me a look in which I saw the whole horror of what
she was remembering. Her eyes were bottomless. I felt myself
flinch. She went on: 'Mal and Betty went to the kitchen to make
tea and coffee and heard a shout—well, more of a scream,
according to Mal. They ran out and found Carol backing away
from one of the small offices. When they looked inside they saw
Rory face down on the desk.'

'Did they touch him?'

'Carol got up the courage and tested his neck for a pulse.
She used to work on reception in a doctor's surgery, so I
suppose she's picked up one or two things. She couldn't find
a pulse so they called the police and ambulance.'

'And they called you.'

'I got there before the police arrived, but I didn't have much time alone with Betty and the others before we were ushered out of the way and all the questioning began. One of the policeman said Rory's neck appeared to be broken.'

'Tell me,' I said, 'were you surprised that Rory was in the office so early?'

'Not at all. He's a bad sleeper. He often arranges meetings at six in the morning. Or he comes in and gets his paperwork done while the office is quiet. But I asked Carol if he had an early meeting and she said not as far as she was aware. If he was meeting someone, it was a private thing.'

'So nobody knew he had an early meeting except the person who killed him. I'm guessing that's not typical.'

'Not really,' she said, sighing. Then, strangely, she brightened. 'Oh, and I've just remembered something else.'

'What?'

She lowered her voice and brought her face closer to mine. Her skin was smooth, her eyes suddenly clear. 'Rory was face down on the desk, and his laptop was open next to him. Before the police arrived, Mal told me what he saw on Rory's screen.'

'What did it say?'

She told me what the consultant had read and I duly wrote it down without having the slightest idea what it meant.

5

WE WALKED BACK to the office, each of us playing back in our mind's eye what we'd seen and heard that morning.

'So what do we do now?' she said. Her voice was small against the traffic. 'I guess we should leave it to the police, shouldn't we? There's even less point you being involved now than there was before.'

'You're right. I can't do anything the police can't do.'

'So I should just pay you for your time and we call it quits.'

I stopped and, sensing this, she turned and looked at me. Her face was strained and unhappy but I was finding it hard to understand what she wanted. After all, she was the one who called me at home and had recently spent half an hour telling me exactly what had happened at the murder scene.

I said, 'If you want me to go away you only have to say so. You're the boss here.'

'Then why do I feel like you're criticising my judgement?'

'I don't know. Maybe you're feeling guilty. I know I am. I didn't particularly like Rory and I don't like this place and I've even got some doubts about you, but I could have treated him with a bit more respect.'

'I suppose I should thank you for your honesty,' she said grimly. 'I'm not used to that from people I'm buying from.'

'I haven't decided yet whether I'm selling.'

'I was forgetting you had a choice.' She blew into her hands and thrust them back in her pockets. For a moment her upward-turned, hard-eyed gaze under the blue beret, and her attitude of forced hostility, made her appear like a schoolgirl putting on a front of sophisticated cool to impress the un-cool adults. It was a disarming look but I armed myself against it.

'I'll go then,' I said.

'I think it would be best …unless you felt there was something you could add to the police investigation.'

'I wouldn't want to raise your expectations.'

'Believe me, they're low.'

'I could ask some questions, check out one or two things.'

'I don't want to trouble you.'

'No trouble,' I said. 'It's my job.'

She turned away abruptly and we continued walking to the office.

'I want to go home,' she said. She suddenly seemed depleted and shrunken inside her skin, as though she could no longer maintain the outsized version of herself that she used to deal with the world. After all, she was still a young woman who'd experienced a traumatic event. At one level, she was a poised and professional business woman, but I saw now that much of her behaviour was a well-managed front. The air practically vibrated as she strained to keep herself together.

I said, 'I'm sure the police will let you go home, as long as you tell them where you are.'

She nodded. 'They say it's going to be the middle of next week before we can get back into the office. I'm going to have to make a lot of phone calls.' Then she stopped again, and looked at me with the still, focused gaze she summoned from time to time. She said, 'When I find out where the funeral is, will you come?'

'I don't like funerals.'

'You'll see Rory's friends and family. It'll give you the bigger picture. Where he came from, where he got to. That kind of thing.'

'Won't the guest list be Mrs Brand's decision?'

'I doubt she'll be up to much. Besides, anyone can come to a funeral. Just don't badger the guests in the church.'

'I do my best work in churches. I'd have to rein myself in.'

'See that you do,' she said. 'I'm still not clear about your role in all this. I worry that you'll be wasting your time and our money. But maybe we owe it to him to do something.'

'Do you think so?'

'Mr Dyke, this is one of the saddest days I've ever lived through. I'm on the point of bursting into tears all the time. But deep down I feel angry. I want to find out who did this, who murdered him.'

'Would it surprise you if I said I'd like to help?'

'Quite frankly, nothing you said would surprise me. But who knows, perhaps you'll shock yourself, and me, and catch the murderer. Whoever killed Rory shouldn't think they can get away with it.'

'Despite my obvious limitations, I'll do my best.'

'I'll bear that in mind,' she said, without a trace of humour.

She did up the buttons on her coat and walked on. We appeared to have struck a deal. I shook my head and followed her down the street, still wondering how she managed to appear human and warm one minute and as cold as a mortuary slab the next.

By the time I reached Crewe the flow of traffic was against me as commuters escaped for home, crawling in a slow evacuation past the railway station and down the hill towards countryside that was getting darker every minute. For an hour or so in the evening of every working day, Crewe wakes up and gives the appearance of being alive and vital, but it's only the excitement created by people glad to be going home. Their pink faces glow in windscreens and against bus windows and over bicycle handlebars as they hurriedly leave the bleak architectural muddle in which they work and head for their commuter homes out in the green Cheshire landscape.

But at least Crewe knew what it was for and had no pretensions. Returning from Waverley, I felt I was coming back to a place that was firmly planted – the metal and steel that underpinned Crewe's life as a centre for the railway and for the production of Rolls-Royce cars gave it a ballast that Waverley, floating free on a tide of new money, simply couldn't match.

In the centre of town only McDonalds was busy, with packs of teenagers standing around dipping into bags of fries and shouting insults at other packs. It was like a mating ritual from White Fang. Kids trying to find their place.

My office is a room on the first floor that I let from the furniture shop below. I have a separate entrance from the outside and a key to the kitchen from the inside, so I can share tea, coffee or toast with the staff. By now the shop was closed. Only a faint security light was illuminated, tipping a faint brown glaze over the sad sofas and chairs that the owner imports from Croatia at a knock-down price and sells to people who can't afford to even walk through the doors of World of Leather.

When I started in business for myself I had no capital and no loan potential, so I was glad to get even these humble premises. Two years on, I liked the privacy and the sense of being in the middle of town. What's more, I had my name and profession engraved in a semi-circle on the outside window, visible from the road. My dad had always said that you didn't make any money until your name was over the door. He was a repository of sayings that he'd harvested over the years as examples of the world's predictability. As I got older I was beginning to see that his reliance on these truisms was a kind of defence mechanism, a way of explaining his reluctance to have adventures or change his way of life. The sayings explained the rules by which the rest of the world lived. And however much he might have wanted to try, he couldn't change the rules, could he, so he couldn't live the life he wanted. In that way, it wasn't his fault. It was a problem with society.

From my computer I could access the Internet and claim the phone bill as a business expense. I turned it on, and when at the desktop ran a Google search on Brands. There were the usual several thousand hits, though only a dozen for the management consultancy based in Waverley. These were mostly press items that were obviously PR releases worked up with a minimum of effort into small pieces in the local newspapers; a couple of them were linked to journal articles written by consultants in the company.

One of the newspaper items described the investment group who had put three million pounds into the company for the development of a specialised IT wing. They called themselves Champion. I printed the article and kept reading. Two further hits were interviews with Rory Brand in management magazines. Even at second-hand, the strength of his personality hit you between the eyes.

There were also several links to Brands' web-site, which described the kind of work they did, offered case studies of clients they'd helped and included a page outlining the company's vision: 'To be the best management consultancy in any discipline in which we operate.' It sounded exactly like the man I'd met.

I navigated to the web-site for Companies House and looked at Brands' entry there. It told me nothing except that their accounts were up to date.

I exited and switched off the computer, then sat and read the article about Champion, the investment group. They were a well-established London company with a track record of investing in young IT start-ups. I recognised the names of some of the companies they were associated with. They had an expensive address in a well-heeled part of London. I thought it unlikely that they'd murdered Rory in a crude attempt to recoup their investment before it matured.

Then I thought back to what Laura Marshall had told me about Rory Brand's computer screen. The words Mal O'Donovan had seen there seemed to make no sense. She'd taken a breath before telling me, as if she needed fortifying before committing the words to the air. But her tone had been level and matter-of-fact. 'It was an open Word document,' she said. 'Someone had typed a phrase using letters that filled the whole screen. The message read, "Who's the daddy now?"'

We'd talked about this for a while but couldn't make sense of it. Brand had no children and, apparently, rarely saw his own family. It sounded more like a bragging statement than a meaningful clue.

I thought about Rory Brand and Laura Marshall and Betty Parsons and Eddie Hampshire—the world they operated in was far removed from the world in which I'd worked for most of my adult life. In Customs and Excise you walked through drab corridors, where bulbs hung naked from ceilings; where the tables and chairs were broken from the legs up; where the walls were covered with cork boards or flyers or government notices; where the people were cynical, tired and contemptuous of most other people they met. Only the adrenaline and the politics kept you going. When was the next hit. Who was screwing whom. Who was brown-nosing for promotion and who was likely to get it.

I'd worked for two years now in the commercial world and I was having to change my outlook. I still saw cynicism and contempt. But I also saw energy and optimism and a willingness to try. A belief that a positive outcome was possible. A recognition that human actions could have monetary value—that it wasn't only cigarettes and booze and pornography, concrete objects, that could be traded. But it was possible for skill, conviction and confidence to be bought and sold. I disliked Waverley as a place and Brands for the kind of business it was, fattening itself on the failure of companies to understand what they were doing. And once I'd got out of C & E I'd promised myself that I wouldn't get involved again in corporate politics and big company disputes – after all, there were plenty of worthy individuals who needed the services of an upright, experienced and honest investigator, weren't there?

But it wasn't as simple as that. To eat you had to go where the money was. And because I turned up my nose at divorce work, I had slashed my potential client list in half.

So I had to work in the business environment. It was not only churlish, but foolish, to spurn the corporate coin. I'd learned to suck up my pride and live with it. Sam Dyke, practical detective.

And then a strange thing had happened. Working on a case involving deceit and fraud by a company director in central Manchester, I suddenly found that I understood how business worked. That it was built on relationships between people, not on the value of a commercial transaction. And in a development that I didn't see coming, it reminded me of the culture that I came from, the northern mining towns where a man's value was seen in what he did, not what he owned or where he took his holidays. I'd never had that experience—the sense that what you did as a profession could give dignity and pride by itself. I'd been a gatekeeper for most of my life, preventing the illegal passage of goods that were without any value except that given to them by society. Finally I'd realised that I'd become a private detective for two reasons: first, there was nothing else I could do after C&E.

Secondly, and most importantly, I had to do it if I was to look myself in the eye each time I shaved.

6

O N THE WEDNESDAY of the following week, I drove out to the church in Knutsford where Rory Brand's funeral was to be held. I parked at a distance from the other mourners, feeling uneasy about turning up without a formal invitation.

The last funeral I'd been to was almost three years ago. When my father had been cremated there'd been a gathering of nearly a hundred people, each one of whom had something good they wanted to tell me about him. It hadn't helped. I still remembered the bleak emptiness that had settled in my stomach that morning and took the best part of a year to ease away. Despite a couple of opportunities I hadn't been to a funeral since, so this was a big test of commitment for me.

It was a barren, windy day and brown leaves swirled like lost souls up and down the pathways that criss-crossed the burial plots. When Laura Marshall rang to tell me the arrangements, she sounded confident and back in control, as though Brand's death had been a minor derailment and not a major catastrophe. I wondered what it would take to get behind her calm, superior façade, to touch an emotion and make it bleed. But now I was here I found myself rather looking forward to seeing her again.

The church was a small gothic relic that was larger than it appeared from outside, its wooden support beams arching upwards into a roof that had been newly renovated, according to an exhibition panel inside the entrance. I sat at the back on a hard pew, next to people I assumed were friends rather than relatives. They shuffled along the bench, making space for me with those blank but sympathetic faces people reserve for public sorrow.

On the front row itself, I noticed a tall, elegant woman with red hair sitting next to a group of elderly people I took to be the inner circle of Rory's family. Aunts, uncles, sisters, brothers. I'd been told his parents were dead. I guessed that the woman with red hair would be his wife, Tara. Several people around me cried quietly into handkerchiefs. Their sniffles were caught by the still air of the church and echoed on and on, becoming a mournful underlying soundtrack to the funeral.

A windswept lady vicar stood before us and smiled reassuringly. Her voice contained the calming banality expected in these circumstances, a rise and fall that soothed and put Brand's death in the context of its equal and opposite, life.

'Rory Brand was a man for all seasons,' she said. 'Talking to his friends and family, it's obvious that there were many sides to this man: businessman, husband, playmate, friend. Everyone knew Rory for his energy, his willingness to take risks, and his ability to say, and do, the unsayable and the undoable.'

I looked around at the congregation. None of them seemed surprised by this description of the man they knew. Rory must have worked his charm on all of them at some time.

The vicar carried on in this vein for ten minutes, then introduced a young man, Brand's nephew, who gave a short reading from a book of poetry. His voice cracked more from nervousness, I thought, than emotion.

Afterwards we sang a couple of hymns, then the pall-bearers stood and gently guided the trolley carrying the coffin back out of the church, like hospital porters performing one last duty with a stretchered patient. We stood and watched as it rattled out of the nave towards the huge wooden door, which was suddenly opened as the coffin approached, admitting a blast of cold air into the church.

At the end of the ceremony Tara, Rory's widow, stood and turned into the aisle, walking towards me. She kept herself upright and her face almost completely still as she walked past. Though her eyelids were swollen and her cheeks raw, there were no tears in her eyes. Perhaps she'd gone past that stage. Perhaps she was focused on revenge, or the next business meeting. But her manner suggested that she knew we were all watching her. The rest of the congregation stood and began to shuffle out in rows. I also stood and waited for my turn. Laura Marshall was in the line, and she lifted her blonde head slightly towards me as she filed past, offering nothing with her eyes. Unlike Tara, she'd been crying. Her emotions had finally surfaced, but only at a time and place where they were sanctioned.

And I thought Tara Brand had managed the event quite well, given the shock she must have had. She'd held herself together, not giving way to loud tears or throwing wild tantrums. She was measured, calm, almost stately. She'd put on a first class performance.

After all, it's not every day you attend the funeral of your second husband and turn to meet your first—me—staring at you open-mouthed with a look of disbelief on his face.

7

THE CONGREGATION moved carefully through the headstones to a distant part of the graveyard. There was now a slight rain and the silence was broken by the riffle of umbrellas being shaken out and raised. I looked around but no one was looking at me. Why would they? They hadn't felt the earthquake that I'd just swallowed and which was still giving off little aftershocks like acid gas in my chest.

At the graveside the vicar said a few more words that were carried off by the wind, and then the pall bearers lowered the coffin on straps into its hole. Two of the pall-bearers went amongst the mourners offering woven baskets containing rose petals. Some of the older women seized crispy handfuls and went to the graveside to throw them in. Brand's extended family seemed to be everywhere, bulky men with short-cropped steel-grey hair and blowsy middle-aged women whose heads leaned forward with the weight of their mascara. Now the main event was over, they stood around in groups smoking Silk Cut and discussing travel arrangements back to town. A pair of blond children raced unhindered around the graveyard, playing loud hide-and-seek behind the headstones.

I found Laura Marshall and stood next to her. She looked up at me clearly exhausted, though there was a kind of determination glinting in the corners of her eyes. I was liking her more and more. She leaned towards me.

'I didn't think you'd come.'

'You asked me to.'

'Do you always do what people ask?'

'Almost never.'

'That's what I thought.'

We stood for a moment and watched people drift away, pulling their collars up against the rain. I breathed deeply and inhaled the ozone.

'I should get back,' Laura said. 'There are some things I've got to sort out in the office.'

Suddenly I didn't want her to leave. 'Anyone here I should know about?' I said. 'Anyone from the company?'

'Well you saw Tara.'

'Yes ... '

I didn't seem capable of adding anything else. I was only just beginning to function properly again after seeing her in the church. Thankfully, Laura carried on without giving me a second glance.

'She seems to be bearing up,' she said. 'I saw her the night she came back from London. She was wiped out. She seems to be doing better now. And one or two of the directors made it. That man over there with the ginger hair–'

'The one who looks like he'd prefer to be propping up a bar?'

' – that's Derek Evans, the Finance Director. Lives and breathes for a deal. Just watch him screw those suppliers until they bleed. He and Rory didn't really get on. Rory didn't understand money, which always exasperates people in Finance.'

Evans had remained in the church doorway, and was moving from foot to foot and blowing into his hands. Like most of us, he wore a full-length dark overcoat but it looked a couple of sizes too big. His hair was thinning on top and he compensated by growing large sideburns that came below the bottom of his ears but didn't travel far enough to join and make the full beard. He glanced in our direction, then went back to staring ahead and warming his hands with his breath.

'He looks miserable,' I said. 'Perhaps he liked Rory deep down.'

'His being here is just a professional courtesy. Don't be fooled. He won't be feeling much one way or the other right now. He'll be calculating the profit and loss associated with losing the head of your company. The damage to our reputation, that kind of thing.'

'He sounds focused, as we used to say.'

'He's being a right pain at the moment, because the other directors want me to take more responsibility and he fancies it himself. He keeps dropping unsubtle hints. Oh God, now he's coming over.'

Evans approached, rubbing his hands together.

'How much do you think this little lot cost?' he said. 'Take into account all the ballyhoo back at Tara's now, I'd say several thousand pounds, thank you very much. Waste of money pure and simple. Come in naked and go out naked, that's my motto.'

'It's something to do with respect,' Laura said.

Evans seemed to ignore her jibe. 'Didn't think you'd be here,' he said. His eyes raked over me briefly but saw nothing worth commenting on. 'Lot of work to do now. Some big money coming in, thank you very much. What did you pay for that coat, by the way? Good colour. Might get one for the missus.'

Laura was irritated. 'Why wouldn't I be here? What did you expect me to do? Sit at my desk and knock out some more advertising brochures?'

'Now don't fly off your famous handle. I just thought you might find it too much.'

'Think again, Derek. I've had to cope with funerals before.'

'So it seems. I'm sorry, do I know you?'

This last comment was directed, finally, towards me, as though I were a persistent buzz in his ear that he eventually had to deal with. The wind gusted suddenly and one of his hands leapt from its pocket and firmly stroked a ginger lock back into place, like a magician hypnotising a dove with a pass of his hand.

'We haven't been formally introduced,' I said.

'Oh.' He waited, expecting more. I let him wait for a while, during which he glanced briefly at Laura.

'I'm Sam Dyke,' I said finally. 'I was about to take on some project work for Mr Brand.'

His eyes widened and he nodded slowly. 'I see. Will it ... you know?'

'Carry on?' I pursed my lips speculatively. 'It's yet to be decided. Miss Marshall and I have some difficult negotiations to work through.'

'I see. Laura, when we're back in the office I need to speak to you.'

'Of course,' Laura said. 'Take a ticket and get in the queue.'

He saw he wasn't going to get much joy from us. With a nod, he wandered away and headed back to his car, a hunched figure slightly below average height who looked and acted friendless.

'Well,' I said to Laura. 'I like a man with his values in place. Anyone else here I should know about?'

'Not now,' she said. Then she turned to face me full on. 'Tell me, you were going to take this case anyway, weren't you? It didn't matter what I said to you.'

'I'm sure I don't know what you mean.'

'Oh don't. You like to be tough and the big man, but you don't fool anybody. You're rude and a bit direct, but the fact that Rory was murdered has really pissed you off. I think there's a part of you that feels responsible, as if you could've done something about it.'

'You think I should have done something?'

'How could you? I warned you against getting involved. If

anyone should feel responsible, it's me.'

'No one could have predicted what happened,' I said. 'Don't blame yourself for what you can't anticipate. Old Chinese proverb.'

She opened her mouth to say something but thought better of it and instead blew her nose.

There was no one left at the graveside now. Even the vicar had walked past us with a small, collegiate smile before re-entering the church. I turned and headed back to my car. Laura Marshall walked with me, carefully placing each foot in front of the other on the rutted path, like an elegant if rather sombre tightrope walker. Everything she did radiated misery and I felt an unprofessional urge to make her feel better.

'I'll send you a rate card,' I said, listening distantly to the sound of my own voice and thinking again about Tara's face as she walked past me. 'Who's going to be paying?'

'I'll work it out.'

'Is this going to get you in trouble? Don't you need agreement from the directors for this kind of expense?'

'Don't worry about me. I'm a big girl. I've got the budget to spend on this if I want.' She sounded irritated so I said no more.

I watched her walk away from me and climb into her car, a black Saab with a soft top. It barely sagged as she dropped heavily into the driver's seat and rested her head on the wheel. I felt a compulsion to turn and go back into the churchyard to hunt for Tara, but caught myself and instead walked away from the church and the mourners, looking neither right nor left in case there was anyone watching who might see the look on my face.

8

I'D BEEN TOLD that the Brands had moved into a converted chapel shortly after they were married and spent most of the last two years re-decorating. The following afternoon I drove there through a light misty drizzle that was more like solidified vapour than actual rain.

I wanted to talk to Tara. I couldn't carry on investigating the murder of her husband without her knowledge – it felt devious. On the other hand, I didn't know what exactly I'd say to her. Rory had said she was involved in a plot to sell his company from under him. Is that what I wanted to tell Tara Brand to her face? And still expect her to keep me on the job? I wasn't looking forward to the prospect.

The chapel was closer to country than town, beyond the suburban sprawl and into the gentle hills and valleys of the Cheshire hinterland. The traffic was thin out here, where you began to move away from the Victorian manufacturing centres still reeking of steam, grime and industrial architecture, and were forced to engage with the secretive beauty of the Cheshire plain. In the failing afternoon light I was aware of the slight rise and fall of the fields around me, like gentle waves in a calm sea.

Stone pillars topped by blue china vases stood as elegant sentries at the entrance to Rory's drive. The vases were empty. The house itself wasn't immediately visible until I'd navigated a couple of bends and crested a small rise, but then it sprawled towards me—a double garage, an outer building that looked like a small office, and finally, facing me head on, the converted chapel itself, with a large wooden door and arched stone windows either side and above. It was made of pale Cheshire stone and was at least a hundred and fifty years old, judging by the wear and tear. The stone-chip drive sparking beneath my wheels gave way to hard-packed earth with the occasional paving slab showing through, and ran out immediately in front of the buildings where small beds of Virginia creeper and ivy sprouted and began their long crawl up the stonework and on to the complicated roofs.

Two cars were parked up against the chapel, both of them facing towards me as though for a rapid exit. One was a large Toyota 4x4 with muddy wheels, the other a square BMW X5 with tinted windows and black bodywork. Red security lights winked inside both vehicles. I reversed into a space at right-angles to them and walked up to the heavy front door, where there was a large brass knocker in the shape of a lion's head, but no bell. The sound of the knocker boomed through the house as if through a tomb, but after a minute no one had replied. I lifted it again and let it fall. The silence this time was even more pervasive.

The two parked cars and light showing in three windows convinced me that Tara was probably in, so I went to the side of the chapel and began to pick my way down to the rear of the building. I didn't know what I expected to find, but I thought there might be a back door or some way of attracting their attention.

The view from here was breathtaking, wandering over fields and past the occasional picturesque farmhouse towards a dim, tree-lined horizon. The air was heavy with mist and the smells of mulching leaves, and the barren trees surrounding the chapel gave off a smoky odour like a natural incense.

Through the silence I felt the presence of people in the house. It was as though I could hear them through the walls, which were clammy and cold to the touch. I pushed myself past hawthorns and ground-hugging plants that tugged at my ankles as I made my way down the side of the house. Now the dark smell of animals and earth fought with the woody burning aroma that issued from the chimney directly overhead.

When I reached the back of the house, I saw that a new conservatory extended out from the brickwork and stretched along the whole length of the rear elevation, attached to the solid, deep-rooted edifice like a flimsy afterthought. I could hear the voices inside the house, though they were still indistinct. I reached out and grasped the wooden sill of the conservatory, then gingerly felt my way around the corner where the ground was a morass of clay and brick shards.

Then I stopped.

I drew back from the conservatory windows. There were two human shapes in the room that backed on to the conservatory. They stood in shadow, facing each other, and were talking animatedly. I stood still and strained to hear. One shape was Tara—her posture and the way she moved her head as she spoke was still familiar after all this time. The other shape was taller, and male. Their voices were not raised but neither was their speech calm. They seemed to be arguing, one cutting off the other before they were finished—it wasn't the steady to and fro of normal conversation.

The discussion got louder and more excited. I caught some phrases but still couldn't hear properly. The couple moved away from the conservatory and deeper into the house, and their voices became more muffled. I stood silently for half a minute, waiting to see if they returned. My fingers were getting tired and I felt my heart-rate increase and heard my breathing growing shallow. I didn't like being exposed like this, especially when I didn't know what was going on inside. I'd half made up my mind to go back to the front of the house when I heard the hollow boom of the front door, followed rapidly by a car door slamming. An engine roared into life.

I turned and raced down the side of the house, leaping over broken bricks and blocks of wood, my arms and legs snatched and hooked by hawthorn briars. I arrived at the front just in time to see the BMW vanishing over the rise in the driveway. The tinted windows did their job and hid the driver from view.

Feeling outwitted, I stood and thought about what I'd just seen. A heated conversation between the widow of my client and an Unknown Person, male. Followed by a swift exit by the unknown man ... someone more suspicious than me might have come to some rapid and unsavoury conclusions.

The air was still, the silence broken only by the sound of my lungs drawing in deep breaths and letting them out. Sam Dyke, athlete. Despite the deep intake of air, my thinking skills didn't improve. I couldn't guess who was in the car. But I thought maybe Tara would tell me herself. I turned to the door, lifted the heavy brass knocker and let it fall.

This time she answered immediately. Perhaps she thought it was her visitor returned. Her mouth was half-open and her face was strained and irritated, but she caught herself and said, 'Hello, can I help you?'

'Hello, Tara. It's me, Sam.'

Her red hair was tangled and her make-up blotchy. Beneath it was still the twenty-year-old I'd known in a seedy boarding house in Leeds, visible now as if seen through a smudged window that added worry, despair, grief and loss to the once-clean outlines of her eyes and delicate nose. Her pinched lips grew even thinner and her expression hardened.

'Oh not you,' she said. 'Not now.'

Then she shut the door on me so firmly that the brass knocker gave a small celebratory leap.

9

AFTER STARING AT the door for probably only ten seconds, though it felt like ten minutes, I went to my car and drove away without looking back. I drove without knowing where I was going, and caring even less. I drove while in deep conversation – with myself. That's just great, I told myself. She comes back into my life and stirs me up, and she can't even bring herself to talk to me. Shows what an impact our marriage had on her. She might as well have kicked me in the stomach and punched me in the teeth for good measure. Perhaps I should just leave her to it and let her sort her life out, if she's so clever ... I carried on in this vein for a good while, letting righteous anger have a good time with me and with my pride that was more than wounded, it was on its last legs and about to collapse, fatally hurt.

Thirty minutes later I'd calmed down and began putting some perspective on it. I could hardly blame her for not wanting to talk to me. I suspected she didn't know what I was doing for a living now. Unless Laura Marshall had told her, she wouldn't know that I'd been hired by Rory. I supposed she'd seen me in the church at his funeral, but she wouldn't know why I was there. As far as she was concerned, I was a bad memory—and judging by our previous history, one that she'd rather forget.

As a way of focusing, I began to consider what I knew of this case—which didn't take me very far. I knew that Rory Brand was expanding his company into areas in which it was inexperienced and had finagled a great deal of money to do so. I was finding out that his management style left a lot to be desired, and that my ex-wife was his ex-wife, in a manner of speaking, but she didn't want to talk to me, which hurt. All these facts might mean something eventually. But at the moment they were disconnected, and if they had a meaning it was well-hidden.

I pulled into a lay-by and rang Laura Marshall. I didn't tell her what had happened with Tara. Instead I asked for details of the people who'd left Brands most recently. I needed to get on with the investigation.

Before giving me any names, she said, 'What exactly are you going to do with these people?'

'Ask some innocent questions.'

'Am I going to get lots of complaining phone calls?'

'Depends on the answers I get, doesn't it?'

Somewhat guardedly, she dictated some names and numbers that I wrote down in my note book.

As I arrived back at my office, two men were squeezing a black three-seater sofa out through the front door, straining and swearing as they tried not to rip its polythene cover. One man was Thomas, the owner, known to everyone as Tommo, a worried, gaunt man whose suits always looked two sizes too big. The other was his shiftless son who never looked you in the eye and gave the impression of laughing at you behind your back. I gave them a hand lifting the sofa into an old Ford Transit. Then a third man who'd stood and watched us climbed into the van and drove it away.

It was a simple task accomplished quickly. No complex reasoning required. And it felt good doing something physical for a change. I needed to get to a gym or start running again; a few months ago I'd stopped my daily five mile run through the fields behind my house because I'd twisted an ankle, and now I was fit again I missed that tingling sense of exhaustion that good exercise creates.

Once inside the office, I took off my jacket, made myself a strong coffee, threw two junk letters into the waste-bin, filed a bill into my red Out tray, and forced myself to concentrate on detail. I picked up the phone and began to call.

I drove past the blue glass pyramid that towers over the main route into Stockport, under the grimy viaduct and up a long hill filled with boarded shopfronts and abandoned warehouses. The roads, buildings, sky and air were grey and everything smelled faintly of petrol fumes. Not for the first time it struck me that Stockport was a town whose time had come and gone. It was hanging around now because it didn't know where to put itself. It was like a poor relation that refused to go away and instead just embarrassed you in front of your fancy friends.

Finally I turned into a grove of newly-built mews houses that were intended as starter homes, and knocked on Gerald Finch's front door.

Some starter. When he opened the door, I saw only as far as his shoulders. He was enormous. He wore dirty blue jeans and a white tee-shirt with *Greaseballs* stencilled on the front that was at my eye level. He ducked his head down and said, 'Come in,' in a surprisingly high voice. I stepped through and it was if I were entering Lilliput. Finch must have been about six foot eight, while the house looked as though it had been built to three-quarter scale. The ceilings were low, the rooms were small, and there was only a narrow passage between black leather chairs through the front lounge into the kitchen, towards which Finch guided me. 'Let's go into the office,' he said. 'I'm in the middle of something but we can talk.'

The office was a white melamine breakfast bar in his kitchen that contained his PC, a printer, one or two pieces of hardware I didn't recognise, and piles of paper strewn at random. Through French windows I could see a tiny garden falling away in paved terracing towards a small stand of trees. I wondered if it was a bonsai garden reflected through some elaborate mirror trickery, and set up to further confuse the weak-minded.

A cat slept on the end of the counter and didn't stir when I sat on a stool next to it. Finch petted it once and then sat down himself. He cleared his screen saver and began to work intently.

'So Rory got it,' he said. 'Doesn't surprise me. He deserved it.'

'No one deserves to be murdered,' I said, as coldly as I could. Finch shrugged.

'He was always heading for a fall, man. You've got to see that. I've worked in this business for nearly twenty years and I've never met anyone who so refused to listen to other people. Time after time I told him we had to slow down, think it through, but no, he had to do the entrepreneur thing—be first to market, beat the competition, you know what salesmen are like ... '

Finch had been the first Operations Director that Rory had hired to run the new IT part of the business. He'd left after only a few months for reasons that Laura Marshall told me were unclear, though there were suggestions there'd been an argument. When I'd phoned he was reluctant to talk to me but became interested when I told him I was investigating Rory's death.

Now he was drawing boxes on his computer screen and then writing text in them. He positioned the completed text box, applied formatting—font style, point size, italic or bold—then saved the document.

'I'm told you had a row with Rory,' I said. 'Is that why you left?'

He looked up at me briefly. 'Wow—is that the story they're putting out? Doesn't surprise me.'

'Not a lot surprises you, does it?'

'You've got to learn to pay attention, man. They always liked

45

to enhance the truth, you know, like putting it through a graphic filter to take out the rough edges.'

'So what's your version?'

'I was sacked. Taken out like a bastard. Oh we did it the formal way, calling everyone together in the boardroom so that they could see me fall on my sword—but it was a sacking. I had to go through that, you see, so they'd give me my payout. Have to toe the party line to get what's rightfully yours.'

'Sounds tough,' I said. He didn't hear the irony.

He said, 'I knew a guy once who was on the management team, like me, and he left with all guns blazing. Told everyone he'd been given the boot. Just wouldn't lie down. So of course they didn't give him the remains of his contract, took his car off him immediately, withheld his holiday pay, petty stuff. But all in all it cost him about fifty grand. So I watched my p's and q's, told everyone in the boardroom that I felt it was in the best interests of the company if I went, and I legged it. Best thing I ever did. In business for myself, now. Hence the web page—just doing a spot of re-design. Supposed to be online tomorrow, so excuse the back of my head.'

'It's excused.'

'So how did Rory get it?'

'I've heard his neck was broken. He was found in his office.'

'Cool.'

He must have heard the silence. He looked up at me again.

'Okay, that's a bit harsh. But you meddle with fire, you get burned.'

'What do you mean?' I said.

'Do I sound bitter? Fucking tough. Rory was an expert at stirring things up. You could never say he was a placid kind of guy. Get yourself some coffee. There's a machine over there.'

'I'm OK thanks.'

'Suit yourself.'

He suddenly stopped working and took his hands from his

keyboard. He turned in his chair and faced me. 'What do you want from me?' he said. 'I didn't like Rory and I don't think he liked me. Is that what you want to hear?'

'Why do you say he stirred things up?' I said.

'His attitude. His manner. Very confrontational. Pissed people off all the time—he couldn't help himself.'

'Anyone in particular?'

'Well, me. Most of the consultants. People who worked for him. Shall I go on?'

'You're not exactly mild-mannered yourself.'

For a second I thought he was going to stand up again, but he shifted his weight back on to his seat.

He said, 'Everyone who knew Rory Brand could tell you a story. Don't pick on me. I'm no different to anyone else.'

This wasn't exactly narrowing down the field. 'What's the problem with the new IT division?' I asked. 'You were heading it up—what went wrong?'

He picked up his coffee cup and sipped from it carefully, pursing surprisingly delicate lips.

'He wouldn't stop meddling,' he said. 'We'd set a project plan for the next year, and as soon as a client expressed interest in a version of the software, he insisted we change the production schedule to incorporate the new request. We chopped and changed every month. Very un-cool. Brand had his finger in everything, even though he hadn't got idea fucking one how this stuff works. So we'd go for a few weeks and it would be OK, then there'd be a sudden meeting of the management team and Brand would have a cow because we weren't delivering what he wanted.'

'Anyone tell him this?'

'I'd argue with him but he's the boss, so in the end I'd back down and go and tell the guys we're changing priorities again. Give Microsoft Project another workout. I tell you, I just got sick of it. Anyway my feelings didn't count, because in the end he fired me. He made it impossible for me to carry on.'

'How did he do that?'

'He talked to Champion—you know, the guys who'd put the money in—and between them they made me an offer I couldn't refuse. Walk the plank or be pushed overboard. I took a running jump, I tell you.'

I frowned. 'Wasn't there any incentive to stay?'

Finch's mood had turned dark while remembering his time at Brands. He hadn't heard my question and instead answered one that I guessed he'd been turning over in his head for some time.

He said, 'It's not as if the program wasn't working, for Christ's sake. Considering the hassle, it was a gem. All we needed was more time. They had consultants testing it and they thought it was superb, so he should have just butted out and let us get on with it.'

'You must have wanted to get him out of the way.'

He didn't hear the insinuation. 'All management's the same,' he said. 'They all have to put their oar in. In the long run there's no point bucking the system. You can't win against the suits. Anyway, in this game you move around a lot. It's not nine-to-five and it's not a job for life. You join, you learn some new licks, you make a bunch of good friends that you   e-mail forever, then you move on to the next start-up or bright idea. Personalities just get in the way. There's plenty of work out there. You just pick up your ball and walk off into the sunset. Portfolio career—that's the name of the game now.'

I looked around the cramped house in the grey town and wondered if he was actually as happy as he wanted me to think.

'One more thing,' Finch said, putting his cup down next to his sleeping cat. 'If you can, take a look at the figures. You've got to remember that the consultancy side of the business is bringing in the dollars, and the IT side is spending them.'

'What does that mean?'

'There'll come a point where breakeven won't be possible,' he said. 'In other words they'll have to sell some product. Each month that goes by costs them a fortune. If consultancy revenues take a dive for whatever reason, they'll slip into the red. The consultants know that. They aren't happy. They've made Brands the company it is, and now they've seen Rory piss it away. Yes they've had three mil in funding, but none of that has gone into the consultant pot, and when it's gone the consultants will be the bankers. Supporting a division they don't understand and whose product will take work from them. Talk about motivation ...'

I made a note and thought of another question.

'What did you think of Tara Brand?'

'Great hair, good with clients. Bit of a cold fish with the rest of us.' He shifted his position and his eyes caught the light from outside. They were palest grey, as though bringing into the room the dead sky outside, and lending him the transparent gaze of someone who really didn't care.

'How do you think she'd cope?' I asked.

'She'd tough it out. There'd be clients to service. She wouldn't let them down.'

'That sounds about right.'

'It might not look like it, but I'm pretty good at reading people. Especially women.'

And I was shortly to find out that I wasn't.

10

'I'D LIKE TO APOLOGISE for my behaviour yesterday. I was taken by surprise.'

Tara sat behind a laptop computer in one of the small meeting rooms. This room contained a high desk with the effect that as she worked, her eyeline included both me and the screen of her laptop.

I was here because Carol the receptionist had left a brief message on my mobile phone that had brooked no argument. I was to present myself in the office at an early hour so that Mrs Brand could talk to me. I pulled a face at the phone but agreed to come nonetheless. Although I wasn't keen to be snubbed by Tara again, I couldn't turn down the opportunity to speak to her. After all, I was effectively working for her company now, searching for the killer of her husband. The least I could do was meet her face-to-face.

Now I stood opposite her and didn't know what to think. Her Yorkshire accent had disappeared. Her dress sense had improved dramatically since I'd last seen her and she was wrapped in a warm ochre jacket over a cream blouse, her mass of crinkly red hair bunched and pulled back into a fiery pony-tail that looked something like I imagined a comet to look, if you got up close. As for her grief, that seemed to be well under control. Her eyes were not red or watery but instead glittered with a hardness that I didn't remember. Whatever she felt for Rory had been parcelled up and put away for the time being. It certainly wasn't on show for the likes of me.

'I'm sorry I intruded,' I said. 'And I'm sorry about Rory's death. I only met him once but he seemed ... full of energy.'

She closed the lid of the laptop and relaxed into her chair. 'Thank you, Sam. I'm sorry if I didn't seem to recognise you yesterday. You look different with your hair shorter. I realised afterwards that it was you I saw at the funeral. I certainly didn't expect to see you knocking on my front door. I suppose I'm still in shock. How have you been?'

'Do you want a rundown of the last eighteen years?'

'An executive summary will do. I'm an executive now, you know. It means I have a short attention span because there's always something more important I have to do.'

At least she was trying to be friendly. But she was using that brittle humour people use when their emotions are not fully in check and they don't understand the impact of what they're saying.

'I moved about, worked here and there.' I gave her the benefit of a small smile. 'I'm in private practice now.'

'So I gather. Married?'

'No.' I looked away. Her eyes had suddenly become inquisitive. I said, 'I suppose you've had adventures.'

'Oh, I did stuff in London once I got away from Leeds—and Dad. The Major.' She'd always had a strained relationship with her father. She shook her head as if trying to get him out of there. 'I found out about marketing. Seemed to suit me. Went to college and did a course. I worked for an international distribution company that you won't have heard of. Then I set up my own marketing consultancy, which is how I met Rory. A conference at a swank hotel in London.'

'Did you know he'd spoken to me?'

'Only after Laura told me. I didn't even know you were in the area. I thought you'd be filling in forms for the underprivileged somewhere in Huddersfield.'

'I broadened my horizons.'

'Good for you,' she said. 'I think I underestimated you, you know …'

'When we were married.'

'Yes, that.' She'd become very still, as if wary of disturbing the air around us. I wondered what she was being cautious about. She seemed to be choosing every syllable she uttered carefully. But then she moved away from these dangerous waters and back into history. 'I hated London, you know. I was glad to come back North. Though I don't know if Tory Cheshire counts as the real North. There are snobbier people up here than you get in Islington—and that's saying something.'

For a moment we contemplated the essential mystery of class differences. Outside the room, a phone rang insistently.

'I know I called this meeting,' she said abruptly, 'but can we make it as quick as possible? I'm still not good for much. I'm trying to ration what I do. Laura tells me you were on a special project for Rory.'

'That was the idea.'

'Now it turns out she's asked you to look into Rory's murder as well. As usual with Laura, I think she's stepping over some boundaries. But my first question is, why did he hire you? What did he want you to do?'

I hesitated. I remembered Rory and his unwillingness to tell her about his suspicions. I said, 'I can't talk to you about that.'

'Why not?' she asked, affronted. 'Rory's dead. Don't tell me your client confidentiality extends beyond the grave.'

'In this case it does. It might cause more problems if I started talking about it.'

She stared at me for a long moment. 'So what am I supposed to do now? You come in to do one job, which you won't tell me about, and all of a sudden you expect me to pay you for working on another.'

'Fair point. Let's just say they might be linked.'

'Or they might not be.' Her eyes suddenly registered a surprise. 'Hang on, am I part of the investigation?'

'I do want to ask you some questions,' I said. 'But we don't have to do it now.'

'Why – are you afraid I'll break in half?'

'Well naturally it's your call, but I don't think you should rush it.'

She reached up and framed her hair with both hands, pulled off the device that held it in a pony tail, then moved her hands away and let it fall. It was a dramatic gesture that gave her time to think. She seemed distracted and unsure how to deal with me. I didn't blame her, because I didn't know how to deal with her either. She looked up at me and smiled glumly. 'History, eh?' she said. 'Who'd have thought we'd end up like this? You a detective, me a—whatever the hell I am.'

'I'm a different person to the one you knew.'

This seemed to interest her. 'Really. How?'

I heard myself saying the words before I knew I'd even thought them. 'I know what I want,' I said.

She rolled her eyes upwards.

'Oh, Sam,' she said. 'Don't give me that new age bullshit. Nobody knows what they want apart from a few obsessives.'

'OK—I don't know what I want. But I know what I don't want.'

'Let me guess—you don't want to work for other people and you don't want to clock on every morning. You don't want to pay a mortgage till you die and you don't want always to be driving second-hand cars. So welcome to the human race. It doesn't exactly make you Captain Freedom.'

'I'd forgotten how compassionate you could be.'

That pushed a button. She smiled to herself and gave a little shake of her head. 'I'm bored with this now. So ask me your questions and let's move on. What do you want to know?'

'I'm not going to ask you any questions now. It's too close to Rory's murder.'

Her clear eyes widened and she leaned back from the table. 'Who do you think you're talking to?' she said. 'What do you think's going to happen? Don't tell me you want sackcloth and ashes. I don't do that sort of thing. I'd have thought you of all people would know that, Sam.'

Our moment had passed. I realised that she wasn't the girl I'd known eighteen years ago. She was still argumentative and direct, which was always a quality I'd liked because of its challenge, but now she seemed to be thinking differently too. There was a brittle shell that covered her like a porcelain shield that I didn't recognise and didn't particularly like. I decided to be as straightforward as she was.

'OK – I'd normally ask about motives,' I said. 'Anyone with a grievance. Any arguments, people he didn't get on with. You might know about those, being the wife and all.'

Her eyes gave nothing away. 'Go on.'

'There's two possibilities here, as I see it. There could have been a personal grudge: an old romance, or envy, or just plain dislike. Someone who had taken against Rory for personal reasons and wanted to prove a point.'

'Rory? Never.' She was being ironic.

'On the other hand, it could have been a professional conflict: a business deal gone belly up, or someone who felt they'd been cheated or put in the wrong.'

She continued to stare at me. 'Don't be ridiculous,' she said. 'This isn't Chicago. We're consultants, not gangsters. I've only been in the business a couple of years, but I'm a main board member and I've been involved in every decision in that time. I told Inspector Howard there was nothing like that going on. Has he talked to you?'

'I haven't had that pleasure.'

'Oh, you should look forward to it. What a delightful man.'

This was said with some disdain—but whether for me or for Howard I couldn't tell.

'Okay,' I said bluntly. 'Straight up. Do you have any idea who might have killed Rory?'

Her gaze was steady, even brazen. 'None. He was a businessman, but he wasn't a captain of industry who wheeled and dealed and toyed with thousands of people's lives. He had fallings-out with people occasionally, but you and I know that happens all the time.'

'So as far as you know there was nobody with a grudge, no threats, no suspicious letters?'

'I've told you. Nothing of any kind. You've got me really interested now. What the hell did Rory say?'

'You know I can't tell you,' I said. I relented slightly. 'We only met once. He didn't tell me much. But he was worried and suspicious about some things that were happening.'

'And then he was killed. Poor Rory.' She sighed. She had the air of a weary schoolmistress dealing with a stupid child. 'There are things you don't seem to have grasped about me, Sam. Although I'm from a military family, I've always wanted to run my own business and I've been self-sufficient since I went to nursing school. You know I'm ambitious. I'm well organised. I'm good at identifying trends and going for them. I specialised in marketing because like Rory I'm very convincing when I'm in front of a client. People tell me it's a joy to see me at work. I'm telling you all this in case you have any suspicions that I had anything to do with Rory's death.'

'You don't need to be defensive.'

'Maybe not, but that seemed to be the direction you were going in.'

She was right and she'd double-guessed me. I tried another tack.

'When I came to your house yesterday, I saw a man leave. Who was he?'

Her cheeks flushed.

'That was bad timing,' she said. 'It had nothing to do with Rory. It was an old friend.'

'Your conversation didn't sound friendly.'

Now her eyes blazed. 'You listened?'

'You were loud.'

'That doesn't give you permission to eavesdrop.' She took the heat from her eyes and they grew cold and distant. I knew what was coming before she said it. I recognised the gesture from many years, and many arguments, ago. 'This isn't getting us anywhere. I can't have you interfering with this company's business. It would be best if you went now. Thanks for your concern but I believe the police have everything in hand.'

She flipped up the lid of her laptop and looked down into it as though I'd already left. I took a step closer so she was forced to look up at me. I found myself reacting to her in exactly the same way I had when we were barely out of our teens. I had to push back. I wouldn't let her win.

'Ignoring these things only makes them more interesting,' I said. 'To me and to the police. It's no way to deal with legitimate questions.'

She stared at me without flinching, almost as though she were looking through me. I'd become an obstacle to her getting her own way, and when that happened to Tara there was only going to be one conclusion. She said, 'When I hear a legitimate question I'll consider your point of view. OK, Sam. Good to see you again.' She looked down briefly at her computer screen, then back up at me. 'Didn't I make myself clear? You're sacked. Submit an invoice and we'll pay it in thirty days. Goodbye.'

11

O N MY WAY HOME I carefully thought over what Tara had said before deciding to ignore it. I reckoned that she was stressed and didn't know what she was saying. It seemed to me that a contract that had yet to be delivered or signed was no contract at all. So she couldn't fire me from it. Besides, my client was Laura, and by five o'clock, after another session on the Internet, I knew I had to speak to her again. There was something she and everyone else in Brands was keeping from me. 'I've been told Tara sacked you,' she said over the phone, her voice echoing from the loudspeaker device she was using. 'I suppose you know she's not happy with what we've been doing. She gave me a roasting.'

'And what do you think?'

'I think you're very high maintenance for someone who's supposed to be working for us.'

'So do you want my report or not?'

'You have a report? I didn't even know you could write.'

'I never said it was in writing.'

'OK, come in on Monday morning. We'll wind it up then. This has all been a big distraction anyway. I can't get any work done worrying about what you're up to next.'

'Don't worry about me,' I said. 'I do enough worrying for both of us.'

I spent the weekend in my garden, chopping wood for the fire and fixing a fence that had blown down two weeks before. I pushed Brands and their troubles completely out of my mind and felt healthier for it. I knew by now the symptoms of obsessive devotion to a client and didn't want to succumb to it this time. You get no extra thanks and very little understanding, so why bother? Instead I relaxed, played some music and got some sleep – not knowing it was the last proper rest I was going to get for a while.

When I arrived at Brands' office on Monday, I parked at the front and went through the carousel door into the lobby.

Betty Parsons, the office manager I'd met on that first day, was standing in front of the lift, staring at its aluminium doors and looking like a staff sergeant waiting for the troops to assemble. She turned her large glasses on me and nodded briefly without smiling.

'We won't keep fit like this,' I said. I didn't know where the impulse to be jolly came from and regretted it immediately.

'They're re-carpeting the stairs,' she replied coldly. 'Everybody's got to use the lift today. I don't use it as a rule because it sticks. I prefer the stairs. And I don't like your attitude, Mr Dyke. This company is in mourning and I think you should remember that.'

'Ah.'

I turned and looked at the lift doors and knew she was examining me. We stood quietly until the lift came, then rose in silence to the top floor. When the doors opened I followed her out and through the main office. She marched briskly to her desk. Although in her fifties and stick thin, she held herself upright and looked the world right in the eye. Just long enough to spit in it.

Laura was on the phone. She waved at me with a pale hand and pointed to a chair, which I took. Around me there were young men and women in jeans and T-shirts seated before large monitors, wearing headphones and intently creating digital media ... whatever that was. There was a low thump of bass coming from one of the workstations—one of the programmers broad-casting his musical taste for the rest of us to enjoy. I wondered how they managed to continue working with their leader having been killed so brutally. What enabled them to carry on even though someone they saw every day had been murdered in an office twenty yards away? What did they think about it and did they care?

I deposited my file on Laura's desk and, seeing that she was still deep in her phone conversation, went over to Betty, who was getting comfortable, re-arranging papers on her desk and organising various foods into drawers—apple, crisps, chocolate bar. She had the furtiveness of a squirrel, her hands moving backwards and forwards like tiny paws. She looked up at me and her face seemed as long and unforgiving as an Easter Island statue.

'Betty, I want to ask a favour,' I said. She stared at me as though performing a favour for me was at the very bottom of her to-do list. 'I'm still finding out about the people who work here, or worked here in the past. I suppose you have CVs of people who Brands have employed—details of their work history and so on?'

She was on the point of replying when her eyes looked up and past me. I turned and saw that one of the young programmers was standing at my back. He was smiling inanely at Betty with his long hair falling down over his face.

'Bets, I've left my card in my other jacket. Can I—you know?' He made a smoking gesture with his hand, taking out and putting in an imaginary cigarette. Betty reached into her drawer and pulled out a small credit-card sized object and handed it over without expression.

'Thanks, Bets. When cancer calls you can't say no.'

He turned and left.

'They stand outside the back door to smoke,' Betty said. 'Rory didn't like them to stand at the front of the building—gives a bad impression, all those cigarette ends, so messy. It's a terrible habit, makes your clothes smell and everything. They need a swipe card to get back in if the door swings shut.'

I nodded. At least she was talking to me. 'Do many of them smoke?'

She shrugged. 'I don't keep count. It's their business.'

She went back to organising the items in her desk drawers. I said, 'So about the CVs?'

She looked up. 'I'm afraid not, Mr Dyke. We keep information like that private except when clients ask for it—when they want to know who's going to be working for them, like, doing the consultancy.'

'Isn't this a special situation?'

'Nobody here murdered Rory,' she said. 'So I don't think we've got to change the way we do things just because you ask me. In the case of the police, like, that was different. They have a right to it.'

'So Inspector Howard already has this information?'

'Of course. Sent one of his men over for it. I'd think it was one of the first things an experienced investigator would do, you know, to narrow down the suspects.'

This was such a clear insult, I smiled.

'So how do you think I could find out more about the people who work here?'

'You could ask them. I understand Miss Marshall has already given you some numbers.'

'You don't miss much, do you?'

'That's my job, to know what's going on with the people around me.'

'But how can *I* talk to them if you won't give me the other numbers I need?'

'I've told you, they're private telephone numbers. I'm not going to give them out. If you want to speak to someone in particular, you should phone into the switchboard and they'll connect you. If Carol on reception can't put you through, you'll be transferred to their voice mail or mobile phone. Leave a message and they'll phone you back.'

'You make it sound easy.'

'We think so.' She looked at me calmly. 'It's a rotten thing what's happened here, Mr Dyke. It's bad enough having police coming in and asking all sorts of questions and disturbing everything—we don't see why we need a separate person investigating as well. We want Rory's murderer caught right enough, but we're not hopeful. Some people think it's exciting having a detective around. As for me, I don't think you're much of a help.'

'We'll see, won't we?' I said. Smiling, I added, 'Any ideas who did it?'

She recoiled as if I'd said a rude word. 'You shouldn't ask me that,' she said. 'Rory was a handful, but he didn't have enemies who'd take things badly enough as to kill him. Not that I know of, anyway.'

'And you knew him well.'

'Seven years I've been here. Seen the company grow from one room to something I'm proud to be part of.'

'I suppose it's different now, though—all these computer whiz-kids and big money coming in.'

'You have to grow. If you don't grow, you stagnate. We can't afford to do that.'

This sounded like something she'd been taught to say. I was about to ask her more when I felt a light pressure on my shoulder. Laura had come up behind me. 'I'm free now,' she said. 'You've got half an hour. Let's go find a room.'

We turned and left Betty staring after us. Her face was

composed and serious, but her words echoed with an absence of passion that I'd heard before in people who weren't telling the whole truth.

12

L AURA TOOK ME to the largest room I'd seen in these offices—an airy boardroom containing one long table, laid out with creamy writing pads and long, sharp pencils. An end wall was almost completely filled by a huge flat screen showing the Brands logo animated as a screensaver. I could barely take my eyes off it. I suddenly realised that Brands had an image that it would be trying to protect in the world outside. The directors and staff would be under extraordinary pressure not to let anything slip that would be detrimental to the company or its clients. I wondered what impact that was having on how people dealt with me and on what they said.

Laura sat with her back to a row of cathedral-like windows, through which there was a view of the roofs of those Waverley houses that would forever be too expensive for the likes of me.

'How are you doing?' I asked.

She looked startled. 'You do surprise, don't you?'

'Don't expect any thoughtfulness from a working-class Yorkshireman? We're not all flat-caps and Yorkshire pudding you know.'

Now she was quietly embarrassed. Her pale skin took on a

tint of rose and she smiled. 'We didn't meet many people from other cultures where I grew up.'

'Where was that? Mars?'

'Might as well have been – Guildford. And I thought my accent was natural, you know, ordinary. When I go back now and hear people talking about going to the 'bas stop' to catch 'the bas' I wonder what the hell they're talking about. And all my relatives wonder what on earth I'm doing up here, near the Arctic Circle. I can't win, can I? You think I'm posh and my folks think I'm tobogganing down-market faster than the royal family.'

'Where do you want to be?'

'Somewhere I belong,' she said simply.

I looked around at the expensive furnishings—the glass-topped tables, the original prints of abstract art on the wall, the personalised coasters for holding china cups full of Earl Grey tea.

I said, 'My dad lived in the same house he was born in till he died. Three years ago next month. Miner's house. Built by the mining companies to house their workers. No inside bathroom. Big jugs of water standing in bowls on tables in the bedrooms to wash in of a morning. Two cooking ranges, one in each downstairs room. One of them not used, because it was the parlour. You only went in there with permission. When I was a kid I'd watch the miners walking home past our gate, black as dominoes, because there weren't any pit-head baths. My mum still lives there.'

'So is that where you belong?'

'I don't think so. I've moved on. Yorkshire and me don't see eye-to-eye any more.'

'I bet you thought you were too good for it.'

'A place like that can really screw up your view of the world. Everyone's got an opinion. It wears you down in the end.'

'So you got out.'

'Some time ago. I went into the Civil Service, then Customs

and Excise as an investigator. Worked in fraud, then drugs, based in Liverpool. Kicked out after ten years.'

'Why was that?'

I stood up and walked around the shiny table to the windows. 'It's high up here, isn't it?'

She followed my gaze. 'I like it. Above the crowds. Does it bother you?'

I felt myself frowning. 'When I was young once we visited relatives in Coventry. I went into town with some cousins and we went up the spire of the old Cathedral. It's right next to the new one with that spindly spire on top that looks like a TV mast. You climb a hundred steps or more. Then you're on a small ledge with a wall that comes up to your waist, looking out over the city. It's cramped and doesn't feel safe and you think it could all crumble away under your feet. I remember just wanting to lean out and fall into ... well, I don't know. There's probably a psychological name for it. Vertigo or something.'

'Most people get over that,' she said.

'Not me,' I said. 'Not yet.' I turned to her. It was time to be frank. 'Brands is in trouble, isn't it?' I said. 'Until six months ago you were winning new clients and new business regularly. Lots of name checks in the business section of the Manchester Evening News. The London papers quoted your managers and sales people and carried interviews with Rory. Your consultants were travelling all over Europe, and you were hiring more people every week.'

'Sam—'

'Now your head count is down and you're not bragging about new business. Some of the companies you listed as clients a year ago aren't shown on your web-site any more or in your company magazine. So far this year you haven't sponsored any charities or any exhibitions, and you're not on the exhibitors list for either the IPD exhibition in Harrogate, or the HRD fair in London, which I'm told are the big showcases for companies like yours.'

'If you'd just—'

'Last year you exhibited at three IT fairs, this year none. And as far as I can tell, no one's bought any licences for Compsoft yet. Is that a fair picture?'

She appeared stunned. She looked down and picked at a thread on her skirt with the embarrassment of a child caught in a lie.

'I'm not going to pretend to you,' she said quietly. 'Trading conditions haven't been great this year. But we're getting a grip now and things are looking better.' Her round eyes gazed at me frankly. 'I didn't really need you to come in and tell me things I already know about this company.'

'You knew these things but you didn't let me in on the secret. I would have appreciated a little more honesty.'

She shrugged. 'I apologise. The financial condition of the company didn't seem relevant to the murder of its boss. Seems odd when I put it like that, but that's what I thought at the time.'

'Never mind. We are where we are. What did Rory think when things began to go downhill? Did he do anything to stop the rot?'

'Not unless you count ranting and raging and sacking people every which way. He met every piece of bad news as if it were a personal slap in the face, and he'd want to hit back.' Now she stood up and walked to stand next to me, staring out over the rooftops. 'We tried to keep him calm, get him to focus on winning business, but he kept interfering.'

'How?'

'Lots of things. He'd call a meeting of the senior management team and we'd all have our backsides kicked. Then he'd go out and meddle again in the software development project. He had all of us testing it when it wasn't in a fit state to test. The consultants hated it because it took them away from their proper job. But Rory couldn't keep his fingers out of the pie. He was a perfectionist in a time and place where it was completely inappropriate.'

66

I looked at her profile, which was straight and clear, her round eyes focused straight ahead. 'What did the consultants think of the program?'

'They didn't like having to put the time in to the testing. But most of them liked the program itself. What there was to see. It wasn't in a useable state and still isn't, really.'

'I've heard Rory was picky.'

'He had to get things right. And he had this habit. One of the consultants called it corrective hindsight. When he talked about decisions he'd made, he could always put them in a context where they made perfect sense. Nothing was ever his fault, despite the fact that everything was his fault. He set things up to fail because of the person he was. It was like watching a ship heading towards an iceberg—you could see it coming a long way off but it was too big to avoid.'

'Did everyone in the company know things were in such a mess?'

'Some knew, others guessed. He liked to think he ran a tight ship, if I can carry on that simile or metaphor or whatever the hell it was—but in fact this is a company of very bright people. And of course everyone had an exit strategy. There were CVs flying about all over the place.'

'What about Tara—what did she do? Was she still the supportive wife?'

She glanced at me. 'Good question. Yes, she stuck by him. But we could see the strain she was under. She's a sales person. She knew we weren't selling enough to keep a pipeline of income on the go.'

I felt a sudden empathy for her. Working in a failing company would sap anyone's confidence. The thought came to me suddenly that I should tell her I'd been married to Tara—but it seemed irrelevant. Besides, she'd learn soon enough.

I said, 'When we spoke the other day you didn't seem happy about Compsoft. But you didn't say anything. Why didn't you tell me the company was so shaky and Compsoft wasn't working?'

She turned and looked at me. 'You've never mixed with consultants, have you?' she asked. 'What do you think consultants do?'

'Tell you things you already know in a language you don't understand.'

'I used to think like that – the cynic's view. But you have to remember consultants come from all walks of life – we've had an ex-jockey, people from the forces, salesman, all sorts. And the reason they end up in consultancy is that they're optimists to the bone. They think things can be improved, so they're always waiting for something to turn up, like that character in Dickens. And of course it's feast and famine in this game. When the feast comes you never think you're going to have enough people or resources to do the job properly. When the famine hits you wonder if you'll keep going till next month. You learn to be hardy—and optimistic.' She raised her arms and let them fall limply. 'Against all the evidence.'

I saw in her again a quality of humour that surfaced when she was talking about difficult subjects.

She said, 'You know Tara says she's sacked you, and at the moment she's the boss. I can't really argue with her, especially in these circumstances.'

'What do you want to do?'

'How am I supposed to know?' she said. 'I didn't want this responsibility. People keep telling me I could do well in this company. But is that what I want?' She threw a look in my direction. 'And you're not exactly helping.'

'How do you mean?'

'You're making me feel defensive about Brands when I don't want to be. I just want everything out in the open. I don't like politics. I don't like keeping things from people in the company— it's the old socialist in me.' She grinned. 'I didn't tell you that, did I? I studied economic history at Uni – turned me into a right

Communist. Never dreamed I'd end up working in the beating heart of capitalism, management consultancy.'

'Everyone has to make a living. The rest is between you and your principles.'

'You're right. I suppose I want you to understand that I don't take all this very seriously – there are more significant things going on in the world than management consultancy's going to fix. But that doesn't alter the fact that every time you have a prod at the company I feel a burst of loyalty.'

'I have that effect on people,' I said. 'I'm told I make it easy for people to dislike me. But I don't want to make things awkward between you and Tara.'

She seemed to make a decision. 'This is from my budget,' she said. 'Keep out of her way and she needn't know. We've heard nothing more from the police, though God knows we're still all over the news. I know they've got an incident room and loads of people out asking questions and so on, but that all takes time. As a business we don't have time. We need to sort this before clients get jittery and pull the plug on us. There are over fifty people working here, Sam. Their jobs are on the line.'

'No pressure, then. But I'm not exactly on Tara's Christmas card list, so how will you get this past her?'

'She won't know if you don't tell her.' She moved to the door. 'All this digging you've been doing—does all the financial jiggery-pokery give you any insights as to who might have killed poor old Rory?'

'I'm making progress,' I said. 'Lots of notes.'

'What do you think is going on?'

I reached out a hand to shake hers, and held on to it for just a moment longer than necessary.

'That's for me to know and you to pay for,' I said.

13

I WAS IN MY OFFICE early the next morning to map out a plan. I cleared my desk, took out a fresh writing pad, found a working biro … and then stared at the lined paper for fifteen minutes.

Since the first day on this case it felt as though I'd been working to everyone's agenda but my own. My old feelings for Tara and the way I was beginning to feel about Laura were confusing me. I needed to take some control. Unfortunately, the universe wasn't listening.

The phone rang at nine o'clock exactly, according to my Bendix wall clock with the red second hand.

A voice said, 'It's Carol from Brands.'

I remembered the receptionist with her sniffy attitude and catwalk model glide.

'Another appointment?'

'That's right,' she said.

'When this time?'

'Mrs Brand would like to see you as soon as possible.'

'What a surprise. Where?'

'At her home—she says you know where it is. Can I tell her

you'll be there this afternoon?'

I hesitated for a moment. This was probably going to be more bad news, given the relations between us. I wondered who had told her. Not Laura Marshall, obviously, but who else would know or would have found out between yesterday afternoon and first thing this morning? Brands' office seemed to be a leaky environment in which to harbour secrets.

In the end I told the woman to go ahead and confirm the appointment. 'Tell her I'll be there for three thirty.'

This was a mistake on many levels.

I stopped to refill the car and bought a stale sandwich from the chill cabinet of the petrol station. I sat in the car and ate it, going over in my head the jumble of relationships in which I was caught up. It had briefly crossed my mind that Tara might have had a murky hand in her husband's death. If he knew she was involved in plans to take over the company, did she in turn know he was suspicious? I didn't like to think of her involved in anything more serious than a bit of light industrial espionage, but I had to be open to other possibilities.

I was also interested by the fact that although I hadn't seen her in nearly twenty years, it seemed that I didn't want her to be responsible for anything truly wicked.

It was getting dark by the time I passed between the blue vases at the entrance to the converted chapel. There were two lights burning in the main building, and past the house, in the distant fields, I could see a remote farm with a bright lamp glowing outside its barn as though acting as a beacon for wayward beasts. The aggressive punch that was the smell of manure told me someone had been spreading in the fields today. I realised how remote this place was when darkness fell.

I parked and walked past Tara's Toyota up to the house and swung the heavy knocker on the door. Its sullen thud reverberated into the house and echoed back past me into the dim courtyard, rolling down the driveway and into the gathering darkness.

A scrabbling noise at the door, then it swung inwards and Tara was standing there, looking dour. She wore a polo-neck sweater the colour of plums, with the sleeves rolled up and set off by tight jeans. As usual these days, her mass of hair was pulled back and held in a pony-tail by a green ribbon. Almost immediately she reached back a hand, tugged on the ribbon and shook her hair free as though clearing her head of nasty thoughts. I wondered if she'd been doing something that required a tidy style but now that was finished with. I was here to add untidiness to her life again.

She hesitated for a second with her hand on the door as if not sure whether to let me in. Then she stood back reluctantly and let me walk past her. I caught the faintest, incongruously erotic swell of her perfume.

She led me further inside. The style of the house was Modern Rustic—clattering York tile floors softened by deep Persian rugs, plump terracotta sofas inviting your company while dark wood bookcases flattered your intelligence. Chopin drifted around us from an expensive sound system whose matchbox-sized speakers I glimpsed here and there as they peeked out from shelves and hidden corners. This was life as lived in a magazine photo-shoot— the romantic converted chapel lightly brushed and baked in a glaze of Italian style, French atmosphere, Moroccan colour and German utility. It seemed to me to be not a house to live in, but to show off—as artificial as the purple tulips that stood on the reproduction rosewood table in the centre of the living room.

'I'd offer you a drink,' she said, 'but I don't want to prolong this meeting any longer than I have to.'

'Thanks anyway.'

She stood facing me, her arms crossed and wearing the expression of a parent disappointed by the latest exploits of an unruly child.

'Last time we talked I thought I'd made it clear that I didn't want you interfering any more with the police investigation. That's why I sacked you. Now I find that not only have you ignored me, but that Laura is ignoring me too.'

'Tricky, isn't it?' I said. I tried to hide my surprise at how much she knew.

'What do you propose to do about it?'

'My very best.'

I could see that she was angry by the way her lips became as thin as knife-blades and her cheeks lost all their blood. I was amused by how well I remembered the expression. But I wasn't about to be bullied by her this time. I moved away and sat grandly on the edge of a sofa that yielded with a professional sigh.

'Tara, I don't want to go round the houses on this. I'm just going to say it straight: financially, you're stuffed, aren't you?'

She kept her temper under control, but at the expense of seeming to rise three inches above the ground. At last she managed to get her mouth to form speech. 'You bastard,' she said in a clipped voice, almost swallowing the words. 'How dare you suggest that I had anything to do with Rory's death.'

'I'm not suggesting anything—'

'You haven't said the words, but I see where you're going. You're saying because we were losing money, I murdered Rory. That's really sick.'

'It's the sort of connection that people pay me to make. I don't have any evidence – '

'No, and you won't find any.'

'I was going to say yet. Others will see it too. The police will be knocking on your door before you know it.'

She threw her head back and looked at the ceiling. 'You dimwit,' she said. 'I talked to Inspector Howard about this the day after Rory was found. The police know all about our financial situation.'

'I see.'

'Do you? Well it's about bloody time. I don't care if you were working for Rory, there's a limit to my patience. Of course I have to honour his memory but I'm not sure I do that by condoning every paranoid half-baked theory he had.'

She was trying her hardest to intimidate me, and I began to wonder why. She didn't have to go through this routine just to sack me again. She could have sent me an e-mail or refused to pay my invoice. There was something else fuelling her anger now.

'Who told you I was still working on the case?' I said.

'None of your business,' she said crossly. 'I asked you to come out here because I thought we could talk in a sensible manner. Well that's not going to happen, is it? In future, I think you'd best keep away from me. I'll talk to Laura again and make sure she understands the situation. As a company we've got to act together on this and leave it to the police.'

'Don't blame her. She's doing what she thinks is best.'

'I'll be the judge of that. Now go home and think long and hard about what I've said. And don't contact us. I mean it. I put you out of my life once, Sam, and I want to do it again. You and me just can't cut it together.'

'What do you mean?' I looked at her closely. 'Is this about Rory or about us?'

'Let it go, Sam.'

'I wish I could,' I said. I felt a pressure rising in my chest. 'I still think you owe me. You went eighteen years without even a telephone call.'

She took this like a blow, as if she weren't expecting to be reminded of her own actions when she was supposed to have the moral high ground. She stared at me for a moment, then said, 'OK, if you want to talk about that, we can. You remember the row we had the night I left for London?'

I nodded. I'd lived for years with the image of us shouting at each other across a kitchen table.

'I never told you why I went, did I?' she said.

'As I remember, you described how you were fed up with nursing and fed up with me. It was a touching scene.'

'You stood there with your sad cow eyes and just let me go, didn't you? You didn't want me to leave but you couldn't say the words. You were so bloody passive.'

'I've become a lot more active.'

'Oh I daresay you've learned a lesson or two in, what, eighteen years? Doesn't alter the facts of the case. When I look at you I see what you were eighteen years ago, and it drives me mad. Two and a half months we lived together and I don't think you had an exciting thought or a fresh impulse once.'

'Not true …'

'That's what I couldn't tell you, Sam. You bored the pants off me. I wanted so much more, and you couldn't give it to me. So I don't want you around reminding me of what I nearly became. A Yorkshire housewife. You're off the case. And this time I mean it.'

As she spoke, the room grew less and less substantial, less and less real. Everything seemed more dim and harder to grasp, while at the same time seeming more solid and practical. I suddenly felt like Peter Pan marooned in a world of hard facts, where before there'd been imagination and dreams. A hard knot began to form in my chest.

She was still looking at me, her eyes blazing and impassioned. 'Nothing to say?' she asked. 'No snappy retort or cynical put-down?'

The words came up and out of me before I could stop them. 'I really loved you,' I said.

She was contemptuous. 'No you didn't,' she spat. 'You were infatuated with me, but it wasn't love.'

'How can you say that?'

'Because you never showed it,' she said. 'You danced around me like a bloody courtier, but you didn't understand me. You tried to fit me into your little world and never knew what I really wanted.'

'And you did?'

'I might have done, if you'd asked the right questions.'

Without realising it, I'd stepped closer to her. Now my hands rose and gripped the top of her arms, and I felt that I could take one more step and pull her towards me and kiss her and something would break between us and things would return to a sensible balance.

'Go on, do it,' she said hoarsely. Her eyes were vivid and scornful. I felt her breath on my cheeks. I held her arms, feeling their tautness, wanting to draw her to me in spite of everything.

Instead I let go of her and took a step back.

'I'd better leave you alone,' I said. 'I don't think this is the right time. You're not in a mood to listen to common sense.'

'You had your chance, Sam. Years ago. I could have stuck it out if you'd paid some attention.'

She looked down at her feet, her hair tumbling forward over her face. I thought she might be on the verge of tears, which would probably have destroyed me. I headed towards the front door, wanting to get out, and quickly. The York tiles rang under my heels again. I stood at the door and she came up beside me and I saw her reach round in front and turn the knurled knob of the lock. For a moment I thought I sensed her hesitate, as if she were reconsidering, remembering our past, not wanting it to end like this. I glanced quickly at her profile, so close I could see the lines under her eyes that eighteen years had put there. But then the door opened and I was faced with darkness, the yard and the countryside beyond made invisible by contrast with the bright wash of light from the house.

'Goodbye, Sam.' She'd hardened her tone again. 'Don't expect any calls from me.'

I smelled her perfume, a taut blend of fruit and acid, as I walked into the darkness towards my car. And going through my mind at that precise moment was how I was going to tell Laura that I was still in love with Tara. That eighteen years hadn't killed the feeling—dimmed it and made it harder to understand, perhaps, but hadn't lessened it one whit.

And then I heard the dull thump of something connecting with the base of my head, and sensed the spreading nimbus of pain, a physical hurt that quickly radiated through my skull and sent me hurtling downwards into an agony that was black, hollow and far beneath my feet.

14

THE COLD CHILL of a damp paving slab on my cheek. The tingle of an arm that has lost its circulation because it's twisted beneath my body. The realization as I begin to open my eyes that it hurts, that this is serious, that I'm in a really bad situation here. The will to move my knee—and it slides slowly along the ground. I bring up an arm and feel the effort as I shove and twist my weight to one side. The taste in my mouth of grit and blood, and the pounding in my head as I become aware of the beat thumping like an urban rhythm in the back of my brain.

As I rise to a hip I become aware of the subdued countryside chirps and rustles, the occasional swish of traffic on the road below, the lowing of a cow and the distant whine of an aeroplane far above, heading for sun.

I'm sitting now, feeling my jaw and rubbing yard dirt from my cheek and the elbows of my jacket. My head is clearing though still painful. I turn to stretch my neck—and see the open door of Tara's house, its light pulsing out slowly into the dark courtyard and illuminating a sad private detective who wishes he were somewhere else.

I rise to my feet and stumble inside. The Chopin études have finished and the house feels even more forlorn than it did when they played. The atmosphere is chill and empty, though all the lights are still on, the furniture inviting and the colours and style still trying to impress the adventurous guest.

Stumbling further into the house, I call Tara's name, but there's no reply. I inspect all the ground floor rooms but there's no sign of life. I find the stairs and gripping the newel post and the dark wood banister I begin to haul myself upwards. The stairs turn sharply twice and I have to hold tight to pull myself up. At last I reach a broad expanse of carpet that I follow, in turn, to three ordinary bedrooms, a master bedroom, a study, and a bathroom. The door to the bathroom is partly open. I lean forward and push it fully ajar, then extend my willpower and walk into the room.

It's relatively small and as green as the inside of an after-dinner mint. There's a sense of bathwater having been run—the mirror is partly steamed and the shower curtains over the bath drip with condensation. The curtains have been drawn together and tucked into the bath, their bottom edges trailing listlessly in six inches of water.

I reach out and pull back the shower curtain, expecting to see Tara curled in the bath—but she's not there. The images I had in my head refuse to go away—images of her slouched lifeless with her wrists cut, or her face blue from strangulation. Suddenly I find myself bent over, breathing deeply, supporting myself with one hand on the toilet cistern. I don't like those pictures in my head.

Then I turn and see a clump of red hair that lies in a tight bunch on a white Lloyd Loom chair next to the bath. On the mirror over the sink there are words that have been written in either lipstick or blood. They read: 'Where's the little girl?'

15

'HELLO, SAM,' HOWARD said. He'd been watching his American cop shows. When you have a suspect you can call him by his first name because you don't have to respect him. 'I wondered if I'd meet you in these environs at some point.'

'Not my choice.'

'I'll be the judge of that, eh?'

My call to the emergency services had summoned five blue-and-yellow checked police Volvos, an ambulance, three other unmarked cars and an hour later, a square forensics van. I was fingerprinted immediately 'for elimination purposes', and eventually a couple of sullen plainclothes drove me to Accident and Emergency in Macclesfield for my head to be stitched. Then I was bundled into the back of another police van and driven the short distance to this station, where I was put in a room until Howard turned up with a pair of his colleagues and began re-arranging the chairs before finally sitting to face me. He was a man in his early forties with neatly-cropped hair the colour and texture of patent leather black shoes, and an unsmiling, sarcastic manner. Laura had told me he was thorough and already I knew that he was shrewd and experienced.

'Ask your questions,' I said.

'Oh, thanks,' he said sarcastically.

He nodded to someone outside of the room and then began to speak formally, introducing himself and me and describing the two other men who were slumped in the corner of the room with their sleeves rolled up. Something was said about an absence of legal counsel under the Superintendent's instructions. He had the right to deny me counsel because of the nature of the crime. I knew that somewhere two tape-recorders had been switched on, and possibly a video camera as well.

And he did ask his questions. We went through my day. Where had I been and what had I done. Who had I talked to, where had I talked to them, what had I said. When did I go to Tara's house, what had we talked about, how did the conversation end, what had happened when I left.

'Good first attempt,' he said. 'Now have another cup of tea and let's go at it again. Oh, and this time, try to mention that you'd been married to the victim.'

I stared at him. 'You won't believe this, but it's irrelevant.'

'You're right. I don't believe it. Convince me.'

We went through it again. I remembered that the sandwich I'd bought had a cheese filling. I remembered the blue Gap tee-shirt of the boy who'd served me, and the number of zits on his chin. I had a better estimate of the time I'd arrived at Tara's. I remembered more of what we'd said to each other. And actually wished I could take some of it back. The more private parts of the conversation I kept to myself.

His two colleagues, who didn't seem particularly interested, asked the occasional question but largely deferred to Howard.

They kept it up for three hours or so. Eventually he pushed back his chair and stood. He rotated his neck.

'What do you make of the note?' he asked. 'Mean anything to you?'

He meant the writing on the bathroom mirror—"Where's the

little girl?" I said, 'I can't help you. I suppose you've checked on the family.'

'You know anything about her parents?'

'Do I get a fee for doing your job?'

'Do yourself a favour, Sam.'

'I've not seen them since we split up. Her dad was something in the Army. Her mother was just someone who stood around looking worried. Have you tracked them down?'

'Not yet. We think he's out of the country.' He yawned loudly and stretched his arms. 'Take him down,' he told his silent partners. 'I'm supposed to be at the golf club tonight. The missus is going to kill me. We'll talk again, Sam.'

'I'll look forward to it. It's a good way to waste a couple of days of my life.'

I was taken to a cell with a thick black door and a complicated locking device and asked whether I had any food allergies. Ten minutes later a beefburger and chips were delivered to me, which I ate with a plastic knife and fork and a raging headache.

16

THEY KEPT ME FOR twenty-four hours, then they had to release me or apply for an extension. My lawyer came and helped them understand. She was a girl called Veronica in her late twenties, as slim and sleek as a racehorse, with long crinkly hair and a no-nonsense attitude that seemed to cut through the procedural delays. I'd signed on with her firm in Manchester a year ago but this was the first time I'd used them. I'd use them more often if they sent Veronica again.

'They can't keep going on this,' she said, 'without actually charging you with anything. No one in their right mind thinks you abducted this woman then boffed yourself on the back of the head hard enough to need six stitches. Give 'em credit for trying, though.'

'I will.'

She picked up her bag and slung its strap over her shoulder, then looked me up and down. 'What do you want to do now? Are you in a fit state to do anything? Anyone I should call?'

'I guess not. Could you take me home?'

She smiled, putting her head on one side so that her hair fell downwards like a crinkly waterfall. 'Ah, that's sad. Walk this way, sir. I will chauffeur you to your place of residence.'

We talked little as she drove me home, then she turned the car round in my drive and whisked back to Manchester to prepare the bill for her services.

I slumped in a chair with a whisky and tried not to think of the events at Tara's house. With limited success. That meant I had to have another whisky to help my concentration. Still no good.

At the point at which I'd been hit, did I smell something? Did I hear something? Was there a shadow cast on the ground that I could recognise if I just thought hard enough? And as I'd left the house, with Tara opening the door for me, I'd glanced at her profile and caught a momentary glimpse of an expression behind her eyes. I realised now what it was that I'd seen. It was deep-seated, bone-deep fear. She was absolutely terrified of something, and I had no idea what it was. And now I would probably never know.

The woman I'd married eighteen years ago had been called Debbie Hoyt, not Tara Brand. She was a trainee nurse, not a sales wizard in a corporate environment. She'd left me and gone to London and I hadn't heard from her since.

She was still the most exciting woman I'd ever known. I'd had longer partnerships with women since, none of which had lasted, but Tara was the benchmark. The one against which all the others were measured. We were twenty years old, living in Leeds. She was a student nurse and I rented a room in the same house when another nurse left the course and created a vacancy. I was avoiding higher education by claiming that I wanted to pay my way in society, and in the meantime acted as a jobbing handyman for my friend, Barry, the painter and decorator. I'd see Debbie at odd hours, flying up the stairs to get changed before she came clattering down again half an hour later looking sleek and shapely, her short dark hair cut in a bob that clung tightly to her head and giving her the appearance of a twenties flapper. She'd charge out of the door and leap into a succession of expensive cars driven, presumably, by doctors with large overdrafts.

God knows what I looked like to her. I was still skinny, though tall, and was usually dressed in a white painter's apron with rainbow streaks drizzled over it as though I'd been coloured in by a child with no aesthetic sense but a lot of big brushes. I gave her a weak grin when we passed on the stairs but she looked right through me, as only the glamorous can.

Then we met a couple of times in the kitchen and talked. I had a sense of humour then, and managed to amuse her for the length of time it took a kettle to boil. She would stand with her back to the sink, tossing her hair and stretching her arms upwards as though unaware of the effect her body was having on me. I quit working for Barry and joined the Civil Service. Started to wear a shirt and tie. I bulked out a little because I took up running and weights. Now she started smiling when she saw me on the stairs, occasionally stopping to talk. The visitors in fancy cars stopped calling as she knuckled down to work, and we sometimes found ourselves in the room downstairs that was a shared lounge, sitting in opposite chairs and reading. At least I was pretending to read, though actually I spent the time thinking about what I could say to her next without sounding stupid.

All this happened in the space of three months. Then I stopped seeing her altogether. I began to hear music from her room, which was above mine. She was spending more time at home when she wasn't at work, slopping around in jeans and a baggy jumper she found in a charity shop. I wouldn't see her for days at a time, then I'd bump into her on the doorstep, where she'd give me a small conspiratorial smile before trotting upstairs—if a gazelle can be said to trot.

Then things happened very quickly. We got drunk one weekend at a party, and an emotion was released between us that we'd known was there but hadn't found expression until then. The pent up feeling gave it an electric charge that I still remembered nearly twenty years later. The union had been fierce, and almost as a footnote to the act, just to show it was more than a passing moment, she got pregnant. Her father—some kind of bigwig in the Army—forced us to marry, though my parents would have been happy enough if we'd decided to live together.

What I remember most is the embarrassed scene where the six of us met in my parents' house. We could barely get in the parlour. My dad was all graciousness and bonhomie, trying to make the guests feel at home; my mother spent most of the time in the kitchen, the other downstairs room, brewing tea and making scones that were hard as slate. Debbie and I sat apart on the sofa, not looking at each other. Her father, the Major, tried to take charge, but was constantly out-charmed by my dad's matter-of-factness: not to worry, these things happened, it would all work out OK, we shouldn't get upset about it, the world was a different place now. Tara's mother, a frail woman you could almost see through, seemed to agree with my dad and was all for a quiet approach to the whole situation. The Major, on the other hand, saw that the niceties had to be observed. Maybe of all of us he had the most to lose—social face, standing, the regard of the men.

So Leeds registry office on a windy Saturday morning. The six of us in best suits. For the wedding before us in the office, the bride went the whole hog—full wedding dress and train, maids of honour, corsage, the lot. Tara and I looked at each other in our plain outfits and laughed, smothering our faces with our hands.

Two months later, she miscarried. Two weeks after that she quit her course and went to London. She didn't tell me she was going until the night before she caught the train. We had a nasty stand-up row in the middle of a kitchen little bigger than a shoe-box, saying things we both regretted at once. She took nothing with her, except a piece of my heart. I hadn't heard from her since, though in quiet moments I'd thought about her. What I thought about mostly was her impulsiveness. She had sex with me impulsively, got married on a whim, left me and our marriage on the spur of the moment. It was exciting, but scary. I thought London would suit her fine.

*

I woke the next morning with a roaring migraine that beat at my head and narrowed my vision to a small tunnel. I staggered to the bathroom and downed aspirin, then fell back into bed and pulled up the covers. The pain was a constant shriek over my eye that I couldn't escape. There was nothing I could do, nowhere I could go to relieve it. All I could do was wait for the pills to kick in and allow me at least to stand up and get things done.

I was lucky—the migraines were coming infrequently now, though there'd been a time three years before when I'd had one a month. The doctors said they were caused by stress, and it was true that when I left C & E they'd almost disappeared. Now I worked for myself the stress was just as great – but caused by the job, not by the people I worked for.

My house stands by itself on the edge of countryside but within walking distance of Crewe railway station. The previous owner had run a car repair business from the garage, which he'd extended upwards to accommodate a hydraulic car-lift. Where the second storey of this extension joined the back of the house he'd installed a large window so you could stand inside the house and look over the garage and into the countryside beyond. To stand there was a test for my vertigo but at the same time a calming influence.

Migraines and vertigo. I wondered why all my troubles seemed to be located in my head. It wasn't as if I used it for much thinking.

For a while I stood with my forehead against the glass and watched the dead fields outside. Within a few minutes, though, I felt ill again, and walked around the house trying to settle down and rest, as the doctor had told me. Whenever I sat, I had to stand up. As soon as I stood up, I had to move around. As I began to move around I understood I was restless and should sit down to stop my head throbbing.

After two hours of this perpetual motion I was finally able to go downstairs and drink a litre of bottled water. Groggily, I collected the newspaper from the doormat, then spread it on the floor and stared at it. I couldn't summon the strength to turn the first page. There was no point anyway; it was too soon after Tara's abduction for any mention to be made in the press.

Slowly I began to function and was able to consider my next steps. I'd had instruction from Tara to quit the case, to leave it to the police. But no one except me knew that. I hadn't revealed this piece of information to Inspector Howard. I'd told him that Tara wanted to see me to explore how the investigation was going. I'd made up some dialogue and created an attitude of supportive encouragement. After all, we'd been married once.

But now I'd had enough. Getting back into Tara's life had caused me physical pain and professional failure. It occurred to me that if I walked away I could tell Laura and anyone else who was interested that it had been Tara's last wish for me to drop the case and leave it to the police investigation. No blame in that. This series of crimes was escalating anyway. Press and television news coverage of Rory's murder had intensified in the last couple of days, making it harder for someone like me to do my job. It was more complicated, more high profile and more difficult than any other case I'd worked on, and it was easier to let go and slip away, leaving Howard and his troops to toil for another six months before giving up. At this point I could just walk away and no one would think any the less of me.

But there were memories that were coming thick and fast now that I'd seen Tara and talked to her.

The day after we were married we'd driven to a caravan site near Filey and spent a week sheltering from an icy wind blowing down from the Arctic Circle. Her father had hired a large caravan for us overlooking the beach. It had two bedrooms, a kitchen unit, a shower and a large sitting area whose cushions unfolded imaginatively to create one huge bed. The smell of Calor gas hung over everything and hit you with a blow to the sinuses when you came inside after spending any time outside. During the week we barely left the caravan for anything but basic supplies and wine. So it was a surprise when Tara asked me to leave her alone one afternoon. She said she wasn't feeling well and wanted to sleep without me walking about and making the caravan rock.

So I wrapped myself in a heavy coat and walked a few miles up and down the east coast, towards Scarborough and back, picking my way over the coarse sand and smiling grimly at other holiday-makers caught up in the same foolhardy pursuit. Exhausted and wet through, I arrived back at the caravan, to find that Tara had cooked a three-course 'honeymoon dinner', as she called it, on the gas-fired four ring hob.

'You deserve it,' she said. 'For putting up with me. I'm probably going to give you hell while we're married, but we might as well start off on the right foot.'

We hadn't been married for long, and she had given me hell, but Tara had become part of me at that moment, and I resented the fact that she'd been taken away. Twice. Resented it enough to want revenge on whoever was responsible.

Suddenly I realised that my fists were balled and that I'd torn the newspaper in half. My thoughts were so disorganised that I hadn't noticed myself doing it. It struck me that this was what I did when I was angry. And I was angry because I was affronted. I knew that I'd been caught out by an expert. Someone who knew where to hit me. Someone big enough and strong enough to overpower Tara and take her away.

Someone like Gerald Finch.

17

AN HOUR LATER and as groggy as a drunken dog, I dragged myself to the train station and made my way via train and cab to Tara's house. I watched the wintry, bare fields trail past the cab window like a succession of Christmas cards, and thought of Tara in the moments after my head was cracked open. Where was she? What was she doing? How had the kidnapper subdued her before taking her away? Had he hit her too? I replaced that image with one of her running down the stairs in the boarding house in Leeds, her short, tight hair bobbing with each step. It made no difference; I was still depressed.

The cabbie could only park outside the entrance to the chapel, next to the two blue vases, because a police car and attendant officer blocked his way. Blue and white police tape wound its way round the site. I paid the cabbie and approached the man on duty.

'Where you going, Chummie?' he said.

I told him my name. 'If it's all right with you, I've come to get my car. Talk to your boss.'

The officer, a young-looking farmer's son with beetroot cheeks and mild acne, stepped back and spoke into his collar. The conversation went back and forth for a while, then he nodded and waved me up the lane.

To walk up to the chapel took much longer than it had taken to drive it a couple of days before. But the weather was trying to break—the sky was a fragile blue and a weak sun came through the oaks and elms, speckling the brown leaves underfoot. There was the same undertone of mulch in the air that I'd noticed before. The clarity of the air began to clear my sinuses. By the time I reached the house I was feeling more like a human being and less like a collection of nerve-ends.

Three large, white police vans and two patrol cars clustered in front of the chapel pointing at each other, and a couple of officers in yellow anoraks stood around keeping a general watch. Forensic staff wearing oversize blue all-in-ones and white gloves and carrying paper jiffy bags walked back and forth from the chapel to the vans, like aliens moving house. I couldn't believe they were still stripping the place, but it was only a day and a half since Tara had gone missing. They would be crawling over the carpets and furniture with vacuums and chemicals and ultra-violet light, hunting down DNA with the relentlessness of train-spotters.

I walked to my car. Howard came out of the chapel talking to a neatly-dressed man carrying a briefcase. I realised it was Derek Evans. Howard stopped when he saw me, then walked over, holding his hand palm up as an injunction to stop. Evans turned away and watched the forensic officers moving between the house and their van. I saw that Howard was tired, but he still managed to summon a supercilious glare to direct towards me.

'You're only here to get your car,' he said. 'No snooping around.'

'What's Evans doing here?'

'Who—oh, him. Colleague of Mrs Brand's. Professional courtesy. Now listen, you've had your go at this, Dyke. You screwed up. You don't get a second chance.'

I said, 'Talk to my client.'

He stepped up close. I could see the tired wrinkles around his eyes and the tufts of hair sprouting like weeds from his nostrils. He smelled faintly of tobacco, though I hadn't seen him smoke. 'I don't know how to make this clear to you,' he said. 'You're beginning to interfere with police procedure. You're in danger of polluting evidence. And what's more, you're getting on my tits. Everywhere I go I seem to be falling over you. You're like a bloody cold-sore that won't go away.'

'I thought we were getting on quite well.'

'I'm giving you a nice warning—stay out of the way. If I come across you again in the next week, I shall not be an happy man. Do I make myself understood?'

'I can't guarantee anything. I'm not responsible for what this villain is up to.'

'I'll have you on a charge for wasting police time.'

'If I hadn't been here it might have been days till someone found out Tara was missing. You've got a head start because I happened to turn up.'

'Funny, that.'

'Spare me the sarcasm, Howard. It might work with your young plods around here but not with me.'

This seemed to upset him unreasonably. He stood with a look of bewilderment widening his face, then got angry.

'You can piss off,' he said. 'I've told you the rules of the game. You keep out of my way. You don't interfere with police business. I don't see you around crime scenes or talking to witnesses. I don't even smell your aftershave. Have you got that in your head? Do you want the stitches tightening to make sure it doesn't leak out?'

'A low blow on an unarmed civilian, Inspector.' I had a sudden thought. 'So now your chief suspect's missing, where do you go from here?'

This caught him by surprise. 'What do you mean?'

'Tara Brand was beginning to look good for killing her husband. Don't tell me you hadn't noticed. She benefited financially from Rory's death and she wasn't keen on the new direction Brands was taking. Now despite all the evidence, I don't think you're stupid. You must have been putting this together in the same way I was.'

He turned away, shaking his head and putting a hand up to feel the shape of his hair.

'I don't believe you,' he said. 'It's true what they say about Yorkshiremen.'

'What's that?'

'They don't understand what tact is because they can't spell it.'

'That's a racist slur.'

'Do I care? Look, whether Tara Brand was a suspect or not is none of your business. What we do next as an investigating police force is none of your business. Your business is keeping out of my way. You can do that as well and as often as you like.'

He moved to my car and opened the driver's door.

'You can go now,' he said.

I climbed in. The seat had been re-adjusted and the rear-view mirror knocked to an awkward angle. There was a faint powdery smell. Forensics had been through here without taking the car in. I re-jigged the seat and mirrors to suit my position while Howard watched from the open door.

'Do we understand each other?' he asked.

'Do your worst,' I said, reaching for the door. 'I've got a living to make. It's every man for himself now.'

I slammed the door shut.

18

I WENT BACK TO my office to get my mail. There was no mail. I called Gerald Finch. But there was no Gerald Finch. I stared at the mailbox and telephone as if they were traitors.

I tried to remember everything I could about Gerald Finch. His small house. His large frame. The cat sleeping on his kitchen counter. He was big enough and I thought strong enough to have knocked me out and overpowered Tara. And certainly he was still angry enough. The atmosphere in his house was like tinder ready to explode, and he struck me as someone who could easily be the fuse.

On the other hand he didn't seem to be someone with the form for it. He worked in design. In computers. He was more likely to find a way to defraud Brands than murder Rory and kidnap Tara.

But murderers don't usually make a career of it. The murder emerges from rage and the murderer's belief that there's no alternative if reparations are to be made for the hurt or bad feelings that he's gone through. I asked myself whether I thought Finch felt that bad or demonstrated that level of rage.

The answer was, I didn't know.

Thirty minutes had passed with me thinking this through when Laura called. I wondered how long I'd been calling her Laura.

I hadn't seen her since the day before Tara's abduction. I should have spoken to her as soon as I could, as my client, but I hadn't worked out what to tell her about the events at Tara's house. She'd also left a message on my home answer phone that I'd failed to return.

'How are you?' she said. I couldn't tell whether she was angry or merely anxious.

'I'm fine, except for a bruise the size of Denmark on the back of my head. Where are you?'

'In the office. Just a skeleton staff today. We're all at sixes and sevens. It was bad enough when Rory was killed, but this ...'

'It must be tough.'

She sighed. I imagined her sitting at her desk, looking out of the windows at the blank, reflective offices in the centre of Waverley. 'You have no idea,' she said.

'Will Brands carry on?'

'I suppose you have to ask that question, don't you? If I didn't know better I'd think you had shares in our competitors. Well there's a meeting of department heads tomorrow to see what we should do. People are still telling me I should take charge.'

'Why don't you?'

There was a pause. 'I don't feel it's my place. It's not my company and I know that. But I don't see how we can stop trading—there's too much at stake for everyone.'

'Laura?'

'What?'

'I want you to do something for me.'

'Oh God.'

'I want you to be with as many people as you can. Don't walk around by yourself. Don't leave your car parked at night in streets you don't know. Am I making myself clear?'

'Why should I be a target?'

'Because you can be. You won't like to hear this, but I haven't got a clue why Rory was murdered and Tara was kidnapped. Personal or professional—I don't know. But I want you to be careful. I mean it.'

There was silence at the other end as Laura absorbed all this. A few days ago she'd have switched into Nazi mode and told me to shape up. Now she wasn't so sure.

'Anyway,' she said, 'I phoned to see how you were, and to give you some information. Champion have refused to give us any more money for the IT development. We haven't made a go of it in the last twelve months, so they're pulling the plug.'

'Do they want their three million back?'

'Not yet. It doesn't work like that. We have a few years before we have to start repayment.'

'So what difference does it make to you now?'

'The first thing we have to do is get rid of—sorry, make redundant—about forty people. We haven't sold any licences of the programme, so we can't carry on with this drain on our finances. Isn't that great timing?'

'It's a money thing.'

'It's a business thing. I hope you're not going to get wishy-washy on me, Sam. And you an ex-member of Her Majesty's Customs and Excise SWAT team.'

'That doesn't mean I ditched my ethics. Don't tell me you're happy about it.'

'Oh for God's sake. These people are used to it. The new economy and all that. I don't say I'm happy, but if it happens, it happens. There's no such thing as a job for life any more.'

'A job for longer than eighteen months would suit most people.'

'I can't talk to you if you're going to be silly.'

'So thinking about other people and their families is silly?'

'You're twisting my words. You really do like having rows,

don't you? Just when I thought we were getting on well.'

'For me, this is getting on well.'

'I guess you're a single man, then,' she said.

And hung up.

19

THE SKY WAS A lead slab scored by a blunt knife. A frigid wind cut through my standard-issue detective leather jacket as I crossed the car park and entered Brands' offices. Within ten minutes a hard-edged rain would be slanting diagonally through the air.

I'd driven up to Stockport and spent a fruitless fifteen minutes knocking on Gerald Finch's door. No answer and no sign of life. I slipped a note under his door asking him to call me. Then rather than drive straight home I thought I'd try to talk to Laura. Upsetting clients is an art, but this could possibly be my masterpiece. I wasn't happy about that.

Laura wasn't in, and I had an even frostier greeting than usual from Carol-the-receptionist. Could anyone else help? Did I have an appointment? Would I like to try again later?

'I'll try again later,' I agreed. When I turned to go, Derek Evans, the Finance Director, was watching.

'Mr Dyke,' he said. 'We met at Rory's funeral. It's fortunate you turned up just now.'

'My timing's always been good.'

'Yes. I thought I ought to tell you that in fact we're not going to continue your contract, thank you very much.'

Well why not? One damn thing came after the other at the moment, and ever since we'd met I knew this confrontation would come. When the bean counters got involved it was only a matter of time. If I didn't contribute to the bottom-line, what was I for?

'Can I ask why?' I said. I saw no reason to make it easy for him.

'On consideration, we think that while the use of a private investigator is on balance a good idea, we're going to use a larger organisation better suited to the way we operate.'

'Who've you got in mind?'

'That's none of your concern, thank you very much.'

'Is it Brannigans?'

He flinched but said nothing. Brannigans was a large and well-established agency that operated in the south Manchester area. They were slick and wore suits and carried laptops to work. Their average age must have been about twenty-five. I'd lost work to them before.

'So,' Evans went on, 'Despite the fact that Laura seems convinced that you have some talent, I'm going to ask you to stay away from our people here.'

'That's a blow.'

'Yes, I can understand you would be disappointed. I won't have you harassing the staff and getting in the way. They've had enough upset lately and I think you should leave them alone.'

'So Miss Marshall knows about this?'

'I'm afraid what I say to her is no longer any of your business.'

I had to give him credit for being upfront. But why not? I was off the clock now. If I carried on with the investigation it would be under my own steam and for my own reasons. Brannigans wouldn't say anything – they had their daily rate to keep them happy.

For some reason I was glad that Laura thought I had talent. Though after our row she might have changed her opinion. Evans was still looking at me expectantly.

'Is there something I can do for you, Mr Evans?'

'We're an odd company, Mr Dyke. I'm sure you'll have realised that from the people you've met. We've got some very mature and responsible people, real grown ups, and we've got a lot of youngsters who are still learning to drive, and living in their first flats and getting drunk every Friday night.'

'I'm sure that's very interesting.'

'I don't want you to leave with the idea that anyone working here could possibly be involved in Rory's murder or Tara's disappearance.'

'As I'm not going to be given the opportunity to find out, I suppose we'll never know.'

I couldn't read the expression that played over his face. It might have been guilt, it might have been relief. He shook my hand again. 'I must go. Thank you for your time.'

He turned and left. So that was it. If the Finance Director had made the decision, it really did seem to be the end of my relationship with Brands. I shrugged and walked to the exit.

This time I reached the doors at the head of the stairs before being stopped by a voice.

'Mr Dyke? Mal O'Donovan. Could I have a word? There's something you ought to know.'

20

H E WAS SHORT AND wiry, with grey hair and sallow skin that suggested he saw the insides of too many offices. He was formally dressed in a dark suit and tie, though his shoes were scuffed. A limp handkerchief dripped out of his breast pocket. He stuck out a stubby hand, which I shook. I looked around for Evans but he'd gone.

'OK, let's go,' I said to O'Donovan, then watched as he took me at my word, turned and sped off towards the consultancy division, his short legs pumping hard. I took off after him. He led me past the desks where I'd met Betty and Eddie Hampshire, and further into a large open-plan area where rows of desks dotted with computers were separated by waist-high partitions covered in blue felt. The space was eerily quiet compared to the hubbub in the other end of the office. It had the feel of a secluded airport chapel removed from the perils waiting on the tarmac outside.

O'Donovan guided me to a table between two shelving units that faced each other, creating a private space that seemed to act as an informal meeting area. The table was served by three tall chairs that looked like modern sculpture—stainless steel tubes and pale polished wood. We hauled ourselves on to the chairs and sat facing each other. I took out my notebook, which he noticed with a small smile before he began to speak.

No one took him seriously. Mal knew that. They thought he came in early to wring brownie points from Rory—but the fact was, he needed the time to think. Time by himself. Away from Vera and the kids and the TV and the dogs ... time when he could gather his thoughts and make sure he knew what he was doing.

So that he didn't cock up again.

He'd only done it once. Four years ago. Made a right bollocks of a proposal so that Brands actually made a loss on the job. To get the project finished, he'd had to work almost twice as many days as they'd proposed, which meant they made no profit. What's more, it threw his timetable out so he wasn't available for the other jobs he was scheduled to pick up. It was a simple sum but Mal had screwed up. He'd told Rory it wouldn't happen again. Worse, he'd told himself the same thing.

That's why he was in early that morning and every other morning that he wasn't actually out delivering. An advantage was that he got one of the parking slots at the front, which he liked. Could get a quick exit then. He usually arrived the same time as Carol and they'd go up in the lift together. He had to be careful now because he'd done his knee in playing Sunday morning football—the doctor told him to rest it as much as possible, so six flights of stairs were out of the question. This morning, Betty walked in with Carol and came up with them in the lift too, staring ahead with her usual concentration and saying nothing.

He'd realised a long time ago that he liked this routine. The life of a consultant wasn't geared around routine. It wasn't nine to five and it often wasn't Monday to Friday. So he liked it when he had a spell driving into the office and sitting at a desk doing paperwork. And he was beginning to realise that he didn't like consultancy anyway. He'd grown more cynical about it over the years. It seemed to him that he'd spent a good part of his adult life working with companies training people who didn't want to be trained in skills they had no use for at times that were inconvenient and at a cost far beyond what it was worth. Brands wasn't a small company any more—they had more money, glossy brochures, a web-site and a big loan from some gullible rich people. But he was doing the same thing now that he'd been doing five years ago. Talking about how people work together. Using ideas that weren't original and might not even have been true. The way it worked was that some academics in America did research and came up with a few concepts that they put into four-box models that were easy to draw on a flip chart. Then consultants and trainers in the UK nicked the ideas and said that what held good for American workers was good for British ones too—and European ones, if it came to that. There was a part of Mal that didn't trust this process and thought it was bogus.

In Mal's eyes, management should have been easy: treat people like individual human beings, talk to them and explain what was happening in the company, ask for their opinion when things were going to change, and don't think that because you were a manager you were better than they were.

That morning, when they got to the top floor, Carol used her swipe card to let them in and Betty went ballistic immediately. There were lights on in the office, which was criminal in her eyes. She was always sending out snotty e-mails reminding people to shut the doors and turn the lights out when they left at the end of the day, or if they were in at the weekend. It was all money being wasted as far as she was concerned. So when she saw the lights she started swearing and cussing and Carol gave Mal one of her raised-eyebrow looks and went to find the relevant light switches. Betty stormed off to the kitchen to put her sandwiches in the fridge and Mal went after her to make a drink, part of his usual morning drill.

He was putting coffee in his cup when he heard a kind of shouting noise from Carol in the main office. He and Betty looked at each other, then went out. Carol was walking backwards out of one of the small offices. Mal guessed she'd been doing her tidy drone thing and was turning lights off one by one. But he saw straight away that this was something serious. There was something out of kilter in the room, something not normal. What's more, Carol had her hand to her mouth and had gone white. She was making strange whimpering noises. Betty was standing beside him now; he felt her push him in the back, telling him to Go on, see what was up. But this was the kind of situation he didn't like. It meant he was going to be in the middle of something important, something with consequences. So he didn't want the responsibility of being the next person to go in that room. He wanted his routine. He wanted everything to go back to normal. And even while he was wanting that, he knew deep down that everything had already changed.

I said to him, 'You any idea who would want to murder Rory?'

He looked away, through the windows, and said nothing for half a minute. 'I've thought a lot about that. I read somewhere that most murders are spur of the moment. Someone loses their rag and the next thing you know they're standing over a bloody corpse with a meat cleaver in their hand.' When he spoke he had a lilting Liverpool accent that coloured his phrasing as though he were suffering from catarrh. 'This doesn't look like that. It's more premeditated. Thought through. Makes me think it was someone with a grudge going back a long time. I reckon someone was sending a message.'

'Who?'

'Don't ask me. But not anybody who works here. God knows there was plenty to get mad about with Rory, but if one of us had done it, he would have been found with his head stuffed under the lid of the photocopier with a waste-bin stuffed up his arse. Sorry to speak ill of the dead. And me a Catholic.'

'He could be tough to get on with.'

'Basically, he kept changing his mind. Then he convinced himself he'd let us all into the secret, and it was our fault for making a bollocks of it.'

'This a regular thing?'

'The longer you worked here, the worse it got. It was like when you started, you were his darling, but he gradually got bored with you, to the point where he couldn't even look you in the eye.'

'Did you ever go through that?'

He gave a small laugh. 'About once a year. I got used to it. It's the others, though. I've lost count of the consultants who left. Some just wouldn't put up with it. They buggered off. Know what I mean? Just wouldn't put up with it.'

I wrote this down in my notebook. I told him Laura had mentioned what he'd seen on Rory's laptop: "Who's the daddy now?"

'Yeah,' Mal said. 'Took me a minute to make sense of it because you don't usually see writing that big on a screen.'

'Any idea what it means?'

'Not a clue. I've been thinking about it ever since I saw it and I've still got no idea.'

'You said something wasn't right in the room,' I said. 'Was that it, or was there more?'

'There was something else. Glad you asked. This is what I wanted to tell you.'

'Now's your chance.'

He gave me a quick grin. 'The police have been putting out stories,' he said. 'They've been telling everyone the office was locked up tight. No ins or outs. But it's not true. See that door over there?'

He pointed to a grey fire door that had a metal release bar running across its middle.

'When I come out of the kitchen with Betty, that's standing ajar. Just two inches. Took me a minute to catch it, but I knew something wasn't quite right.'

'You've got a good sixth sense.'

He shrugged. 'When you come in every morning you get an idea of what the place should look like. I reckon that's how the murderer got in. Either someone left it open, or he forced it somehow. Comes in, does the dirty, walks out.'

'Where does it go to?'

'Small door on the side of the building. Nobody's going to see you early in the morning. Anyone could wander in or out. Absolutely anybody.'

21

THE BUMP ON THE back of my head was tender and made it difficult for me to sleep, so I rose early the next morning and went out for a run in light drizzle. There were four weeks to go to Christmas, and it was cold and bleak in the fields behind my house, the ground unyielding and hard as concrete, despite the rain. I ran around the edges of two ploughed fields, crossed a wooden stile greasy with dew, picked my way over an abandoned railway line and then climbed the short rise that led to a municipal playing field in which two sets of white goal posts loomed out of the morning mist. Then I turned for home, crossed two roads busy with early traffic, and tracked drying pebbles of mud over my carpet as I headed straight into the shower, where I stood like a penitent, head bowed, waiting for some kind of judgement.

Eventually I took a deep breath and phoned Laura's mobile phone.

'Well well,' she said, when she heard my voice. 'It's the solitary man.'

'Aye, well.'

'I'll take that as an apology.'

'I'm not always careful what I say.'

'You do come on like a beefy bully sometimes.'

'Is that how you think of me? I like to think of myself as a sensitive wallflower.'

'With those shoulders? I don't think so.'

This was promising. 'Where are you?' I said.

'I couldn't face work. I'm weary, Sam. All those sad faces. I've been working from home.'

'I'd like to meet you tonight—perhaps on neutral ground.'

'Given how people are feeling, that's probably a good idea.'

'Where?'

She suggested one of the large country pubs on the road that connects Waverley to Alderley Edge. I had no reason to argue, this time.

It was Friday and the place was heaving. It was a young Waverley crowd—an expensive haircut, a sleek car parked outside, a confidence borne of a large bank account and a good school. I didn't take to them much. It seemed to me that the glamour was unearned, the result of daddy's money smoothing a path through life and solving any problems that arose along the way. I pushed through the taut, shiny skin and open neck shirts to the bar and ordered a pint of the guest beer. When it came I took a deep slug and tried to forget how old I was.

I'd found a table in a corner behind a screen, so I saw Laura enter and look around before she saw me.

She made quite an entrance. She'd changed from the office formality into something a lot racier—dark purple leather trousers coupled with a simple black top, this covered by a black lace bustier that swooped around her neck and ran down her bare arms in a series of lacy swirls to her wrists. She was very slim and tall, and edged easily between the crowd as she looked past them, finally catching my gaze; that can't have been difficult, as my eyes must have been on stalks.

'Thanks for coming,' I said. 'You must be exhausted.'

'It's good to get out of the house. I can't stay home and stare at the four walls every night.'

'I bet they stare right back.'

She smiled and sat down, and I went to the bar and bought her a drink. When I returned she was on the phone. I sat quietly until she'd finished.

'Sorry about that,' she said. 'Mothers have a great sense of timing. They always call just when you're leaving the house, or about to have a drink with a man in compromising circumstances. Oh, perhaps I shouldn't have said that.'

I took another slug from my beer.

'I'm sorry I caused you problems with Tara,' I said. 'Sometimes you have to confront things head on. Cause a fuss. See what falls out of the tree.'

'Is that your standard practice? It's not what I had in mind when I asked you to investigate.'

'What did you think I'd do?'

'In my last company we called in an investigator because we thought one of the managers was salting money away. This guy, the investigator, just followed the paper trail.'

'It might come down to that in the end.' I took a sip from my drink. 'Has Evans spoken to you?'

She gave me a dim smile. 'He told me he'd asked you to leave. I told him to go boil his head.'

'I like your imagery.'

'Ignore him, Sam. It's coming out of my budget. It has nothing to do with him.'

'You really get on with him, don't you?'

'Old wars. But it would be useful to have something concrete to show. Any ideas?'

'It's still early in the investigation. It can take a while to get your bearings.'

'At our expense.' She caught herself. 'God, listen to me. I sound like our clients. Wanting to know they're getting their money's worth for every hour that's billed. Sometimes I feel like sending them copies of Das Kapital and asking them to read it and then debate the true value of labour. If it wasn't tragic you'd have to laugh.'

I looked at her closely, leaning forward to get her attention. 'Laura, I do have some questions I need to ask.'

She leaned back in her chair as if to distance herself. She didn't appear pleased. 'Is this how you work, then—trick people into thinking they're having a night off, then interrogate them?'

'It won't take long. First question. Did you get on with Rory and Tara?'

'Me? Am I a suspect now?'

'It would be a good ruse—the perpetrator of the crime hires someone to investigate it. Like something out of Agatha Christie.'

'Thanks very much for thinking I'm that clever—or devious. I've told you how I got on with Rory—all right in small doses. Tara I could take or leave. I suppose we rubbed along OK but you couldn't get close to her.' She smiled grimly. 'But then you must know that, of all people.'

This felt like a mild dose of retaliation. I felt my cheeks buzzing with blood. 'When did Howard tell you?'

'Yesterday. He came by the office. He took great pleasure in letting me in on your dirty little secret. Did Rory know?'

'Not that I'm aware of. Unless he was a damn good actor.'

She took this in. 'Howard thinks you need to be watched. He's suspicious—on two counts, really. First that you'd been married to her; second, that you were there on the night she vanished.'

'My turn now—do you think I did it?'

'You seem to have convinced the police, so that has to be good enough for me.'

'Thanks for the vote of confidence.'

'You started it.'

We both sipped from our drinks, unable or unwilling to look at each other for the moment.

'So why did you split up?' she asked.

I described the circumstances of my so-called marriage to Tara and explained that I hadn't heard from her in eighteen years, apart from when I received the divorce papers, which I signed and sent back in a fit of righteous anger.

'So was she hard work back then?' Laura asked.

'I think we both were. I couldn't give her what she wanted.'

'Which was?'

'I couldn't help her become the person she wanted to be.'

'Tough one. And do you feel guilty now?'

'What do you mean?'

'The feeling I'm getting is that you think you failed her somehow.'

I looked away uncomfortably. That was something that I'd never fully explored, even in the worst moments of despair after Tara left. Laura had got there quickly.

'I'm not a great one for responsibility,' I said. 'It's something we spoke about.'

'You and Tara.'

'She wanted me to commit to her. In some way. I thought it was because of her dad, the Major. But maybe it was the way she was—she wanted me to show something, some dedication. To her. It was always to her.'

Laura shook her head. 'That's pretty lousy. She comes back all these years later, makes you feel guilty, then vanishes.'

'Thanks. I hadn't looked at it like that.'

'Do you think she's dead?'

This was something else I'd been trying to avoid thinking about. 'Maybe not,' I said. 'But if it's the same man who killed Rory, why not leave her the same way he left him? Why take her?'

She looked down guiltily. 'Sorry. I shouldn't bring this up here. But it's hard not to. I worked with her but I didn't know her. It's a shock she's gone like this, but I don't really know what I think about it. I've never had to deal with anything like this. In

111

marketing you tend to look at the upside of things and avoid negative thinking. Not very helpful for dealing with real life.'

I didn't want to talk about Tara any more. I've always thought it was unhealthy to dwell on a past that couldn't be altered. Also, I didn't think it fair to involve Laura in the twists and turns of my relationship with my former, possibly dead wife.

I changed the subject. 'How much do you rate Mal O'Donovan?' I said.

'Oh, he told you his story, did he? Good. He's OK, as consultants go. Lots of experience. Good with the boys—when he's away on courses he gets down with the delegates, becomes one of the lads. Always gets good feedback, though I don't think Rory liked him.'

'Why not?'

'There's just something creepy about him. Untrustworthy.'

'He told me he's spoken to you about his theory of the open fire door. What do you make of it?'

'I couldn't say. I didn't notice whether it was open or not. I know the lads use it to go downstairs for a smoke. It could have been left open from the night before.'

'But what about when you get downstairs—the door to the outside. Would that have been left open too?'

'Probably not. They're pretty security-conscious. They have to be with all the gear lying around. Everyone knows it's a security door and has to be shut properly.'

'So it's unlikely it was left open the night before Rory was murdered and someone used it to get inside?'

'Unlikely, but not impossible. It's all very casual there. You must have noticed. It's the new rock and roll—office life is the same as being on tour with the Stones, now. You can call people dude, smoke dope and play music all day long.'

'It wasn't like that in our day,' I said.

'Certainly not. We wore shirts and ties, pulled up our socks and saluted the manager as he parked his Bentley and walked in.'

She raised her glass then and drank her red wine in great gulps and waggled the glass in front of me. I took it from her and headed back to the bar. I was glad that we seemed to be on an even keel again.

When I returned to the table, two young men were standing over her and talking with raised voices. I recognised the one doing most of the talking as the man who'd asked Betty if he could borrow her swipe card before going out for a smoke. His lank hair hung down over his face like a straw-coloured veil that was parted in the middle by the protrusion of his long and bent nose.

'I don't care what you think, Billy,' Laura was saying. 'Sam's working for us and he needed to ask me some questions.'

Billy stood back as I approached. The man with him was tall and skinny and made entirely of angles, and had a clear, open face across which no thoughts seemed to travel; he said nothing but mimicked Billy's tense body language.

'You've got to work out whose side you're on, Laura,' Billy said, pointing a nicotine-stained finger at her. 'Let the police do their job and stop pissing about with amateurs.' He turned to me. 'Nothing personal, mate, but you weren't exactly a lot of help to Tara, were you? I'd think you'd want to bugger off before you made another cock-up.'

'Can't do that,' I said. I put Laura's drink down, then stood to my full height and took half a step towards him. 'Why don't you leave us alone before we all get in trouble?' I smiled calmly.

'Is that a threat?'

'Might be.'

'This is the way you do business, is it? People disagree so you puff out your chest and try to look hard.'

'Never fails.'

'I don't trust the pair of you,' he said. 'This company's going right down the plughole. Someone's got to say something.'

'You've said something. Now why don't you and your friend here go and pull the wings off some flies.'

He hesitated a moment, looked at his friend, then backed off, pulling his colleague's arm as he turned. They filtered back into the crowd.

'Great work, Beefy,' Laura said when I sat down. 'Two more pissed-off people with a grudge against me.'

'They're not the ones to worry about. At least they're obvious. It's the ones who keep quiet I worry about.'

At that moment, I didn't know how pertinent this statement was about to become.

22

O N MONDAY, DEREK Evans went missing. Laura called me at eleven o'clock with the news, her voice a little breathless. She told me he'd failed to turn up to work and didn't phone in. He didn't answer his mobile phone or e-mails.

'He never does this,' she said. 'You've met him. Winner of the boring fart award. He was due for a nine-thirty meeting with the management team and didn't turn up. And we can't raise him or his wife at home.'

'Have you reported it to the police?'

'They're on the way. Given what's happened around here lately, they're moderately interested.'

I thought for a moment. At this point there was no knowing whether this was a red herring or was directly related to everything else that had been going on with Brands.

'Where did he live?' I asked eventually.

Laura gave me an address that she said was between Alderley Edge and Macclesfield—she described a large house set back from the road with solar panels on the roof. I told her I'd go look.

I arrived at the house and parked opposite the entrance to Evans' drive, which snaked upwards from the road and curved behind a row of leylandii. There were no cars on the drive and no sign yet of the police. Two wooden plant pots stood either side of the front door, their soil neatly turned but containing no shrubs or flowers this late in the year. I rang the bell and knocked loudly on the door. No reply. There was a large wooden gate painted black that stood to one side and presumably led to the back garden, but this was locked too.

The house was one of a row of four built together some time in the 1920s but not attached to each other. They had gables and bow windows and ivy climbing up under their eaves, but were also equipped with satellite dishes and alarm systems in the best suburban style. Through fences at either side of the front garden I could see the front porches of the neighbours—and as I did so I saw an elderly woman looking back at me quite sternly while gripping an umbrella in one hand. She looked like she could turn it into a weapon with the merest flick of her wrist.

'What do you want?' she said. 'They're not in. You're not selling dusters, are you? We're sick and tired of you people coming round selling cleaning materials. Now go on home.'

I put on my warmest smile and walked towards her with a hand raised.

'Hi,' I said. 'I'm Dave—Uncle Derek said he'd be in this morning but I can't get an answer.'

She continued to look suspicious, but was a little less certain of herself. 'Who did you say you were?'

'Dave—Dave Underwood. I haven't seen Uncle Derek in ages. I rang him last week and he said he'd be in this morning because he was working from home. I've come over from Norwich. I farm out there. Have you seen them round this morning?'

She lowered the umbrella and came a little closer to the fence. She was tall and sharp-eyed and was nobody's fool.

'I was walking Biggles, my dog, this morning,' she said. 'Emily was packing the car.'

'Crikey,' I said. 'That must have been a sudden decision. We were supposed to go out for lunch. What time was this?'

'I told you, I was walking Biggles. About seven o'clock.'

'Did Aunt Emily say where they were going? Perhaps I should try and meet them.'

'She didn't say and I didn't ask. We don't pry into other people's business around here.'

'No, quite right,' I said, looking around. 'Oh well, if you see them when they come back, tell them Dave called in.'

I made to go, then had an idea and turned back. 'Oh—I think they have a place in ... where was it? Down South somewhere? Could they have gone away for the weekend?'

She looked puzzled. 'Well their Brian has a place down in Narberth, but I don't know that there's anywhere else.'

'Of course—Brian. Well never mind. I daresay they'll be in touch. Thanks.'

I gave her a wave and then left. As I was getting into my car two police Volvos pulled up in front of the house and four uniforms climbed out. I hoped the neighbour gave them the same grief she gave me.

Narberth was in the bottom Western tip of Wales, about 250 miles of motorway and country roads from where I was, and the last place I wanted to be. I drove back to my house, threw some things into a bag, and got back into the car.

23

BEFORE LEAVING CREWE I'd used a CD-based telephone directory to track down any existing Brian Evans in Narberth. I found half a dozen Brians or Bs and rang them all, but none of them admitted to being the son of Derek Evans. That either said something about him as a father, or that the Brian Evans that I wanted had an unlisted number and I'd have to try a more direct route. My usual trick was to ring the person's doctor, pretend I'm the missing person, and tell the nurse who answers that I'm waiting for a hospital appointment and that I want to check they've got the right address and telephone number to send the appointment to. Always works. But this time I didn't know Evans' doctor and had no way of guessing without access to a Yellow Pages or the internet.

It was almost four o'clock, so my hunting time was running out. I parked on the high street and put on a thick fleece, then started to get my bearings. It had grown dark quickly and I had a sense of the life of the town being sucked out of it as people arrived home from work and retreated behind their curtains. Kids on bicycles gathered on corners next to the mini-supermarkets and looked at me territorially as I went past.

My first stop was the Post Office, but the lady in there either couldn't or wouldn't help me. If Evans wasn't in the telephone book, the postal system was blind. 'I'm sorry, love,' she said. 'We're not supposed to go around giving out that kind of information, see.'

So I hit the street again, working my way on foot around the main stores.

I tried the ironmongers and the insurance company, but no one could help. They looked at me through narrow eyes and had we been in Texas I would have seen them reaching for the shotgun under the counter. But in the third shop I entered, a woman with wiry grey hair that sprouted in all directions, and teeth that looked as though they were wearing thin, drew a deep breath when I mentioned the name of Brian Evans.

'Ooh yes, we know him,' she said liltingly. 'Nice young man but we don't like his wife. She comes in to pay the newspapers and never a hello or how are you.' Her eyes took on a shrewd look. 'Why do you want him then?'

'Some of his old college friends are throwing a surprise party.'

'I see, it's a secret.'

'For a surprise,' I said. I didn't like lying to this woman, whose face was maternal and trusting while at the same time seeming to look straight through me.

'We've never been to his house,' I said. 'I was roped in to find out where he lives. We're going to wait in his garden and surprise him when he comes home from work.'

She nodded slowly. 'That'll be cold, see, in this weather.'

'We don't mind.'

'Known him a long time, have you?' she asked, resting her elbows on the counter.

This was getting too serious. 'If you don't know where he lives, I can ask someone else.'

'Oh I know where he lives. And I'm wondering why you have to come in here and start telling me all these fibs so you can find

119

out.'

'I'll go now.'

'I'll tell you,' she said suddenly, standing up straight, 'because I don't think you're a bad man. I don't think you mean him any harm. What is it, then? Does he owe money or something?'

I looked at her. 'You're very bold. You don't know who I am.'

'Perhaps. But I used to be married to the Police Sergeant down here, over at the station, see. I met a few bad people in my time, and Arthur told me about plenty more. Before he died, God rest him. You're not one of them, are you, but you're not being straight with me.'

I looked around her shop. It was a small newsagents and tobacconists that carried one wall of glossy magazines, a carousel of postcards and a glass cabinet of speciality cigarette lighters. I didn't understand how anyone could look at these objects all day long and not go crazy. But maybe she had.

'It's his father,' I said. 'I'm trying to find Brian's father. He's gone missing up in Cheshire and this seemed a good place to start. Do you know him?'

'Derek? Oh yes, I know Derek. What's that thing about knowing the price of everything and the value of nothing? That's Derek. Never liked him or his mother. Brian turned out all right, but Derek was always shifty.'

'What else should I know?' I asked.

At this she shook her head slightly. 'I've done my gossiping for the day,' she said. 'Very nice too, but it's not Christian to go on about others, is it?'

I stared at her. 'So how do I get to Brian's house?'

'Come out here,' she said, 'and I'll show you.'

Her name was Ruth and she knew most of what had happened in Narberth for the last twenty years. And didn't like it much. Too many immigrants from England; too little for the kids to do; too little work for their dads. She gave me this commentary as she pulled me down the street and at the second corner, pointed up a road that headed north and was bordered by large white-fronted houses that gave directly on to the pavement.

'Up here two hundred yards, then take the first left,' she said. 'The road opens up and after a while you'll see a row of three houses set back behind low brick walls. Brian's is the middle one.'

'You've given me a hard time,' I said.

'Are you laughing at me, young man?'

'I guess I am. But you like it, don't you?'

She punched me lightly on the arm. 'Just don't tell him I told you.'

'Sealed lips,' I said.

She turned and walked away, limping slightly on fat legs encased in thick stockings. Strange the people you meet in this job, I thought.

I cut across the road, started my car, then drove back and followed her directions. I parked opposite the row of three houses she'd described. Lights were on in the downstairs rooms of all three, but the curtains were drawn only in the house belonging to Brian Evans. A dented Rover 420 was parked in its driveway—a car that I thought was unlikely to belong to a Financial Director at a swish management consultancy in Cheshire.

I sat in my cold car and wondered whether I was on a fool's errand. Derek Evans could be at the opposite end of the country, or in the Bahamas for all I knew. But there was something about his cowed bellicosity towards me that made me think that his ambition would be small and that if he were running away, he wouldn't have the guts to run far—at least not to begin with. He may not even have told his wife yet, saving up that task for when she began to ask questions.

And there was, of course, the question of why he'd run away in the first instance. If that was what he'd done. Maybe he'd turned up at Brands this afternoon. Maybe if I phoned Laura now she'd tell me that he'd arrived in the office at three o'clock wondering what all the fuss was about—wasn't a man allowed to have a round of golf on his day off ... ?

But somehow I didn't think so. Things were too tense and at the same time too controlled at Brands for someone in Evans' position to simply take a day off without letting anyone know what he was doing. There was something guilty and furtive in his actions.

Any further thoughts I might have had about this were cut short when a long Audi 8 pulled up silently outside Brian Evans' house. Derek Evans climbed out of the driver's side and waited while a woman I took to be his wife, Emily, got out the other side. Satisfied she was out and her door was shut, he pressed his key and the doors of the car locked with a flashing of indicators. They had no bags and walked straight up to the front door. Evans looked around and then knocked quietly and after a moment the door pulled back and they slipped inside.

I sat watching for ten minutes. What now?

24

I SPENT THE NIGHT in a cheap bed-and-breakfast where the bed was too short and the breakfast consisted of stale bread brutalised into toast and cornflakes that were as soft as confetti left in the road.

By 7:30 I was outside the younger Evans' house again, yawning into the back of my hand and chewing gum to get the taste of stale bread out of my mouth. Fifteen minutes later Derek Evans and a younger man I presumed was his son came out of the house and climbed briskly into their own cars. Derek Evans drove off and Brian reversed his old Rover on to the road and followed. I waited a few seconds and then pulled out behind them.

The weather had turned wet, and it was difficult to follow their greasy tail-lights as they drove further north, away from the suburbs and into hillier and wilder country. Rain slanted down into my windscreen and turned the whole world outside into a grey mess that seemed to get no lighter even as daylight proper began to break over the hedgerows. We drove for twenty minutes with me wondering what the hell I was going to do when we arrived at our destination, wherever that turned out to be.

The tail-lights ahead burned brighter momentarily as they

braked, then both cars turned left. When I reached their turning point I slowed down and saw that they'd turned into a gravelled courtyard surrounded on three sides by low grey buildings capped by tin roofs and entered through wooden doors. I drove past, found a gated field opening a hundred yards further on, turned, and came back. I waited five minutes, then drove through the entrance and pulled up next to the two cars that stood together and were still ticking like grandfather clocks as they cooled down. They were parked outside the central one of the three buildings, which had a wooden sign nailed over its door that read, 'Floordamp Ltd.' I climbed out of my car and looked more closely at the other two structures. They were warehouses, each with large double doors at one end serviced by loading ramps. This was a working day, but there were no other people around and no cars except those belonging to the three of us parked on the gravel. The smell of freshly-cut timber and wood-smoke floated towards me from another industrial unit behind this one, then the sudden whir and grind of a sawmill erupted into the air.

The door of the middle building opened and Brian Evans came out. He was probably in his mid-twenties. He was as slim as a racing dog and almost vibrated with pent-up tension, like a shaken soda bottle. His Adam's apple protruded above the collar of his shirt and his wrists, too, showed knobbly bones where they emerged from his suit jacket. His face was pinched tight and ruddy, as though he'd been engaged in a shouting match, but I think this might have been the result of him creating an internal pressure so that he could deal with me.

'We're not open,' he said. 'Please leave the property.'

I took a step towards him and he visibly flinched.

'I'm here to talk to your dad, Brian,' I said. 'He knows me.'

'He's not here ...' he began, but couldn't help his eyes sliding sideways to the Audi squatting five yards from him like an open rebuttal to his words.

This was getting me nowhere. I walked past him as though he

wasn't there and went into the building, which was as grey and dismal inside as it appeared from the outside. It was one large space that had been subdivided into three office cubicles by hip-height screens along the far wall, the rest of the space seeming to act as a dustbin for torn cardboard boxes, fat rolls of bubble-wrap, sheets of corrugated cardboard and boxes of those plastic filling shells that look like marshmallows and cling to static electricity. Derek Evans was standing to attention by a chair in the central cubicle, staring at me as though I'd dropped in to put him through a formal inspection—which, in a way, I had.

'I thought I'd fired you, Dyke,' he said, his voice sounding forced and unconvincing. He looked tired, his eyes showing pink rims and with dark half-moons emerging on his pale cheeks. Those eyes now flicked over my shoulder at Brian, who had come in behind me and shut the door.

I ignored his comment. 'So what's going on here, then, Mr Evans?'

'What's that supposed to mean?'

'You know as well as I do. You've gone AWOL from Brands and then turned up here as though butter wouldn't melt in your mouth. I'm sure the police team investigating Rory Brand's murder would find this all very interesting, not to say enlightening.'

'What's he saying, Dad?' asked Brian.

I turned to him. 'Left you out of the picture, has he? What is it? Running a dummy company for him, but you haven't a clue what's happening? Listen, Brian. Get out while you can. Walk away.'

'Don't talk to me like that, whoever you are.'

I looked around the room. Despite the temporary feel to the buildings the floor was concrete, and in the far corner a rug had been rolled back and a thick metal door about a foot square had been opened out of the floor. Next to it lay a small tan briefcase, its lid open but turned away from me.

Evans saw me looking. I realised that his upright stance when I entered had been an attempt to distract my attention away from the safe, like a child moving away from the scene of an accident in order to show his innocence. He really was living on the edge of his competence.

'You take the cake,' I said to him. 'How long has it been going on?'

'What?

'Okay, if that's the way you want it I'll go phone Inspector Howard now.'

I heard a sudden shuffle of feet behind me and on instinct moved to my left. Something heavy glanced off my shoulder and I turned to see Brian standing with a square marble ashtray in his hands, his eyes wide open, a fleck of spittle on his bottom lip. He began to raise the ashtray again so I stepped forward and popped him with a medium strength punch on the point of his jaw. He staggered and fell backwards awkwardly into a metre-high roll of bubble wrap, which unfurled a tongue beneath him and exploded with a thousand little exhalations as he fell to the floor. He dropped the ashtray and raised a hand to his jaw.

'Ow! You bastard, I'll get you for that.'

'Sit still, Brian,' I said.

I turned back to Derek. He had collapsed and was sitting on a plastic office chair. The rain outside came harder and drummed on the tin roof like an overture for his confession.

'Well?' I said. 'Do we have to carry on with this nonsense?'

'All right. If you're going to be a bully about it. Where do you want me to start?'

'You and Rory Brand.'

He sighed and looked away from me. 'Rory knew nothing about money,' he said. 'It was almost criminal to see the waste after we got the venture capital. New cars, new equipment, staff we didn't know what to do with or even what their job descriptions were.'

'So you thought you'd get in on the action.'

Brian spoke up from the floor, his voice nasal. 'This is a legitimate business.'

'I can see that,' I said. 'All your workforce on holiday today? Go on, Derek.'

'Brian already had this company registered. It never really got off the ground. So I got him to send invoices to Brands periodically and I made sure they were paid.'

'Damp-proofing? How much damp-proofing did Brands need?'

'I bought a ready-made company name,' Brian said. 'Floordamp Limited. It was cheaper. Actually, we supply IT services and consultancy.'

I looked around at the cardboard boxes and wrapping paper. I remembered the hardware stacked in boxes in Brands' offices and had a sudden realisation. 'So let me guess—you buy PCs and computer gear cheap off the net, then re-package it and re-sell it to Brands at an inflated price. Together with maintenance contracts and a help-desk service. Didn't your IT buyer smell a rat?'

'I made sure we recruited a junior who bought what we told him to.'

I walked over to the tan briefcase and turned it towards me. It was half-full with bundles of high-denomination notes; there were more in the floor-safe. 'Jesus,' I said. 'How much?'

'Two hundred grand, thank you very much. Perhaps we can come to an arrangement ...'

'The police will be here in a few hours, if they're doing their job. Won't do me any good to be caught with my hand in the cookie jar, will it?'

Derek and Brian looked at each other. 'So what's next?' Brian said. I felt sorry for him. I guessed he thought his dad was helping him out, not getting him deeper into the mire. I wondered if he'd known how much his dad was creaming off the top. Derek was the accountant, after all. And we all believe what our accountants tell us. I ignored Brian's question and turned to his dad.

'So why did you kill Rory? Did he find out about your little money-laundering scheme?'

His eyes widened. 'I did no such thing!'

'Then why the runner?'

'I thought ... I thought with Rory gone and Tara missing, the company wouldn't last much longer. I wanted to just get away, go away from it all, I mean.'

'You didn't think it would look suspicious?'

'I had no motive and I'm not that kind of man.'

'And of course the police knew this and would therefore leave you out of their investigations. You really are a dolt, aren't you? This kind of malarkey is exactly what would bring them hot on your heels.'

'I wasn't thinking about them.'

'So do you know anything about Rory's murder or Tara's disappearance?'

He sighed deeply. His ruddy cheeks were regaining some of their colour and he rubbed his hands through his mutton-chop whiskers as if pushing life back into them. 'Absolutely nothing, I swear,' he said. 'I didn't really like Rory, if you must know. He could be a brutal man.'

'In what way?'

'You're an investigator. Find out.'

I closed the briefcase and lowered the lid on the safe. 'I don't think you're in a bargaining position,' I said. 'You have a couple of options, though.'

Brian was standing now and watching us from the other side of the room. 'What options? Aren't you just going to snitch on us?'

'You're not on the radar,' I said. 'I'm after whoever's got Tara. Not interested in this lot. That is, so long as I get some cooperation.'

Derek Evans stood up, running his sweaty palms down his overcoat—the one he'd worn to Rory's funeral. 'I've told you, I

128

don't know anything about Rory's death. As far as I was concerned, it was just the last in a long line of bad decisions. As for Tara, I'm worried about her, but I know nothing about her disappearance. You can tell the police about us or not, but I can't help you.'

I looked from father to son, the sad gang of white-collar thieves who could barely stand up without an instruction manual.

'You said Rory was brutal. What did you mean?'

'He took no account of people's feelings.'

'And being a Financial Director, you did?'

'Talk to Andy Braithwaite. Talk to Eddie Hampshire.'

'Who's Andy Braithwaite?'

'The computer man Rory stole Compsoft from.'

'I've met Eddie Hampshire. Why should I talk to him?'

'Didn't you know, Mr Clever-Dick private eye? Rory fired him two weeks ago. He's working out his notice.'

No, I didn't know that, I thought.

25

I LEFT THE EVANS gang stewing in their own juices and drove away. I didn't want to have to explain to Howard how I'd tracked Evans down, and I certainly didn't want him suspecting any involvement from me in the money-laundering scam. If the police found them, it would be without my help.

I drove home the long way, directly north through the Welsh countryside, rather than heading east for the clogged motorways. I drove up towards Carmarthen on the A40, then through Llandovery and Builth Wells, and stopped for elevenses in the grandiose surroundings of an old hotel in the centre of Llandridrod Wells. Once seated in its vast lounge, my coffee poised on a small table alongside a tray of biscuits, I phoned Laura, who answered immediately.

'Where are you?' she asked, her voice sounding both impatient and tired in the earpiece of my mobile phone.

'I don't think Evans is coming back,' I said.

'You've seen him?'

'Don't ask me that question. It might get you in trouble. But take his name off his office door.'

'Do you always talk in riddles?'

'Professional obligation.'

'You'll need to talk plainly if you want paying.'

'Meet me tonight and I'll say more.'

'I don't respond well to being bribed,' she said crossly.

'Then think of it as an incentive. Something to look forward to.'

Personally, I was looking forward to seeing the leather trousers again.

She met me at a restaurant near the railway station. Unlike most restaurants near railway stations, it was upmarket and glamorous, with two large rooms decorated in a pale cream, waiting staff like trainee undertakers all in black, and offering a curious mixture of French and Mexican cuisine. As usual, the clientele was young and wealthy. There seemed to be no one in Waverley over the age of twenty-five and with a less than six figure income.

'You have something to report,' Laura said, slipping into the space next to me at the bar. The leather trousers had been replaced by a pencil-skirt in navy blue, with a beige halter top revealing her slender arms and prominent collar bone. Her face shone in the half-light and her make-up was subtle but well-defined. I signalled to a barman and Laura asked for a Perrier with ice and a slice.

I hadn't given much thought to what I was going to say about Evans' scam, but I reasoned that as a client she deserved to hear something. It was also good for my professional reputation to have had a success, however small.

'Evans was ripping Brands off,' I said.

She went very still. 'How?'

'His son had a company through which they sold computer gear bought cheaply and marked up before it was sold on to you.'

'Bloody hell,' she said. 'We've spent something like six hundred grand on IT in the last two years. Networks, servers, PCs and continual software upgrades.'

'You paid about a third more than you should have done. He was walking off with two hundred grand under his arm.'

'What have you done with him?'

'I'm not martial law, you know. I haven't "done" anything with him. If Howard asks me nicely I might tell him, but as Evans isn't involved in Rory's murder I've got nothing to say.'

She turned on her swivel stool to face me more directly. 'I hardly think that's your call,' she said. Her eyes were glittering in the reflected light from the bottles and mirror behind the bar, as though full of a dark intense fire. 'What if you're wrong and Evans is involved somehow in Rory's death and Tara's disappearance?'

'He's not.'

'How can you be sure? You're suddenly an expert on Derek Evans and what goes on in his head?'

I took a hit from my beer, turning away from her gaze. 'I didn't come here to argue,' I said. 'Evans is a creep but he's a scared creep. He doesn't have the ambition or the guts to kill Rory. White collar theft, where he doesn't have to put anything personal on the line—that's his strength.'

We were both silent for a while, like surfers waiting for the waves to arrive and burst overhead before paddling through them, arms flailing. She broke first. 'If I'm paying for your time, I want you to put this stuff about Evans into a report. That money belongs to Brands, anyway.'

I conceded she might be right. 'I'll mention it when I write my report. You can show it to whomever you like.'

A smile touched her lips. 'Whomever?'

'All the best detectives are literate,' I said. 'We have to take courses in business writing to get our badge.'

A group of women came into the room, hooting and talking loudly to each other and wearing paper hats. A birthday party. I wondered where Tara was and what she was going through, if she was still alive. I felt momentarily guilty for being here with Laura, flirting a little, drinking, feeling good that I'd solved a problem and generally having a good time. Surely I owed it to Tara to be taking things more seriously?

'Deep thoughts,' Laura said quietly. I snapped back into the room.

I said, 'Did you know Eddie Hampshire had been booted out by Rory?'

Her eyebrows rose. 'Evans tell you that?'

'You didn't know?'

'I had suspicions but Rory hadn't said anything. So he's working out his notice, I guess.'

'Seems pretty happy about it, doesn't he? Or is he the kind of guy that nothing puts a crimp in his tie?'

'Nobody likes to lose their job,' she said. 'Unless he's got something else to go to.'

A waiter told us our table was ready and led us to a dark corner. A long-stemmed rose erupted proudly from a slim vase placed in the centre of the table.

I looked at the other diners sitting at round tables and having a good time. There was a glitter and sparkle in the air from the healthy skin and bright jewellery of the élite band eating here tonight. I continued to let my gaze drift around the room. Through the dark windows, edged with silver in anticipation of more serious Christmas decoration, I saw the blue flash of a police car's roof light. There seemed to be no escape for me these days— everywhere I turned I fell across a policeman. Another blue flashing light joined the first and went past the window. Waverley was obviously enjoying a mini crime-wave tonight.

Laura patted my hand. 'So do you have a plan, dude? Want to share?'

'Sharing is for softies. Is Waverley a hotbed of crime?'

'Not that I know. Why?'

'Building a picture. Context is all.'

'First you threaten some colleagues of mine with physical

violence, now philosophy. You have a wide range.'

The blue flashing lights stopped outside the restaurant. I turned and saw Laura looking at me. 'What's wrong?' she asked.

'Nothing,' I said. 'Just experiencing déjà vu.'

'I knew you were going to say that.'

'You seem to be in a good mood tonight.'

'Given everything that's happened? Well, I can do moody, but not for long. That's why they're called moods. After all, what's going to happen now, tonight, that could be worse than what's happened in the last couple of weeks?'

I started to say something to her, when a movement caught the corner of my eye. I turned towards it—and saw Inspector Howard edging sideways between tables. Two uniforms trailed behind him, looking embarrassed in these glamorous surroundings, their cheeks pink and their eyes fixed straight ahead. Howard arrived at our table, and looked down at Laura. He had the stern look of a disappointed father etched into the lines of his face. The two uniforms came and stood either side of him and also looked down at her.

'Hello, Miss Marshall,' Howard said. 'Sorry to disturb you.'

'Well I am disturbed, actually.'

'I realise that,' he said. 'I'm afraid I'm going to have to ask you to come with us to the station.'

Her mouth opened slightly and she looked at me, her eyes round and completely shocked. I started to rise, but Howard put out a hand to keep me seated.

'What's all this about?' Laura said.

Then Howard turned slowly and looked at me. He spoke deliberately, savouring each word. He said, 'I'm arresting Mr Dyke, and we'd like you to come with us in order to make a statement.'

26

THEY PROCESSED ME through the custody officer and put me in a dank cell that smelled of bedding that hadn't been washed in a month, then left me for an hour with only my thoughts and a pair of shiny shoes for company. I sat on a bench made more comfortable by a bright blue plastic mattress and watched a spider make connections between two grey bricks in the top corner of the cell. I wished I could make connections as easily. I had pieces of information but nothing linked. I was suddenly aware of the size of my ignorance, an awareness that moved like a poison down my chest and settled in my stomach.

It also began to kick off another migraine. I laid back on the bunk and put my hand over my eyes, trying to settle my breathing and calm the tumbling thoughts that I only became aware of when one of these headaches started up. Instead, I began to feel sick.

What did the phrases left with Rory's body and in Tara's bathroom mean—'Who's the daddy now?' and 'Where's the little girl?' Was there any significance in the fire-door being open in the office where Rory was murdered? What impact did the fact that Brands was losing money have on the people who worked there— particularly on their morale? And their potential for murder? Was

Derek Evans as uninvolved in the murder and kidnapping as I thought he was?

I didn't have answers to any of these questions.

After an hour the cell door made several metallic noises and then swung open. Howard stood in the doorway with his hands in his pockets, staring at me through pouched eyes. I sat up slowly with my hands on my knees and my head down. I didn't give him the satisfaction of showing him my face.

'We found some fingerprints,' he said. 'Round the back of the Brand house, on the windowsills.'

'Aren't we supposed to be in an interview room with two of your mates?' My voice sounded hoarse and distant.

'I don't recall any part of the story that has you going round the back of the house.'

'You should talk to my solicitor about these interesting facts.'

'You'll remember we took your prints when Tara was kidnapped. So we were able to match these new ones to you.'

'Lucky.'

'Anything to say?'

'Not that you want to hear to your face.'

My migraine began to pound more fiercely behind my eyes. I stared down at the floor and imagined myself in a calm, quiet place. It didn't help. I heard my voice echoing in my ears as I tried to make Howard feel bad. 'What have you done with miss Marshall?'

'Took a statement and let her go.'

'You know she's my client. That's her only connection with all this.'

He shrugged. 'What's a few questions between friends?'

'Enjoy it while you can, Howard.'

I looked up and he smiled without saying anything. After a moment he turned and left the doorway and the cell door swung closed again. I lay down and closed my eyes. I thought about Laura and what Howard had said to her. I hoped she didn't listen too closely.

Eventually they led me upstairs to a green interview room that smelled of crushed cigarettes and grilled me thoroughly—with the occasional break for the legally permitted meals. I gave my version of events and felt my stomach sink each time they asked me to repeat it. I told them about visiting Tara and hearing voices inside the house; I mentioned the big BMW, whose driver I never saw; I described that first meeting with Tara, when she'd slammed the door in my face without saying anything.

'How did she appear?' Howard asked.

'Tired. But then she'd just buried her husband.'

'When you say "tired", what do you mean?'

Interview techniques have moved on from the bullying tactics of years gone by. The modern style of interviewing is to ask the suspect to go over his story while looking for inconsistencies and holes that you can probe. There are specialist, trained interviewers who speak quietly and in an understanding fashion, trying to build rapport. It's effective, eventually, but God it's boring. I told Howard that 'tired' meant exactly what it sounded like. He looked at me dubiously.

'What do you know about Derek Evans?' he went on.

'He's the Finance Director of Brands. I've met him.'

'Do you know where he is?'

'Not at this moment.'

'Have you spoken to him?'

'I've met him, so I've spoken to him.'

'I mean recently.'

I hesitated. 'Yes.'

'When?'

'Earlier.'

Howard leaned forward in his seat. 'You went down to Wales?'

I nodded.

'Say it,' he said, glancing towards the recording device.

'I talked to him today, in Wales.'

Howard smiled, folding his arms. 'He said you found him this morning. We just missed you.'

'Did you find Brian and the money?'

The smile vanished from his face. 'What money?'

'Check the airports and the ferries,' I said.

Howard glanced at one of his colleagues, who left the room hurriedly. Far from being grateful, Howard became more grim. 'You've been a bad boy,' he said. 'You've got to learn to tell the truth.'

'Will it do me any good?'

'If it fits.'

'The facts as you know them.'

'You didn't tell us about seeing Tara at the house beforehand. You didn't tell us you'd been married to her. You didn't tell us about the mysterious stranger in the big BMW. Is there anything else you didn't tell us?'

'I'll have a think.'

'Well have a think on your own time,' he said, and gestured for me to be taken away again. 'People do their best thinking while staring at the back of a cell door.'

As he turned to go, I said, 'Have you spoken to Gerald Finch?'

He looked at me over his shoulder. 'The man Brand sacked?'

'One of them.'

'What's he got to do with anything? He was alibied for Brand's murder.'

'He's a big man. He could have knocked me out and taken Tara under one arm, like Shrek.'

Now Howard turned fully to face me.

'Got any evidence? Motive?'

'He and Rory disliked each other. It's worth a punt.'

He shook his head. 'You take the biscuit, Dyke,' he muttered. 'This is your finest hour. Back to the wall and you try to throw the blame on someone else.'

'So you'll give Finch a call?'

'Finch is out of the country,' he said. 'We told him to tell us of his whereabouts and he did. He's in Belgium on business. He checked in with our colleagues in Ghent. Happy?' He couldn't help a condescending smile twitching the corners of his lips.

'You mentioned motive.'

'So?'

'What's my motive for killing Rory and kidnapping Tara? Why would I do it?'

'Grow up, Sam. Envy, revenge, lust – they're all in there. You've known Mrs Brand a long time. When you found out Rory was married to her it must have hurt. Who knows what goes on in the mind of a crazed killer?'

'That's me all right,' I said.

We both knew they didn't have anything more to go on than my brief marriage to Tara and the fact that I was there the night she was taken. Admittedly both of these were worth a poke, and I couldn't blame Howard for trying. But there was no more physical evidence and no real motive that held up. They knew I hadn't seen her in nearly twenty years.

I could tell Howard was frustrated but his heart wasn't in it. He had the air of someone going through the motions for the sake of appearances, and possibly to appease the press. He had to be seen to be doing something, and I was It until something better came along.

I slept briefly and in the morning I was feeling better and ate the food when it came. At lunch time, when I might have been expecting more food, Howard solemnly took me out again and went through it all one more time. He was beginning to look tired—his eyes were dark and his shoulders slumped forward so far they almost met in front of his chest.

By late afternoon I was back in the cell and was on nodding acquaintance with the uniform who locked me up. He looked at me without letting a single emotion show on his face. But I knew deep down he was on my side.

Finally Veronica was able to weave her legal magic again. It seemed that when forensics took my prints the first time, after I was knocked out at Tara's house, they were taken as elimination prints to exclude them from consideration alongside any others they found. They couldn't then use those prints as the basis for an arrest just because they had a match. I could almost hear the fireworks from my cell. I was unprocessed by my friendly uniform and got my possessions back.

'They knew all that,' Veronica said to me when we were outside. 'They were trying it on just to throw a scare into you. What the hell have you done to piss Howard off?'

'I breathe,' I said.

'Well try to do it more quietly,' she said.

Then she zoomed off again, hair flying behind her like a superhero's cape.

27

I'D BEEN BANGED up for almost twenty-four hours. I had no cash, no change of clothes, little self-respect and was suffering from the aftermath of institutional food. I'd let Howard brow-beat me into talking about Evans and I wasn't proud of that, though God knows I didn't owe Evans anything. Worse, I'd involved Laura in some of the messier aspects of private investigative work and probably implicated her in concealing evidence of a crime. Way to go, I told myself.

Despite these misgivings, I phoned Laura and asked her to pick me up from the station. Half an hour later she arrived and smiled grimly as she leaned over to open the passenger door. It was dusk, and in a fanciful moment the weather had decided to burn the edges of the sky red; her face glowed as it caught the last of the light.

'Where to, Beefy?'

'Home,' I said, and she pointed her Saab convertible and drove like a bullet out of the car-park.

'Howard doesn't like you very much,' she said after a while.

'What did he say to you?'

'He told me about the fingerprints at the Brands' house and

what the implications were for you.'

I glanced at her. 'He's trying to strongarm us.'

'I know.'

'We're embarrassing him so he's trying to frighten us off.'

'I know.'

'He didn't have anything on me, he's just frustrated.'

'I know, Sam. It's all right, I'm not frightened off. I understand what's going on here. Howard's trying to clear the decks and keep us out of the way. When I say "us" I mean you of course.'

'That's what I thought.'

'As long as we're not breaking the law I'm willing to carry on with your investigation.'

'That's all right then.'

She drove for a few miles in silence, handling the car as if she were stroking a big cat, with a calm attention to detail. Outside, the dark Cheshire countryside flickered past, hiding its secrets behind high hedges and a sense of its own superiority. I thought how far my relationship with Laura had changed. I was almost at the point where I considered her a friend. Where once I'd seen an efficient businesswoman with a drive to achieve, now I saw a young woman who hid her vulnerability beneath a show of calm professionalism. I was beginning to see that I could depend on her, which wasn't something I'd done with many people. I felt myself relaxing into the leather passenger seat.

'You don't talk much, do you?' she said eventually. 'Nothing to get off your chest?'

'I'm a seething mass of internal passions,' I said. 'But I keep them hidden so they don't get in the way. In fact I shouldn't tell you this, but I've been accused of playing the tough guy to keep people at arm's length.'

She thought about this with the air of a Buddhist considering one of the four fundamental truths. 'You don't play at being tough,' she said. 'I think you're the real deal. With fries.'

'Thanks. I'm touched.'

'So what do we do now? Have you eaten? We could go somewhere.'

'I'm OK. The one thing the British justice system does is keep you fed. It's procedure.'

Another pause for thinking. I was beginning to enjoy this leisurely conversation, and I was beginning to enjoy being in Laura's company.   She said, 'I've been thinking about this whole thing.'

'I would hope so.'

'You're going through a lot of hassle at the moment, with no guarantee of a pay day at the end. If you want to give it up I'd understand. Brannigans are beavering away in the office every day—they've been given their own room.'

'That must be interesting for you.'

'They're going through the accounts like train-spotters, writing down mysterious numbers and talking to each other in code. Do they go to special detective school to learn that?'

'It's a secret wing of the accountants association—special forces division. Their motto is, He who adds, wins.'

She looked sideways at me.

'You could sack them,' I said, 'now that Evans is out of the way. I take it he is out of the way?'

'We haven't heard from him. I don't know if Howard has any plans to charge him with fraud on the company. I suppose there has to be an investigation and so forth. I hope they hang, draw and quarter the little bastard.'

'In answer to your question, I don't want to quit. First, I'm having way too much fun. Then there's the glamorous life style to consider. There's also the fact that I'm starting to get huffy. I've been knocked out, locked up twice and humiliated in public. Howard is pulling my chain and people keep talking to me as if I'm a moron.'

Laura smiled. 'I just love it when a Yorkshireman expresses vulnerability. It's like sunshine on a rainy day. So what are you going to do? Do you have any leads?'

'A couple.'

'Is that all?'

'It's not quantity, it's quality.'

'So you speak detective too.'

'My dad used to tell me stories when I were a lad. He spent nearly all his life down the pit or at the local workingman's club, but he knew hundreds of stories. Things that had happened to someone he knew, or someone's cousin, or to the friend of a friend. God knows where they came from.'

Laura looked at me but said nothing.

I said, 'None of them were true stories. He had an active imagination and he just made them up to make us laugh. It's the same thing here. So far I've heard lots of stories from people. Their ideas about what was going on with Rory, with Tara, with the company. But they're only stories. I'm still nowhere near the truth.'

'I get the impression you're worried.'

'I am. Rory's dead and Tara's missing and probably dead by now. And we don't know why any of it has happened. So the murderer can take his time covering his tracks and tidying up any loose ends.'

'That means you.'

'Right enough,' I said. 'But not just me.'

28

I RANG ANDY Braithwaite. At first he listened, wary and distant, while I explained who I was. Then I told him that Rory was dead, and if anything the line went even quieter. Finally he said that he'd see me. After some negotiation, we arranged to meet at Sandbach Service station on the M6 motorway.

Laura had given me a thumbnail sketch of how he and Rory had met, and between them had set up a multi-million pound business venture off the back of a couple of casual conversations in a McDonalds restaurant. Braithwaite had been developing the programme that became Compsoft for several years, working on it at nights after spending his days supervising data security for an IT consultancy. He was single, living in Manchester, and eager to find someone with the money to develop his brainchild. Brand operated with his usual charm and Braithwaite thought he was partnering up with God. Laura made it sound as though he'd been naive and easily disadvantaged by Brand, who saw the potential for the new program immediately. Over time Braithwaite had become disillusioned with what Brand was doing—particularly when the company started to spend the venture capital as if it were about to self-combust—and left, but not before having a couple of Olympic-standard rows with Rory over the division of the spoils.

I arrived at the service station early, swooping brazenly down the service slip road as dozens of people did every morning on their commute up to Manchester. I sat by the picture window that looked out over the car park. Scrapped lottery tickets and sweet wrappings drifted and tumbled across the concrete, then launched themselves on to radiator grills and hub caps that they seized like desperate orphans hoping for escape, unwilling to release their grip.

There was a threat of rain in the grey air, and I realised grimly that whenever I found myself alone and waiting for people I was usually depressed. This time I was more than depressed—I felt as though I were letting down all those people who were dealing with me as if I knew what I was doing. It struck me that on this case I'd been acting like a blindfolded bear trying to keep his feet while baiters snapped, growled and laughed from a position of safety. Apart from finding Derek Evans, I hadn't made many inroads into the mystery surrounding Rory and Tara, and I was now seriously worried about what might be happening to her. The weather was turning wet and cold and if she were being held outdoors, her condition would be worsening every hour. What's more, we'd heard nothing from her captor—no hint of a ransom, no boasting telephone calls, no requests for interviews with newspapers. The silence was worse than any of these options, and was beginning to set my teeth on edge.

I pulled myself back into this meeting, dragging my eyes from the grey skies and wind-whipped hedges beyond the cars and lorries parked just the other side of the glass. I supposed Braithwaite had every reason to be suspicious of contact from Brands, or from anyone connected to them, and I had no idea what he expected from me. Perhaps there was a sense of unfinished business—Laura had said that he'd left Brands feeling bitter. Maybe he saw this as an opportunity for some small-minded gloating.

If I was expecting a nerd, I was mistaken. A fit-looking man who was probably older than he looked stepped into the entrance to the café and inspected the room. His grey suit was tight on the shoulders, the knot of his tie refined to a small point positioned exactly on his Adam's apple. His head was square-cut and chunky, as though hacked out of limestone by someone using crude tools. He noticed me noticing him and walked towards me with the spring and single-minded intent of a big game hunter. He juddered to a halt and thrust out a hand. 'Andrew Braithwaite,' he said in a firm voice. I shook the hand, impressed by its grip. This was a hand that had dealt with more than keyboards in its past.

I fetched us both coffee then told him again who I was and what I was doing. He concentrated fiercely, his pale eyebrows pointing down towards a surprisingly delicate snub nose. He had the weathered, freckly skin of someone who had spent a long time abroad.

'Got you,' he said when I'd finished, as though I'd been giving him a complex set of instructions. 'So you're not on the payroll but sense of duty and all that. Find it hard to believe you've got a debt of honour to that scoundrel Brand, but I suppose it takes all sorts.'

'Why do you call him a scoundrel?'

'Bit of an old fashioned turn of phrase, I suppose. If the cap fits, though. Never trusted him. Or rather I did trust him once, and look where it got me. Stuffed.'

'Weren't you paid for your work?'

'I suppose technically yes. Got a handout like everyone else. But it's the principle of the thing, isn't it? I come up with something that stands to make him pots of money, and he finds a fancy loophole to stiff me on the copyright. "Intellectual property rights vested in the company not the individual" — what malarkey. If I could have been bothered I'd have taken him to court.'

'Why didn't you?'

'Life's too short, old man. Got to move on. Leave your dead behind. They'll find their own way to the Pearly Gates.'

I drained my coffee. 'Where did you serve?'

'Ireland, Cyprus. Here and there.'

'You learn a trade, though.'

'Stood me in good stead, Signals. Know my way around a black box.'

'How did you come across Rory?'

'Met him at an exhibition. Plausible sort of guy. Big ambitions. I'd been working on the software by myself for a few years and he offered to put in some money. Never say no to money, do you? Threw in my lot with him.'

'When was this?'

'About eighteen months ago. Not long after he married the little woman. Very strange relationship that, you ask me.'

'Let's pretend that I did ask you.'

He paused. 'Did you know them?'

'A little.'

'What did you make of them? Did they seem like the kind of people who'd want to work together and spend their lives in each others' pockets?'

'My opinion doesn't matter,' I said. 'What's your point?'

He looked away, into the car park where a huge lorry changed up and rattled the windows as it passed. 'Mine's an outsider's point of view,' Braithwaite said. 'But they weren't much of a couple, were they? They barely saw each other, and then later he had one or two other things going on the side, if you get my drift.'

I sat up. 'Can you be more specific?'

'All seems rather besides the point, what with recent events.'

'Do you have any names? Anyone else I can talk to?'

'No, I don't. It was just gossip in the office. Generally don't listen to that kind of thing, but I was angry. When you're angry you look for another rod to beat them with, don't you?'

'Do you?' I said. He didn't back down from my gaze. 'So were you angry enough to do something about it?'

Now he smiled grimly at me. 'The bitter artisan enraged to murder by the hard-hearted businessman? Really, Dyke. Give me more credit. He was about to receive a letter from my lawyer. Hardly likely to bump him off in those circumstances.'

'You said there was gossip. Who was gossiping?'

His look became steely and direct. 'No one in particular,' he said. 'Look here, I'm not sure where this is going.'

Despite his rigid manner, he had suddenly become very uncomfortable, as though he were tip-toeing into a field laced with landmines. I didn't have much sympathy. He'd obviously thought he could come and have a good time bad-mouthing Rory without facing any consequences. His military bearing now seemed forced and rather pathetic.

'Why was he interested in what you had to offer, Andy? He was in charge of a consultancy. You were—what? A programmer?'

His already stiff back stiffened some more. He put down his plastic cup as if it were bone china. 'My partners and I consult for some of the largest companies in the North West. I had expertise that he needed. He put some capital into my business. I put some expertise into his. Now I think I ought to be going. I'm meeting some people in Liverpool this lunch time and I don't want to get caught in the traffic.'

'Aren't you interested in who might have killed him—and taken the little woman?'

He stood up. 'That's rather your business isn't it, old man? I'm just a programmer.'

'I'm sorry if I hurt your feelings. I didn't realise there was a hierarchy.'

'There's a hierarchy in all walks of life, Mr Dyke. You see it more plainly in the forces, but it only makes overt what everyone knows deep down.'

'I'm from Yorkshire. We don't have a lot of time for hierarchy.

When I hear the word hierarchy I reach for my machine gun.'

'Very droll.'

'But mention the word whippets and we could have a conversation.'

29

NOW I WAS CONFUSED. No one else had mentioned that Rory was seeing someone—but of course there was no need for anyone else to have known. Brand probably ruled his private life with the same ruthless hand with which he ruled the public one. But did Tara know, or suspect? Were they playing out some bizarre ritual, where he accused her of trying to steal his company and she had him murdered?

It sounded needlessly melodramatic—but then the newspapers were full of melodrama being acted out in every suburb.

Ever since Derek Evans had told me that Rory Brand had fired Eddie Hampshire, I'd been trying to get through to him. But his phone was either engaged or left on answerphone. After I met Andy Braithwaite I tried again from the service station, got no reply, and drove back to Crewe. I had just climbed out of my car and was walking towards my office when my mobile rang. Hampshire was driving and talking very loudly into his hands-free set, over the rush of wind and traffic.

'Can you talk?' he said. "I've got a free moment.'

I thanked him for returning my call. He said he was sorry for not seeing me in person, but given that he was working as an independent now, he had to keep up his client contacts. I was surprised that he was happy for me to know he didn't work for Brands any more. His voice was confident and even over the phone was as large as I remembered him in the flesh.

'I'm told you and Rory didn't see eye to eye,' I said. 'Was that why he sacked you?'

'Good God,' he said. 'Don't be such a tosspot. That was a misunderstanding.'

'Care to straighten it out?'

'Why bother?' Hampshire roared into the phone. 'As a matter of fact, I was looking for an excuse to leave. Deliberately over-reacted to some feedback he gave me, so I could look noble when I left. He was within his rights, absolutely.'

'What did he say?'

'That's rather close to home. I don't talk about private stuff, Dyke.'

'Rory's death was close to home, too.'

'OK, I hear you. Well it was the Personal Development review we had every year. A chat when Rory would tell you what he really thought of you, and pretend he was giving you honest and unbiased feedback. Never got any himself, though. Not part of the deal. Anyway, he said that a client had objected to my behaviour. Said that I'd behaved in an 'inappropriately macho' way when I'd been working with these tosspots in a hotel in Wales. I mean to say, it was a storm in a tea cup. Are you there?'

'Yes, I can hear you.'

'Thought I'd lost the signal. These bloody hills. Anyway, these sods worked in a paper mill or something. We'd worked all morning in the grounds of this hotel, doing abseiling or potholing or some such, then we came in to eat at midday. These bastards just headed for the bar and we couldn't get them out. Never ate a thing but drank a good lunch. So I issued a couple of gentle threats and they came back in quick sharp. But they weren't happy and one complained—hence the feedback from Rory. I told him he was a stupid tosspot and how I dealt with delegates was my business. Didn't like that, did he. Didn't like his authority questioned.'

'Does anybody?'

Hampshire barely paused to think about his reply. 'There's something you need to know about consultants, Dyke. We're pretty damned confident people. We have to be. There are sods out there just waiting to have a go at you if you say something they don't agree with. This isn't a game for kids. You need balls and a hide of leather. Hold on, just coming to a roundabout. Need to concentrate.' The line went quiet for a moment. 'That's better. Where was I? Oh yes, consultants. I don't know what you know about this game, but we're a weird bunch. Got to be to enjoy the fight. Every day trying to persuade people that they've got the wrong end of the stick. Life isn't as easy as they think it is. They've got to try harder. Some people can't take it, and they bite back. Anyway, Rory and me have this set-to. And there we are for a couple of weeks, with him making it harder and harder for me.'

'How did he do that?'

'Subtle things. Attitude mostly. He loses the smile. He gives you the dead-eye stare when you're talking to him, and then when he says something it's got a little bite in it. Well I can take that, I'm a big boy.'

'I'm told he had you testing the software.'

'Waste of time that was. Didn't work properly and looked like one more nail in the proverbial coffin, for me. But I was past caring by then. I'd decided I wanted to leave. So I took umbrage and played the drama queen. Resigned in high dudgeon. Handed in my swipe card and company mobile. If I'd been really serious I'd have claimed constructive dismissal, because he was making it pretty bloody hard by then.'

'Surely he was the same with everyone,' I said.

'You don't get it, Dyke. He had a killer instinct. He was

famous for it. Couldn't help himself. Spotted a flaw in a person and went for it like a terrier.'

'So who might have killed him?'

'Haven't a clue. Did he have any secrets? Gambling or women? Maybe he owed big money to someone. He always seemed stressed to me, but that could have been anything.'

The air was silent between us. I felt as though Hampshire had an answer for everything, like a champion swordsman parrying every thrust with an idle flick of his hand. I said, 'Where were you when you found out he'd been murdered?'

He laughed. 'Ah, the sixty-four-thousand dollar question. Rest easy, I was in London.'

'Who told you he'd been murdered?'

'I had a phone call from Betty. I think she phoned everyone. Strange, isn't it? Knowing there's someone out there with a grudge against you bad enough to excite them to murder. I guess we're all supposed to be careful now, until they find this guy. And in case you think I have a motive for doing anything silly, I should tell you I was supposed to see Rory this week anyway. We were going to discuss my doing some associate work for him. So he can't have thought that badly of me after all.'

The phone in my hand went dead. I assumed he'd found some more hills to go behind.

30

I PHONED LAURA and asked her to meet me. What I'd learned from Braithwaite and Eddie Hampshire had cast Rory the entrepreneur in a different light. He seemed more driven, self-centred and ruthless than I'd been allowed to see by the people who still worked for the company. Protecting his reputation, I thought. Also, I wondered if Laura knew anything about the extra-marital relationships that Braithwaite had suggested.

She walked me to a pub that had recently been converted into a modern wine-bar-cum-lounge affair, with large televisions blasting out music videos of black men wearing heavy jewellery surrounded by women in bikinis, and garish neon lighting attached to the plasterwork coving high on every wall. Even at late lunch time it was filled with a young, honking crowd who ate Mexican wraps with small crinkly French-fries and disposed of blue and green drinks at a frightening rate. She seemed perfectly at home.

I told her about my meeting with Braithwaite earlier that morning. She wasn't impressed. 'Andy never had any ambition,' she said. 'He needed someone like Rory to point him in the right direction and give him a kick-start.'

'We know Rory could be hard to get on with. Might he have stiffed Braithwaite? Cheated him?'

Laura looked at me levelly. 'We're in business, Sam. When you enter a partnership like this you draw up a contract. Lawyers from both sides go through it with their eyes wide open. It's not like spitting on your palm and shaking hands, you know.'

'Braithwaite was genuinely upset. If everything was in a contract and dealt with rationally, why was he so arsy?'

'Just because you have a contractual arrangement with someone, it doesn't mean you're not emotionally engaged. Andy loved the code. The stuff that he wrote. He's probably sorry it hasn't worked out as he wanted. What can I tell you? I'm not a psychologist.'

A chill had settled on the table between us. But I had another question to ask.

'Braithwaite also suggested Rory was playing away.'

'What do you mean?'

'Seeing other women. Did you know anything about that?'

She gave me that appraising look again. The one where the dark edge of her irises bored into you and let you know she was judging, thinking.

'There are always rumours about powerful men like Rory,' she said at last. 'But I didn't see any telltale lipstick on his collar. None of the girls walked into work wearing the shirt he was wearing the day before. I've seen that happen elsewhere. People cotton on pretty quickly.'

'Is there anyone who would have known?'

She sighed. 'Are you sure this is all relevant?' she said. 'We started with Rory's murder and the threat to steal his business. We've moved onto Tara's disappearance. Now we seem to be bringing in adultery. I don't want to be telling you how to do your job, but shouldn't you be concentrating on one of these at a time?'

'Unless they're connected. Second law of private-eye school: keep joining the dots until you make a pattern that you recognise.

Then try and see what it means.'

    'And is there a pattern emerging?'

    'Oh yes. Definitely.'

31

I WALKED LAURA back to the office and said I'd be in touch. I'd
seen a plaque in the foyer which told me that the company
Brands leased their offices from was based in Warrington. I
wanted to know how security at the offices worked, so I climbed
in my Cavalier and headed north up the M6, crossing the Thelwell
Viaduct with hundreds of other pilgrims and peeling left
immediately to exit the motorway and weave through
Warrington's suburban hinterland. Two miles of low concrete
warehouses, petrol stations, bleak housing estates and roadside
hoardings crawled past my windows. The grey detritus of an
industrial neutron-bomb — the people were gone, but the
buildings, such as they were, remained.

I parked in a shopping centre that seemed only half-finished
and walked to the grey sixties office where the leasing agents were
housed. It looked like a slightly worked-up gigantic breeze block,
with windows. Pale sunlight struck the side of the building but
like me seemed reluctant to enter.

At the reception desk I asked to speak to someone about
security in the buildings that they leased. The woman behind the
desk put down her crossword magazine and gave me an odd look.

She dialled an extension, spoke briefly, and told me to wait. I sat in a soft plastic chair that exuded the musty smell of furniture that's been stored in a damp warehouse. Glossy magazines on a low table advertised the range of high-tech offices leased by the company throughout the North West. An air of tragic banality lay over the whole enterprise. I supposed someone had to lease buildings, but it seemed like a seedy business in these surroundings.

Five minutes later a man with a distended stomach opened a glass-paned door into the reception area and lifted one of his chins towards me. I followed him down a corridor painted institutional beige, then into his office. A single fluorescent strip overhead sent out a flat light that barely crept over his desk, a bookcase, his computer and two wooden chairs.

In this small room I began to smell the rank odour of the man's sweat gathering in the folds of his nylon shirt. It reminded me of the fat boy at school that we all bullied.

'Micky Turbot,' he said, holding out a stubby arm. I shook his hand briefly—it had the firmness and consistency of a bunch of Lincolnshire sausages. The effort of walking down the corridor seemed to have exhausted him. He fell into the chair behind his desk and sipped from a plastic beaker of orange juice. I waited for him to regain his breath.

I told him my name and said that I was working for Brands on some investigative work.

'Who are Brands?' he said.

'Tenants of yours in Waverley. They pay you a lot of money every month.'

He took the insult. 'We lease over three thousand properties in the North West. Don't get shirty because I don't recognise one name.'

'They've been in the news lately.'

'Oh them. Poor buggers. Man and wife, wasn't it?'

'I'd like to ask you some questions about security in the offices they lease from you.'

He had a round face in which the eyes were small and never looked directly at you. Now they darted away as if hunting down a swarm of invisible wraiths in all four corners of the room. 'What kind of questions? Why should I tell you anything?' he said.

'There's a swipe card system. You swipe to get in and out.'

'That's not a problem, is it?'

'Can the cards be duplicated?'

'No way. Each card has a reference for the building, for the lift and for the main office door. They're good as gold, matey.'

'Who makes them for you?'

'Do them ourselves. We get the cards printed up with the magnetic strip laid on. Then we just magnetize them as and when.'

'So you have batches of blank cards lying around somewhere, just waiting to be magnetized.'

'Each one's individual, of course. Different strokes for different folks. Ha!'

He was beginning to feel more cocky now, confident in his expertise. He took another sip of his orange juice. 'If you use 'em properly there's nothing safer,' he said. 'Worked for a company once used keypads—you know, type in your security number. What a bloody disaster. They gum up, stick, get dirty. Too many moving parts. Course, next on the agenda is eyeball recognition. Look into this mirror, quick scan, buzz, you're in. Dutch are the ones ahead of the game. All the best talent over there. Mate a mine's earning a fortune, sitting on his arse in Zuider Zee, coding for Microsoft. I tell you, matey, we're always behind the curve over here. Never catch up.'

He sat back in his chair, breathing heavily. His navy suit was shiny at the elbows and his shirt showed dark patches in ridges across his belly.

'So if I'm Brands,' I said, 'and I take on a new recruit, what do I do to get a swipe card?'

'Easy. You phone up, identify yourself and we send one out in the post.'

'So I could be anyone ringing up?'

'Don't be silly. We have your name registered and you have to give us a code number. We weren't born yesterday.'

'So who does the ordering for Brands?'

'That's confidential, matey. I don't know you from Adam. You walk in here cool as you like and start asking questions. How do I know what's going on?'

'That's just the point,' I said. 'You don't seem to get it. One person's been murdered and another one kidnapped, and the one who was killed was sitting in a room that was supposed to be secure because of your cards. If I were you I'd be wanting to find out what's going on, not playing the Jobsworth with me.'

'Now hold on—'

'Are you going to give me that name or do I have to go and talk to the Senior Investigating Officer? He's always on the lookout for people to help him with his enquiries.'

He stared at me, then turned to his computer and gripped his mouse. A few clicks later he turned back to me. 'It's someone called Gerald Finch,' he said coldly. He must have seen the expression on my face. 'Don't get excited, though. I don't suppose they're recruiting any more. They haven't had a new card in the last six months.'

32

THE SUN WAS SETTING as I turned into Brands' car park. The watery light had strengthened during the course of the day and a honeyed glow softened the edges of the red-brick office. I was struck by the contrast between this world of sophisticated urban wealth and the environment that I came from. My father wouldn't have been able to hold a conversation with the confident, educated, experienced people that worked for Brands, though his sense of right and wrong, his ability to take the measure of a man, and his determination to provide for my mother and me, whatever it took, gave him enough sophistication in my eyes.

When I entered the office, I could see Laura through the full-length glass windows of one of the small meeting rooms. She was standing and talking animatedly towards a tele-conference machine that stood on a low table. I moved away and waited for her to finish.

Mal O'Donovan walked by and winked at me. I called his name and caught up with him.

'What's up?' he said.

'If I were a consultant,' I said, 'and I'd just started working for

Brands, what would you expect me to know?'

He was taken aback. 'How do you mean?'

'What would I be asked to do? How do you go about things when you're training people? There must be some basic stuff that you use, some presentation material or handbooks or something. Every consultant I've ever known has got their own hobby-horse, some method that they swear by.'

His face took on a cunning look. 'Ah, the big secret,' he said. 'The magic bullet. Wait here a sec.'

He walked off and came back a minute later with a slim paperback book. He gave it to me like an offering, both hands outstretched.

'Handle with care,' he said. 'The holy grail for consultants who work in the behaviour business. I'd say everyone who works here has used this some time or another. We always build it into our programmes. It's easy to understand and makes sense to people straight away. We like things that are easy for people to understand—makes our jobs easier. Know what I mean?'

'I'll handle it carefully.'

'Don't worry about it. We've got dozens of copies.' He backed off with a cheery wave.

I looked at the book. It was a slim Penguin paperback called Games People Play by someone called Eric Berne.

When I looked back at Laura, she was standing against one of the windows, wide eyed and gesturing with a hand for me to join her. Before I reached the door, she opened it and put a finger to her lips. A dull voice without any inflection was coming from the conference device.

' … and I know you've got the police involved, but that was to be expected. I don't expect any more from dull little creatures like you, actually, without the resources to try something different. Are you listening, Laura?'

She stepped to the table and bent down to the machine. 'I'm here. Tell me what you want and go away.'

She turned her face up to me and her eyes were round with fear and a kind of supplication. She glanced at the machine and shook her head at me, as though she knew I was about to say something.

'What I want, Laura, you can't give me. It's the satisfaction of having that little shit dead, for one. Everything after that is gravy, including this touching conversation. You can't believe how much I wanted him to suffer, and in fact he didn't. It was over much too quickly. So I've still got issues, as our American friends call them. Unresolved feelings of anger and resentment. And I guess you're the standing target at the moment. Bad luck.'

The voice was male and it was muffled, as though his mouth was half-hidden behind a gag or a cloth. It also sounded as though it had been treated, moving up and down in pitch and volume as though passing through an electronic device.

'If there's nothing I can do,' Laura said, 'then I guess there's no point us having this conversation, is there?'

'Oh I disagree there,' the voice said. 'I need to impress on you the urgency of my situation. You see I know that you have someone on the case, as they say. I think I need to convince you that it's not a good idea. Listen.'

There was silence for a moment, then a scrabbling sound close to the microphone. The man's treated voice came back. 'This is what waits for you, Laura.'

Then came a sound that was hard to make sense of at first. It started in a high register, a high-pitched note of intense, piercing shrillness that was difficult to place. The speaker in the room couldn't handle the prolonged intensity, warping it and edging it with white noise. Only when the unmistakeable sound of a sobbing breath interrupted the shriek was it evident that the noise was a cry – an awful, human, shattered screech of pain. It shut off abruptly as the man yanked Tara away from the telephone mouthpiece.

'There you are,' he said. 'Don't say you weren't warned.'

Then the line went dead.

Laura collapsed on one of the two armchairs in the small room and put a hand to her eyes. I stood next to her and put a hand on her shoulder. We stayed like that for nearly five minutes, until I felt her breathing calm down.

'What did he say?' I asked.

She looked up at me, her eyes rimmed with red, her lower lip trembling.

'He terrified me, Sam. He said we were playing a dangerous game. He said we should butt out. He mentioned you personally. He said he'd wanted Rory to suffer, and he wants Rory's family to suffer, and he wants the company to suffer. But if we got in the way he'd make us suffer too. You and me.'

I nodded. 'He had a lot to say for himself. He's obviously deranged.'

She sighed deeply. 'Poor Tara. What's he going to do with her?

I didn't answer. Nothing I said would be good.

She stood up and looked at me. 'I don't know what to do. Should we tell Howard?'

'At the moment we do nothing. We definitely don't tell Howard — if this caller knows about me then he's getting information from somewhere. We shouldn't rattle his cage more than necessary. Besides, I don't see what Howard could do. There was nothing in the phone call that you could identify? Nothing in the background, nothing in the man's tone of voice or his vocabulary?'

She shook her head. 'I'm frightened to death, Sam.'

'Well that's good. It means you're unpredictable and potentially dangerous. My old dad used to say shit or get off the pot. This man's still on the pot. I think Howard was right. He's warming up.'

'And did you ever listen to your old dad?'

'Not as often as I should have done.'

I calmed her down by telling her what Micky Turbot had said about the swipe cards. She listened intently and then raised her eyebrows. Although the lighting was harsh in the small room, it only emphasized the angularity of her cheekbones.

'So you've been all the way up to Warrington and think you have to report in,' she said. 'Even though it's less than three hours since we spoke. You don't have to prove yourself to me, Sam. You don't have to let me know when you've got a clue—if that's what this is.'

'The office is on my way home. No extra charge for the house call.'

Half an hour later we left the room. Laura stopped suddenly to reach round behind me to turn off the light switch on the door frame, brushing an arm against me as she did so. Again her perfume tantalised my senses. An emotion that was almost physical stirred inside me, so strong that I had to hold on to the door handle. I was briefly ashamed of myself for the feelings I had, given the emotions that Laura must have been feeling.

Not that you would notice. She had gathered herself and seemed to have recaptured the icy calm that I'd seen before. She strode back towards her desk, talking over her shoulder. 'I still don't think this swipe card information is enough evidence. I don't know what it proves. If anything, it just makes things more difficult.'

'It proves that whoever was in here with Rory when he was murdered was either let in by him, or had a swipe card. My money is on him already having a card. Then he has the element of surprise. So the question is, where did he get it?'

'People have quit the company, they don't always return their cards. You know how these things are.'

I stopped. 'No, I don't. How are they? If someone leaves, don't you make sure they return their card? And when they do, what happens to the cards—are they left lying around in the office for anyone to steal?'

'You don't seem to have a very high regard for our professionalism.' There were pink spots on her cheeks.

'I need some help here. You know a lot about management consultancy, doesn't mean you're whiz-kids with security. Don't take this the wrong way, but I wouldn't trust you to look after my comb.'

We were out in the main office by now. Laura looked around and grew flustered. 'The people we deal with are decent people. That goes for everyone—employees, clients, everyone.'

'Everyone steals a pencil when they need one.'

'I don't want to argue with you, Sam.'

'Then just say I'm right. Security's been lax around here. It takes a murder and a kidnapping to wake you up. How can I find out what's going on with the swipe cards?'

She looked away, breathing deeply. 'I don't know. I don't know who looks after them now Finch has gone.'

Two other people sat in this part of the office—a young woman with long crinkled hair and a deep tan, and a middle-aged man with a vague resemblance to Dustin Hoffman; both of them were deeply engrossed in their computer monitors. I stepped closer and reached out a hand to touch her arm. She looked up at me from under her pale lashes.

'I know you're scared,' I said. 'But being angry with me won't help.'

'Maybe not, but it feels good.'

'Depends on which side of the desk you're sitting.'

*

When I was certain that she was OK, I decided it was best for me to leave. Laura walked me out of the office and we found Eddie Hampshire standing in reception, being greeted by one of the women consultants I'd seen on my first day. His black hair curled over his white shirt collar and his neck bulged under the constraint of his tie. The consultant murmured something softly, then turned and headed towards the part of the building where she and her colleagues were holed up. Hampshire turned and gave me a white-toothed grin, then reached out to shake hands with Laura and then with me. He clasped my hands with both of his, his huge paws smothering my fingers and crushing and holding them for a long moment, until finally he relaxed his grip and I took my hands back. His eyes glittered with recognition.

'You're the sod who asked me lots of impertinent questions while I was driving through that armpit they call Leicestershire.'

'You're still drumming up work, then.' I said, nodding past him into the consultancy division, where the woman was standing waiting.

He looked briefly uncomfortable. 'I had a phone call—"We need you desperately"—who am I to resist? Now that some tosspot's seen fit to take Rory and Tara out of the picture, the company needs lots of warm bodies to put in front of clients— sorry, that's an unfortunate turn of phrase.'

'You don't feel embarrassed about coming back, after the way you were treated?'

'That was Rory. As I told you, I was looking for an excuse to leave. Rory was his usual insensitive self and I took the opportunity to walk away. Things are different now.'

'Why—because Rory's not around?'

'No, because the company's in trouble. I still have some friends here. If there's something I can do to help out, then I'm willing.'

'For a fee.'

'Well nobody does anything for free, do they? I'd be a stupid sod if I did, wouldn't I?'

I let the silence hang for a moment. Laura looked at me as if she were wondering how she could throw a bag over my head.

I said to Hampshire, 'Is that your BMW in the visitors slot

downstairs?'

'Why do you ask?'

'I was out at Rory's house to see Tara, not long after he'd been found dead. Someone driving a BMW had a row with her and left at full pelt.'

'And your point is?'

'Just asking.'

Hampshire smiled his toothpaste smile. He looked at Laura to share his amusement.

'Good god, man, don't be such a tosspot. Look around—this is Waverley, spiritual home of the BMW. You'd be more in line looking for someone who wasn't driving a Beemer.'

'You might have a point. Colour's the same, though.'

'I don't know what all this is leading to. I already told you I was in London the day Rory was murdered. Can't be in two places at the same time, can I? Listen to me! I'm talking like I'm a suspect.'

I turned to Laura. 'What do you think, Laura? Is he a suspect?'

'Well he's always suspicious, if that's what you mean.'

Hampshire took this as an opportunity for a hale-fellow-well-met bout of laughter, during which he bent to pick up his briefcase. I saw again the leverage in his shoulders. He leaned forward and gave Laura a dry kiss on the cheek.

'Not my car,' he said to her with a grin. 'Came by train today. Much simpler.' He turned to me. 'Nice to meet you again, Dyke. Especially in your true colours. I've never met a private detective before. You're not half as seedy as I expected.'

'I have my moments.'

Another bout of laughter and he was gone, following the woman consultant and laughing jovially with her as they moved out of sight. I watched him vanish and wondered why he made me feel uneasy.

Laura asked, 'What was all that with the car?'

'Trying something on, that's all.'

'Is there even a BMW down there?'

'I haven't a clue.'

She smiled grimly.

'And what are you going to do about the swipe cards?'

'I've got an idea, but I'll need some help from an unlikely source.'

33

I DIDN'T TELL LAURA that the telephone call worried me. It was the villain's attempt to get some kind of respect for his actions. But there was no way to acknowledge them publicly, with the result that he could end up feeling even more hurt. This was a downward psychological spiral we couldn't afford. If Tara was still alive, there was no telling what he might do to her just to make his point. There might be an ear delivered in the post, or a finger ... I had to do something to get closer to this madman. If I couldn't catch him, I might as well give up this line of work. After all, I'd never again work on a case where I knew the people involved so intimately. If I couldn't solve this, I couldn't solve anything and didn't deserve to be in business.

At least I had a plan. But as usual I wasn't allowed to put it in place without something else getting in the way first.

The next morning my mobile phone rang and a woman's voice asked if I were the private detective looking into Tara Brand's murder. She was a friend of Tara's who'd got my number from the receptionist at Brands. Melissa Ball sounded efficient, intelligent and keen to talk. She lived in Knutsford and agreed to meet me in one of the coffee shops nestled between the estate agents and charity shops that crowded against each other on its main street.

Knowing the new Tara, I guessed at the kind of woman who would be her friend, and when I entered the coffee shop I picked her out immediately—hyper-well-dressed in a black polo-neck and cream jacket, blonde hair pulled back into a pony-tail, good make-up and finely-detailed nail manicure. The perfect Cheshire-set hostess with a husband probably working in finance in the middle of Manchester and a second home either in Spain or Tuscany. Tara would have liked the world Melissa moved in, and would have been dazzled by the freedom represented by so much disposable wealth. Melissa, on the other hand, would have liked Tara's independence and her willingness to run her own life.

I was ready for all this. What I wasn't ready for was the anger.

'Mr Dyke,' she said, shaking my hand. 'Well it's about time someone took this seriously. Before you settle in I'd like to show you something.'

She stood up and walked towards the door I'd just come through. 'Come on,' she said. 'It's down here.'

We went out on to the street again, a row of dark Victorian buildings that bent over each other to keep daylight at bay. She strode purposefully ahead, her blonde pony-tail bobbing rhythmically. We walked for twenty yards and then she stopped in front of another café and looked into its large window. I followed her gaze. The café was not much different from the others—a counter selling cakes and eccentric sandwiches made from Italian bread, an old-fashioned till that popped up square tickets when you hit a key, and behind the counter a hissing coffee machine made from lots of shiny metal. Further back were immense picture windows and a raised section where people sat at round tables and looked out on to a complex garden. Melissa Ball pointed.

'That table, there,' she said. 'That's where we'd meet. That's where my last memory of Tara is. Very ordinary, isn't it? So can you tell me how something as ordinary as this can be turned into something tragic, something awful, and no one seem to care two hoots? What the hell's going on? Why aren't I seeing nightly bulletins on the news? Why aren't I reading reports every day in the local papers?'

'Police investigations are long and dull,' I said. 'Nothing happens for a long time, then someone's arrested.'

She folded her arms and squinted up at me, used to being in charge and getting the answers she wanted. 'So where do you come in? I understand you're a private investigator being paid for by Tara's firm. What does that have to do with the official investigation?'

'Very little. I'm following my own line of enquiry.'

'And by complete chance I call you out of the blue because I want to talk. I'm very impressed by the depth and intuition shown by your detective work.'

'My methods are my own. But I usually get my man.'

She threw up her hands. 'Well that's very reassuring—a small-time investigator who thinks he's a Mountie.' She turned and walked back to the place where we'd met. Once inside she ordered a cappuccino and I asked for water. She seemed to have calmed down.

'As you can tell, I'm not happy,' she said. 'It's the first time I've had anything to do with the police, and I'm not impressed. I might become more involved with our local people if this is the general standard one can expect.'

'You know Tara well.'

She gave me a look that could have withered granite. 'I suppose you could say we were best friends. In fact I'm probably her only real friend. She has lots of acquaintances, but I don't believe she speaks to them in the same way she speaks to me.'

'Where did you meet?'

'We both took part in a charity walk five years ago, in Kent. We got on well and stayed in touch. When my husband was transferred up here, we started to meet regularly. Tara is very good once she trusts someone. She always organises our meetings. It's as though she needs someone outside of work to talk to and keep her sane.'

'Is that all you do—meet and have lunch?'

'We play squash occasionally, but she developed a bad back and it's difficult with timetabling. In the end it seems easier to meet and gossip over a pannini and latte. You know how it is as you get older, Mr Dyke. The simple pleasures and the routine are enough to keep you going.'

'You seem rather young to be falling into routine.'

'Bless your little Mountie heart. I admit that I get a lot from my meetings with Tara. She leads a far more exciting life than I do. Yes I'm married to a nice man who's happy for me to drive a fast car and decorate the living room when I feel like it, but it's not exactly independence.'

'And Tara has that?'

'Independence in a practical way, of course. But also in a spiritual or philosophical way. Let's face it, she does more or less what she damn well pleases. I didn't know Rory that well, but from what I hear he deserved everything he got.'

'He was married to your best friend.'

She made a gesture with her mouth that was a metaphorical shrug.

'Doesn't make him a nice man.' She looked at me coolly over the top of her fat white coffee cup.

'If I can be personal for a moment,' I said. 'you seem very angry. In my experience people with that kind of anger are frustrated that they haven't been able to do something. It burns them up inside that they had a chance, an opportunity, but wasted it. What's getting at you, Melissa?'

'You're more shrewd than you look,' she said. 'You come along with your wrinkled leather jacket and your 'Ah were this' and 'Ah were that', but you're not so dumb, are you? Well in

174

answer to your question, I think Tara was having an affair.'

I looked at her for a long moment and she looked right back without blinking.

'Do you have a name?' I said.

'No. She almost came right out once and told me what was going on, but she never quite made it. I didn't want to push it because—well, because I've been in that situation myself and I know when it's best to keep quiet. If she wanted to talk she had people she could use.'

'Can you tell me anything about this man? Was it up here or down in Kent? Was it still going on or had it ended?'

'If I could be more helpful, I would be. I'm afraid I don't know any more than I've already said.'

'If you did, would you tell me?'

She took out a packet of cigarettes and lit one without offering them to me. She blew out a stream of smoke before answering. 'I don't believe in this not speaking ill of the dead nonsense,' she said. 'Not that I believe that Tara is dead. She's my friend and I'm more sorry than you'll know that I didn't pay more attention. But there's no point in trying to hide what was going on for the sake of appearances—that's just ridiculous.'

'You make a strong case.'

'You have to have people whole or not have them at all.'

'Have you got any idea who might have wanted to kidnap Tara—or kill Rory, for that matter?'

She stared past me through the window and into the street. 'Don't think I haven't been over and over it in my mind. Going through everyone we knew, everyone she might have mentioned, any hint she might have dropped. But Tara is strange like that— she gives the impression of intimacy but you never really get through. She has all the social tricks when she wants. She can ask questions and encourage you to witter on, but she never gives much away herself. It's almost as though she wants you as a friend to fulfil the functions that friends do—but she doesn't need you, the real you. I suppose she uses me, if you want to think of it like that.'

'I'm sure you're more than someone she uses,' I said.

'Why? What could you possibly know about it?'

I hesitated. To say anything about my marriage to Tara seemed irrelevant to what Melissa was feeling.

'There you go,' she said. 'You can't say anything, can you? If I want to believe that Tara uses me, then that's something I have to deal with. Don't try to comfort me when you don't know what you're talking about.'

She tapped her cigarette on an ashtray that had miraculously appeared at her elbow. I poured out the last of my expensive bottled water and drank it down. It seemed to me that Melissa was happy to hold on to this anger for the time being. Perhaps it replaced the loss and pain that she would otherwise be feeling. Tara had probably been the only person who gave her some hope for escape.

'How was Tara when you last saw her?'

'Happy. Very happy. Things were going well for her. New business was coming in. Brands was doing well.' She hesitated for a split-second.

'And what else?'

'I don't know—she was more alive than even she usually was. There was more energy. More eye-contact, more excitement. She didn't say anything, but I knew something was going to happen. Something good. She was worked up, excited. I asked her what was going on but she wouldn't say. Except she was quite cutting about Rory, which was different. I don't think they were getting on particularly well in the last few months, but she usually defended him. This time she took chunks out of him, like a shark smelling blood. It was all done as though in fun, you know, being a bit scathing about hubby—but I thought this time she meant it.'

'What did she say?'

'I can't remember. It was two months ago. But I came away

thinking she was different. She seemed to have let go of Rory, if you know what I mean. He wasn't quite as important any more.'

'You sound like you approved.'

'Do I?' she said. 'Well, Mr Dyke, the thought of someone getting out of this rat-race is always exciting, isn't it? We all want to break out from time to time, if only to see what it's like on the other side of the fence.'

We looked at each other for a moment. She was doing her best to let me see the emptiness of her own life. The fact that someone she knew had tried to fly free and had possibly been murdered as a result wasn't lost on her. A life of long afternoons stretched ahead.

I broke the silence. 'I've heard that Rory was having affairs as well. Did Tara say anything about that?'

Melissa Ball delicately wiped the corners of her mouth with a fat ivory cloth napkin, and smiled for the first time.

'Well now,' she said. 'You'd have to talk to the people he worked with, wouldn't you?'

34

WHEN I LEFT MELISSA Ball I went home. I felt I needed a shower and a change of clothes after all the innuendo I'd heard in the last two days.

I started to read some of the book that Mal O'Donovan had given me. In it Eric Berne described his theory of how personality was created. His ideas seemed obvious and simplistic, but I could see their attraction to consultants working in management training.

He said that people's personalities depended on what they'd seen and heard in their childhood. If they were treated well they developed 'nurturing' behaviour that they copied and used themselves when they grew up. But if they were treated badly they developed 'critical' or 'controlling' behaviour, which they could also copy and perpetuate themselves. The kinds of behaviour that grown people then exhibited, according to Berne, might depend on the way others interacted with them—so if someone used 'critical parent' behaviour towards me, telling me what to do, pointing at me or raising their voice, I might react as I did when I was a kid going through the same experience for the first time. What I might demonstrate could be either 'adapted' or 'natural' child behaviour—that is, willing to give in and let things slide, or likely to be argumentative and emotional.

The way out of these parental or child-like reactions was to be in 'adult'—which Berne described as a condition that's more interested in gathering information and being rational than playing out 'games' learned in childhood.

I thought of how this had worked with my own dad. I recognised that most of the time he behaved in an adult state: rational and logical and apparently open-minded. He could appear very reasonable. At other times, perhaps because of something I'd done or said, he'd get really angry and eventually he would slap me, which made me angry too. It was interesting to think that the way we dealt with each other might have been the result of these shifts between us—that we brought out the worst in each other, as well as, sometimes, the best.

I thought Berne's ideas were superficially plausible in a pop-psychology way. After all, I recognised my own behaviour in some of the games that he described.

It was dark outside when I stopped reading. I took half a pound of mince from the fridge, fried it with onions and added tomatoes, peppers, paprika and chilli powder. I put some brown rice on a low heat and forty minutes later I ate while watching the television news. I was washing up when the door bell rang. I went downstairs and looked through the spy hole in the door. A man in his sixties with short grey hair, hollow cheeks and a prominent nose stood absolutely still, looking back at me as though he knew I were inspecting him. He was familiar but I couldn't put a name to him. I opened the door.

'Well, Samuel,' he said, 'I've tracked you down at last.'

Realisation came to me. 'Major Hoyt, come in.'

I stood back and let Tara's father into my house.

Like many men I've met from the forces, Hoyt was only average in height but squatly built. His shoulders almost brushed the walls as I guided him towards the kitchen. He wore an extravagant waxed raincoat with extra shoulder panels like something Sherlock Holmes might have affected, and before we reached the kitchen he stopped and began to shrug himself out of it, folding it neatly down its spine, pulling out the arms and levelling them together before collapsing it flat over his forearm. Composed, he then walked into the kitchen.

We sat facing each other across the kitchen table. When Tara – Debbie – and I had married, the Major was the chief architect of the wedding. Her pregnancy drew out of him all the middle-class resentment towards youth and change that he sublimated, I presumed, in the Army. He stood for no argument while making the wedding arrangements, and while it was painful for his wife— a long-suffering, almost mute partner in this shotgun wedding— to do without a church ceremony, we were guided towards the registry office with martial efficiency. Tara and I had shifted the axis that the Major's world rested on, so it was important to put it back in balance again as quickly as possible.

After Tara left for London, I hadn't seen him again until today.

I knew the Major didn't think much of small talk, so I got straight into it.

'Not the best set of circumstances for us to meet again,' I said. 'I'm sorry it happened like this.'

It was as though I hadn't spoken. The Major ignored my attempt at ice-breaking and went directly to what was uppermost in his mind.

'Samuel, I'm told you were there on the night Deborah went missing,' he said. 'I have several things to say about that. There are some thoughts going round in my head. Primarily, it seems you're always in the wrong place—especially where my daughter is concerned. You seem to have brought me nothing but grief for the last twenty years. Why do you think that is? What have you got against me and my family?'

The notion of 'family' was strange coming from him. Tara had told me that throughout her childhood and adolescence he'd been no more than a distant provider—someone she saw at Christmas and possibly on her birthday, carrying gifts but with little enthusiasm in his eyes. Maybe it was guilt that made him cling to the idea that they'd been a family in anything but name.

I was irritated by his sudden aspiration towards a kind of moral high ground.

'I'm working as an investigator these days. I was following up on the murder of her husband.'

'I know her husband,' he said, casually dismissing Rory with a small gesture of his hand. 'She had very little luck with men. Meeting his family at their wedding was the most dispiriting thing I've ever done. I counted my fingers after shaking hands with his father. Nothing I've met in the Arab countries could outdo them.' He shook his head. 'So you were hired as an investigator to look into his murder, but it seems you didn't know who was actually paying the bills. That's to say, Deborah.'

'I was asked by Mr Brand to investigate a private matter. If I'd known he was married to your daughter I would have refused to take him as a client in the first place. Then I wouldn't have become involved at all.'

'But you did become involved, and you went to her house. And when you left, someone kidnapped her.'

'I was attacked from behind. I didn't see a thing. Major—'

'Oh for goodness' sake don't call me that. That's what Deborah called me, in fun, but I was never a Major. Of course you never talked to me long enough to find that out. You had no idea what I did.'

'I was a young man. You were quite intimidating.'

'Rubbish. I've never met such a backward youth as you were. You jumped at your own shadow. My wife and I used to despair of you and Deborah making a go of it.'

'How is your wife? She was very kind to me.'

He looked away, his eyes taking in the details of the room.

'She died five years ago,' he said. 'She suffered terribly from cancer.' He drew a breath and turned back to me. 'But never mind that. I want to know more about what's happening with this so-called investigation. I've talked to Inspector Howard, but he's less use than a condom on a porcupine. What can you do?'

'As an investigator I have to look at things in a different way to the police. They have access to forensics that I don't. So I look at motives, relationships, the reasons behind the crime. The police usually assume the murderer was known to the victim. They start by thinking the murderer's a member of the family. Then it's a question of elimination. I've got more of an open mind.'

'Any results?'

'Nothing concrete yet.'

'Excellent work,' he said, standing up and beginning the long process of unfolding his raincoat so that he could put it on again. 'Much as I expected, given your track record. Now I have a train to catch. I just wanted to see you before I left. You know, Samuel, that was a very strange time in all of our lives. Deborah was very unhappy, very confused. Marrying you, leaving for London, changing her name—I wouldn't say it was typical of the girl her mother and I brought up.'

'From what I saw of her, she'd changed quite a bit. She seemed more in control of what she wanted.'

'You didn't know her particularly well. She was quite a serious and ambitious child, which is why she was beginning to do well with this man Brand and his consultants.' He paused a moment. 'I'm a consultant now, you know. I left the army after my wife died. Couldn't stand it any more. But they ask me back from time to time for some specialised jobs. I've been in the Middle East until two days ago, which is why I'm only just getting involved in this. You can expect to hear from me again.'

He was now fully armoured once more, his raincoat with its shoulder panels and waxy surfaces ready to repel all attacks. He stood looking up at me, a somewhat lonely and wistful presence that he tried to play down with a show of military bluffness.

'Incidentally,' he said, 'I suppose there's something else you should know. When Deborah went to London, she was still pregnant.'

I had been opening the door for him. Now I stood with my hand on the door knob, staring at him.

'What did you say?'

His demeanour became even more brusque, as though he didn't want to get involved in a discussion of this topic, but had to transmit the message. 'She told you she'd had a miscarriage, didn't she? Well, she very nearly did. But in fact the baby survived. That's why she asked you not to visit when she was in hospital, if you remember. Didn't want you finding out the baby was still alive. Then she went to London because she didn't want you to be the father. Once she'd had the child, she gave it away for adoption. A boy. I think she called it Daniel. He doesn't know who his real mother is. I don't even think he knows he's adopted. I'd like you to keep that to yourself. Now, which way do I go to the train station?'

That night I dreamed I was lost in a desert, searching for water. My mouth was parched, my legs as heavy as pig-iron. A pitiless sun burned down on the top of my uncovered head, and sweat ran down my face in rivulets. Wherever I looked, all I could see was turquoise sky and yellow sand.

I fell repeatedly into an oasis—the same oasis each time, and each time it was dry, its bed yielding only more sand to my grasping fingers. I stood up and stumbled away to keep looking, and every time I stood I was suddenly surrounded by hundreds of women who encircled me and observed me calmly. I knew that the women had red hair, though they wore veils to hide their features. That didn't fool me: I knew that beneath the veil every one of them was Tara. I turned and ran away, my feet sinking in the sand, trying to escape the stares of these women.

Then in my dream I stopped and turned to face them. They stopped running too, and in unison reached beneath their desert robes to pull out a small, silent child, whom they threw pitilessly to the ground. There was a moment of terrible silence, then they all began to laugh with gaping mouths, the sound of their laughter like fingernails being scraped down a thousand blackboards.

I woke sweating in my cold bedroom, seeing blood and red hair floating in my vision until I rubbed my eyes and brought myself back into focus.

My subconscious mind obviously didn't like surprises. The next day brought another.

35

AMONG THE OFFERS to loan me more money or give me twenty-five thousand pounds a year for life, there was a brown envelope lying on my doormat.

Inside it were printouts from a computer-based diary—one week printed on one sheet of A4, with seven boxes for each day of the week. Every box except the occasional Sunday had something written in it.

There was no covering letter and no sign whose diary it was, but a small footer at the bottom of each page said 'brandr' in a small font, followed by the week's number. The printout listed one appointment after another in a hectic schedule of times and locations, naming clients and now and then adding lists of actions to perform before a meeting took place.

I spent an hour going through the diary—which covered the last two years of his life—but there was so much information it was almost impossible to take in. There were company names, the names of individuals, initials that presumably stood for one category of meeting or another, and occasional reminders such as birthdays or anniversaries. Nothing seemed to have more importance than anything else—it wasn't a personal diary in the sense that Rory would even have filled it in himself. It was more likely to have been kept by someone responsible for his schedule and making sure that he wasn't double-booked or spread too thinly.

Rory was obviously a busy traveller. He'd had appointments in Singapore, Detroit, Edinburgh and Paris, as well as local ones in Manchester and London. The far eastern appointments seemed to be associated with a multi-national Bank that I'd heard of. The ones in America were related to a car manufacturer. The rest were scattered between numerous smaller and less well-known clients, and usually took place in hotels or conference centres.

Then I noticed a number of appointments where a hotel was mentioned, but no client. That was so unusual that I trawled through the hundred or so pages for another half hour, until I had a list of fifteen hotels in the Manchester area where there was a stretch of six months of appointments with no name given for the client. Presumably he'd entered these details himself, to avoid being double-booked, but didn't want to use the name of the person he was meeting.

I didn't know what this meant, but I was sure it meant something.

That afternoon I went to the gym. I worked on my legs and stomach, pushing and curling with a row of sweating men fifteen years younger than me who seemed to take the effort in their stride. Afterwards I swam thirty lengths in a languorous crawl, watching the speed merchants thrash past me in a riot of noise and energy while I coasted slowly from end to end, taking deep breaths and feeling the oxygen course through my bloodstream.

My mind kept returning to what the Major had told me—I had a son called Daniel who knew nothing about me. There was someone out there who possibly looked like me, who perhaps thought about me, who probably hated me. A boy of about eighteen who had already lived a life and was starting on his adventure into the future.

I turned on my back and did a couple of lengths in slow backstroke, looking up at the arched ceiling of the swimming pool. I felt older but no wiser. In fact I felt as though I knew nothing at all about what had happened to me in my life.

I shopped on my way home, then grilled some lamb chops with mint potatoes which I ate at my kitchen table while reading the book on Transactional Analysis. I was intrigued by the 'games' that Berne described. They had odd names like 'Schlemiel', 'See What You Made Me Do' and 'Now I've Got You, You Son of a Bitch'. I particularly liked 'Cops and Robbers'. In this game, Berne suggested that some criminals were in it for the money; others were in it for the game. This made a lot of sense to me. In C & E we dealt more often than not with hard-faced villains engaged in strictly for-profit activity. But from time to time you came across someone who smiled when you told them who you were—you weren't their best mate after all, but an undercover officer. These types seemed to shrug and accept the fact that they'd been caught. They'd played a game and lost. Berne said that this type of criminal often wanted to be caught. Like the child who squeals with laughter when found in a game of Hide and Seek, the pay-off was in the finding, not the hiding. Similarly, for a certain kind of criminal, the pay-off was in being caught—the fun was in deferring being caught for as long as possible, to heighten the sensation of the final capture. It was no good to evade being caught forever. That was much too sensible and destroyed the psychological basis for the activity. No—it was far better to include everyone in the game: victim, policeman, perpetrator. These were the criminals who liked to think they were 'toying' with the authorities by demonstrating their superiority. Phoning up and taunting the investigators. Sending messages to the press.

Leaving clues such as cryptic phrases written on computer screens and steamed-up mirrors.

First thing Monday morning I called Carol-the-receptionist. She seemed surprised to hear from me. 'Mr Dyke' she said coolly, 'What can I do for you?'

'We started off badly but I'd like to thank you for your help.'

'What do you mean?'

'You've put one or two people in touch with me.'

'If you're talking about Melissa Ball, I had no option. She was very determined. The police haven't been helpful, so I thought of you.'

I wasn't going to push it. But an idea occurred to me. 'I'm beginning to understand how Rory and Tara worked,' I said. 'But I need to talk to more of their friends. People who knew them well. Who else is there who'd give me an honest view?'

She barely gave it a moment's thought. 'Dominic Michaels,' she said.

'Who's he?'

'Someone Rory used to go to the football with. He runs a recruitment company in Manchester. Hold on, I'll give you his number.'

She went away and a moment later returned with a telephone number, which I wrote down.

'Thanks, Carol,' I said. 'I appreciate your help.'

'My job is to help Rory and Tara.'

I hung up. Neither of us had mentioned the diary, but we both knew that we'd talked about it.

36

DOMINIC MICHAELS RAN a recruitment advertising agency from offices located in a large Victorian pile in the centre of Manchester. The building had been recently renovated and the fresh paintwork and replastered colonnades suggested a wealth and stability rooted in history and the triumphs of Empire, though these days most of the companies renting offices had Arabic or Asian names. A board in the echoing marble foyer listed these companies and the floors they occupied. I rode up in a futuristic lift that announced my floor and swished open with a sound that wouldn't have been out of place in Star Trek.

When I was shown into Dominic Michaels' office it was getting dark outside; he was standing by a large window looking down on one of Manchester's wide streets packed with slow-moving cars and buses. I wondered if he was one of those people who consciously made gestures that demonstrated their importance: here he was, the captain of industry, looking down on the struggling masses. I'd once had a boss who constantly pulled out his shirt cuffs below the length of his jacket sleeves, straightening them out. He seemed to think it made him appear smart in more ways than one.

Michaels was younger than either Rory or me, somewhere in his early thirties, and wore a dark pinstriped suit that seemed to flare out at the wrists and waist like something that might have been worn by an actor in a sixties TV show. It was probably a new Mancunian fashion that I hadn't caught up with yet. He had a full head of elaborately sculpted black hair that sat above a relaxed and supercilious face that was almost handsome but not quite. He spoke with a London accent that was similar to Rory's. I wondered whether they'd known each other when younger, in the wilds of south London.

Like many entrepreneurs I'd met, his listening skills were terrible. He'd forgotten nearly everything I'd said to him over the phone, so I had to go through it again. When I finished, he looked at me and said nothing for a while. He was jowly for someone so young, and his mouth hung slightly open when he wasn't speaking, as though there were a half-chewed stick of gum occupying his lower jaw. He sat down behind a rosewood desk.

'So tell me again who you're working for,' he said when I'd finished explaining myself. His eyes were steady as he scrutinized my face. He had a laptop open on the desk and he typed into it without looking at the keyboard. I felt myself become guarded.

I told him Brands had hired me but neglected to mention that I'd been replaced by a more expensive outfit. I got the long stare once more. 'Sorry,' he said. 'I'm trying to work out what's going on here. Rory is murdered and Tara is missing, and their company hires an investigator who's then arrested himself for kidnapping her. I'm your average man in the street when it comes to these things, but it seems odd to me. Do you get my point?'

'The police were following up what they thought were clues. They asked me a few questions and let me go. We're on very friendly terms.'

'I doubt that very much.'

I shrugged. 'Wouldn't you like to find out who murdered your friend?'

'And you're saying I should put money on you to do that before the police. Look at it from my perspective. Is that likely?'

'Point taken, but it wouldn't do any harm to talk to me, would it? I'm not asking you to say anything you wouldn't say to the police.'

Now he lifted his arms, honest John, showing he had nothing to hide. I had a sudden vision of him standing on a stall and selling plates in a Saturday morning market.

'You've got to understand where I'm coming from,' he said. 'My job here is to match people up with what they want. Clients tell me who they're looking for. I go out and find them. I take a fifteen percent cut. It's a straightforward transaction. Now this situation between you and me is just the same. At the end of the day, I'm giving you something for free and I need to know how you're going to use it.'

'So you want cash in return for what you know? That's very cheap.'

He held up a hand, keeping at bay such a harsh and commercial thought. 'Don't get the wrong idea. At the end of the day, information is only worth what someone will pay for it— that's true. But I'm not a mercenary man. I just want to understand what you get from this.'

'A fee. Satisfaction in a job well done.'

'Now you see, I understand that. That's what it's all about, isn't it? Getting paid for what you do in fair exchange. And, of course, doing a good job. My philosophy is that you can't do better than that.'

'Seems to me you're trying to work out what commercial value the life of your dead friend has. Not much of a philosophy.'

'That's a bit harsh. At the end of the day you and me are going to have a conversation, aren't we? I know that. You know that. I just need to get the rules of the road laid out so we both know where we're coming from. When you've been in business as long as I have, you've got to make sure both parties to the deal know what they're signing up for. That's right, isn't it?'

'If you say so. I just want to ask you some questions about Rory. I don't want to enter a contractual arrangement with the party of the first part.'

He sat back, closing the lid of his laptop, and I suppose the look that passed across his face was dismay, as though I'd contravened some unspoken negotiating regulation. He appeared to give up on me.

'Ask your questions,' he said. 'This is about trust, and if you don't trust me we might as well do it and get it over with.'

I was too irritated to get into an argument with him. It was better to get what I needed and leave.

'Did you see Rory in the last six months?' I said. I had my notebook out to give the questions and answers a level of formality.

'Three or four times,' Michaels said. 'He used to come in and we'd go out to Rusholme for a curry. He liked to try different places. And he liked the buzz. You know those places out there— neon paradise. Always heaving. If it was midweek we'd try to arrange it so we'd go to a match afterwards.'

'Did he ever talk about business?'

'Of course. Practically nothing else. We nearly worked together at one point. His consultants often helped companies to recruit. As I might have mentioned, that's what we do here. But we couldn't sort it out. At the end of the day, we place recruitment ads in the papers and do the occasional piece of executive placement. His consultants were working at a different level. Expensive level. His charge-out rates were phenomenal. My clients wouldn't wear it.'

I wondered if this made him envious. 'And what about Tara?' I asked. 'Did he ever talk about her?'

Michaels' face took on a cunning look, as though he knew this was the vital fact and there should be some way of realising its value. The cool air in the room suddenly seemed quiet and tense. I saw calculations passing behind his eyes. But after a moment he breathed out and let his shoulders sag. He looked moodily towards the big office windows. 'He was giving up on her,' he said. 'He hardly saw her. She was away as much as he was. It wasn't a marriage—more of a joint venture. Right from the beginning. At the end of the day, they were both getting something from it, but it wasn't romance, was it? They had their own ways of getting their jollies, you know. The relationship was all about winning. They both liked to win. I think romance was too ... out of control.'

'Were they going to split up?'

'Let's face it, they already had. It started as a business relationship and they always go sour, don't they? And as for the other side—Rory was pretty certain she had someone else tagging along in the background. And for all I know, so did he. He never said.' For once he closed his mouth fully and edged a little closer across the table that separated us. 'He thought he was being followed, you know. He hadn't seen anyone, up close, but he knew they were there. He told me he felt the eyes. Looking straight through him. I know what he meant.' He raised his heavy eyebrows, as though trying to astonish me with his insight. 'It was true in his case, though, wasn't it?'

'Do you think someone's following you?'

'For ages. Not everyone's as trustworthy as I am, so I take care. The world of commerce is a jungle, you know. And that's not just a fancy what-do-you-call-it, metaphor. There are predators, traps, slimy creatures and rats out there. You've got to keep your eyes open.'

I suddenly understood why he looked out of his office windows onto the streets below. He was Tarzan, safe in a tree house, safe from the dangers which bothered the rest of us. He must have led a very interesting life. In his head.

I asked him if he knew anyone who'd want to kill Rory Brand. He surprised me by giving it some thought.

'Manchester's a rough town,' he said. 'It was going to spill over to Waverley eventually. They can pull their lace curtains together but they can't keep out the jungle.'

'I'll take that as a no.'

Michaels lifted both hands from the desk, raised them to his face and rubbed the flesh of his cheeks until they were red. He suddenly had the air of someone who was drained of ambition and bereft of answers to any of life's questions.

'In my experience, you don't have to go far when there's a big crime like this.'

'In your experience?'

He shrugged, as though making reference to a hinterland of involvement in crime and illegality that I could never comprehend. 'The police will tell you the same.'

'You don't sound hopeful.'

'If that means I don't trust people, you're right,' he said. A dark energy entered the corner of his eyes. 'Knowing Rory, your best bet is to find the women. He was never discreet. They'll know something.'

'Is that true?'

'As true as the fact that I've been taping this conversation. Just in case.'

37

WHEN PEOPLE LEAVE an office at the end of the day they suck from it any life and atmosphere that it might borrow during working hours. Michaels' office had that dead and sterile air as I passed through it on my way out. The secretary who'd signed me in and two other young women I'd seen through a glass partition had gone for the night. The lights were on a dim setting, casting a grey pallor over the quiet space.

Out in the corridor a cleaner pushed a vacuum around as though she didn't care whether it was sucking or blowing, and the talking lift had only me to chat to on its way down. The whole building was like a velvet-carpeted and well-lit tomb. I thought about Michaels upstairs in his cavernous office, looking down on me as I tapped down the steps and headed back to the multi-storey car park. I thought what a strange view he had of the transactions between people—that there was rarely anything more involved than the transfer of information for the gain of one or other of the parties. It was a philosophy, I thought, that might lead a sane man to hang himself from a lamppost.

Before I left my office I'd stuffed in my pocket the list of hotels that Rory had visited during the last couple of years. So being in

Manchester I thought I'd act like a proper detective and do some field work.

The first hotel was in the centre of the city, still a twenty minute drive in rush hour traffic. It was small but stylish, with a lighted balcony overhanging the front entrance. A white ceramic pot shaped like a globe held a superannuated pampas grass, and an imposing doorman with close-cropped hair and pierced ears rocked backwards and forwards on his feet as if waiting for some action to start. He nodded me through warily and I went in and explained what I was looking for to the balding man who stood behind the reception counter.

He bent forward, pointing a pink ear towards me. When I finished he said he wasn't allowed to talk about guests, and anyway he only covered the evening shift. Midday and afternoons were someone else's lookout. I thought better of arguing with him and left, nodding casually to the doorman on the way out. He stared at me as though I'd just slapped him in the face with a leather glove.

It was the same routine for the next two hours. If people talked to me they couldn't help because they weren't on duty at the right times; if they were on duty, they wouldn't talk, full stop.

Almost the last place on the list was out by the airport. I took Princess Parkway out of town, hit the M56 motorway, then turned off almost immediately on to the looping slip road that sucked me into the network of roundabouts scattered between the three neon temples that were the airport terminals. After a couple of false turns I found the Ascot Lodge, an old-fashioned country hotel that looked like it offered no more than half a dozen bedrooms behind its shuttered front. It was spot-lit from below, and I cast hulking shadows on its doors and windows as I crunched across its gravelled car park.

I knew my luck had changed as soon as I saw the family photos on the wall and the pram in reception. It was a family-run hotel and more than likely had the same staff on duty throughout the day. The woman behind the desk was in her forties, wide-armed and stolid, like a comfortable armchair. She had the rosy cheeks and innocent smile of the eternally optimistic. She believed anything I said before I opened my mouth.

I went through my routine. I mentioned Rory's name, said she might have heard he'd been murdered recently.

She took me seriously at once and widened her eyes. When I finished, she bent underneath the reception counter and pulled out a thick register, turning back several pages with a fat finger. Within seconds she found Rory's last entry, over two years old.

'There she blows,' she said triumphantly. 'Never forget a name, me.'

'I don't suppose you'd remember the client he was with?'

She turned coy and her red cheeks flushed a deeper shade of plum.

'Not a client,' she said, in a nasal Manchester whine. 'His usual meeting. He used to say they were business meetings, but he always hired a bedroom, you know, instead of taking one of the conference rooms downstairs. Never let us interrupt with tea or coffee.'

'When you said "usual meeting", what did you mean?'

'Shouldn't really be saying all this, should I? Getting people in trouble.'

I gave her a serious look. 'You could save lives,' I said meaningfully.

'Put it like that,' she said. 'Went on for about six months. That's why I remember. Used to turn up with the same young lady. Very nice, she was. Blonde lady, very slim. Very well-dressed. I liked her, me. She used to wear these lovely leather trousers. Purple, they were. I fancy a pair meself when I've got me weight down a bit. She seemed very nice.'

'Yes, you said that,' I murmured. 'So it must be true.'

38

I RANG LAURA Marshall's mobile phone from the Ascot's car park, pacing backwards and forwards on gravel that was slowly whitening under a night frost. Planes took off and passed overhead every couple of minutes like an insistent metaphor for the passing of time.

There was no reply from Laura, so brooding over what the receptionist had said, I drove home and drank three whiskies in a forlorn attempt to bludgeon myself into sleep. I only managed a couple of hours before my alarm dragged me back into a world that was becoming less and less predictable.

I rang Laura from my office as soon as I got in and drew another blank. Carol-the-receptionist told me she was on leave and would be out until the following day. But she gave me Laura's address and home telephone number when I convinced her it was urgent. Then I had another task for her.

'Carol,' I said, 'I'd like to ask for your help.'

There was a pause. 'I've already done as much as I can.'

'You can do more,' I said. 'Tara's still missing.'

'I know that.' This time the pause was lengthier. 'All right. What is it?'

'I'd like you to email everyone in the company and ask them to hand in or post their swipe cards to you. Say that the police want to check the electronic signature on the cards.'

'I can't do that.'

'Why not?'

'It's dishonest. I won't lie for you, Mr Dyke.'

'So stay honest and feel good about yourself when you're crying in the back row at Tara's funeral.'

'That's not fair.'

'Fairness has got nothing to do with it.'

'You can't track people's movements through the cards anyway.'

'Not everybody will know that. Do you really want this murderer to get away with it? Is that being loyal?'

'You can be a bit of a swine, can't you?' she said. 'Very well, I'll do it.'

I spent a couple of hours making notes on what I'd learned so far, but by early afternoon I couldn't distract myself any more and got in my car to drive to Laura's house. A computer mapping programme put a location to the address that Carol had given me, and I set off towards Nantwich and the bypass system that would swing me round towards Chester.

It was just over three weeks to Christmas, and the weather had been slowly deteriorating. The sky to the west was yellow with the prospect of cold rain as I headed towards it, into the flat countryside that led eventually to the grey desolation of the Irish Sea. By the time I reached Tarvin, the small village on the Crewe side of Chester where Laura lived, it was already dark.

She was in her driveway unloading her car. The house sat in a row of squat sixties semis, each one different to the one next door. There was a lot of slate cladding, angled roofs and tall chimneys. Very chic forty years ago. Garages were built into the front of the houses, and some of her neighbours had converted them into living rooms or kitchens. It was a sizeable property for a single person. From her front room she would have seen nothing beyond the laurel hedge that shielded the houses from the main road into the village.

I watched Laura make two trips as she unloaded supermarket bags from the boot of her Saab. When she came out to push down the boot and lock the car, I got out of mine and waved at her through the gloom. She took a step back before recognising me.

'You frightened the life out of me,' she said. 'I'm already seeing shadows everywhere.'

'Good. I want you to be careful.'

She turned towards the house and I followed. Even walking on gravel in sensible shoes and wearing jeans, she was elegant. Her straw-coloured hair bushed out like a beacon for me to follow.

Inside, she pointed me towards a room decorated in a modern style that still had enough wood, framed pictures and leather to capture that late Victorian feel that the Cheshire set seemed to prize. I sat and allowed a large sofa to swallow me up. She asked if I'd like a drink and I told her water was fine. She went through to the kitchen and came back with water for me and what looked like a gin and tonic for herself. She sat down facing me. For a moment the fizz of the tonic in the glass was the only sound in the room. I looked at her for a few seconds.

I said, 'So tell me about your affair with Rory.'

She didn't look away or give any indication of surprise. Eventually she took a deep breath and began.

'It was over a long time ago,' she said. 'It's got nothing to do with his murder.'

'I'm glad you're so confident. We're not the ones to make the judgment. It's not my job and it certainly isn't yours.'

'Oh come on, Sam. Pot and kettle. Are you telling me you're not making judgments all the time? Yeah, right, you're the objective recorder of factual evidence. In a pig's eye. You're no less judgemental than the rest of us, but you can dress it up and call it detective work. Inferences based on assumptions. Isn't that called circumstantial evidence?'

She'd become more agitated as she spoke. Now she stood and went to the window, looking out across her gravelled garden.

'So prove me wrong,' I said to her back. 'Talk to me about you and Rory.'

'It was a mistake,' she said. 'We both knew it. We'd been working together for a couple of years, and there was always, you know, a little something there. He was a pain to work with, but he could be charming. I suppose that made him a challenge.'

'Ah, the old women-like-a-bastard routine.'

She ignored me. 'We went to an exhibition down in London one week—this was after Gill left him and before Tara swanned in—and we were staying in the same hotel and we got a little drunk. It was a thing that happened.'

'But it carried on happening.'

She turned to face me, eyes burning.

'I don't report to you,' she said. 'We were both adults. We were both single. I'm not proud of sleeping with the boss, but there you are. It happens. As far as I know he never let it get in the way of working with me.'

'And you?'

'If anything, it made me stricter. I wouldn't let him so much as shake hands with me at work. God,'—she let out a sigh full of weariness—'even in the middle of it I knew it was a bad idea. But it's easier to carry on with it than go through the trauma of calling it off.'

'Who did call it off?'

'He did. He'd met Tara and was completely captivated. I suppose you can understand that, can't you?'

I looked up, expecting to find her gloating. But her expression was resigned and humorous.

'We get ourselves into these things, Sam, when we're not at our strongest. When we're vulnerable. You can't always expect good judgement.'

She dropped back into her chair as if the effort of remaining upright was too great.

'The test of character,' I said, 'is how you get out of them.'

'I failed, then,' she said. 'Rory was polite but strong. I was a wreck. He was completely professional, which I have to say surprised me. I expected him to lash out when I started to give him a hard time. It was tough when Tara came into the company. But I've been here before. I'm thirty-two, Sam. Rory wasn't my first affair. It's what we career girls do, now. We have affairs. We've got too much to lose by giving it all up for a man. But we can still have affairs and think we're in charge, in control.'

I went and sat next to her. I'd arrived full of anger and wanting to punish her. Now she seemed alone and somehow exhausted, as though any kind of emotion had been drained from her. Without looking at me, she leaned her weight sideways against my arm. I moved it and placed it around her shoulders. I felt the strength in her square-set torso, and then she seemed to soften and melt and leaned into me with all of her need. Her rich blonde hair was under my nose, and smelled how I imagined South America to smell, filled with a raw and vibrant sensuality. I took a deep breath and was lost in its voluptuousness.

Later, when she took off her clothes, I was surprised by the implicit sexuality of her body. Although I'd thought of her as slim and rather angular, her nakedness revealed a firm but rounded fleshiness that moulded itself perfectly into my hands. She gasped when I touched her hip and, in the shadowed darkness of her bedroom, I saw her move into the curve of my arm and after a delicious moment of suspense, the tips of her breasts gently touched my chest. Her lips came to me and found mine, and we lay gently on the bed and began to find the places in our bodies and our minds where we made an acceptable fit.

When I woke the next morning, she was already up on one

elbow looking down at my face. Her hair was perfectly arranged while I knew mine would be displaying its usual morning dishevelment.

'This doesn't need to have happened,' she said. 'I have no one to tell, and I guess you don't either.'

'I like a client who's sensitive to my needs.'

'I'll say.' And she rolled on to her back to stare up at the ceiling. Her shoulders above the covers were as smooth and rounded as the rest of her body had been.

'Laura, I've taken advantage of you.'

'I know. But that's okay, because I've returned the favour. You needed it as much as me.'

'It's not the kind of thing I usually get up to with clients.'

'What—the half dozen clients you've had in the last two years?'

'I think you misunderstood that. Most of them were long projects.'

'Who for?'

'I can't talk about them.'

She raised herself on one elbow again. 'Why not?'

'Official Secrets Act,' I said. 'I'd have to kill you.'

She nodded slightly but seemed unconvinced. Her eyes moved over my face. 'Tell me—you said you were kicked out of Customs and Excise. What was that about?'

I stared at the ceiling. 'There's a lot of nonsense been written about them,' I said. 'They do great work there, day in, day out.'

'Will the witness please answer the question?'

'Let's just say it's sometimes hard to be completely honest. There's too much temptation.'

'So you ... '

I turned to her. 'No. Not me,' I said. 'Not me.'

Realisation sparked in her eyes. 'People you worked with. It was the people you worked with.'

'Not even them,' I said. 'Think higher.'

We were quiet for a while. Then she let out a breath to change the subject. 'Don't think for a second that you've done the dirty here,' she said. 'I've been thinking about this for some time.'

I said nothing. I'd been thinking about it too. But also, I'd suddenly thought about Tara. For one night I'd been able to forget about her and her situation. Now I felt a spike of guilt in my stomach. Despite the years of absence and the depth of her dislike for me, I couldn't seem to prevent myself having feelings for her.

Laura said, 'What are you thinking?'

I turned to look at her and found her gaze and held it. 'How good people can do bad things when they forget to be good.'

She looked at me with an expression that I couldn't read as I climbed out of bed and got dressed.

39

LATER THAT MORNING Laura and I drove in convoy to Waverley, with me following behind at a respectful distance. I could see her blonde head sitting up pertly in the driver's seat, her eyes occasionally wandering to the rear-view mirror and smiling at me when we were close enough to exchange glances. I wasn't sure how I felt about this shift in the relationship. She was vulnerable and probably not making the best judgements she could. I hadn't exactly made it easier for her to keep a distance from me.

Over breakfast she'd asked me to talk about what I'd learned to date. I told her I was sure that what had happened to Rory and Tara was done by someone they knew. Rory was in the office early—probably for a pre-arranged meeting. I didn't tell Laura that there was nothing in his diary for that day. I said that I guessed the murderer had let himself in beforehand using a swipe card that he'd stolen or kept or got hold of in some other way.

Plus, my gut told me something else was going on. There was the person in the BMW that I'd heard arguing with Tara, and then driving off so quickly I could only swallow his dust. There was the man Melissa Ball was convinced Tara was seeing. Were all these the same person? It seemed likely.

Plus I didn't believe this was an unmotivated murder, but neither of the usual motives for kidnapping Tara seemed relevant—sexual assault or ransom. So it must have been motivated by something else.

I believed Rory and Tara knew the person responsible for their fates, and he might know me. So I had to do something. Going from one interview to another was one thing—but it wasn't the same as throwing down a gauntlet. That's why I'd asked Carol to collect the swipe cards. There was no way I could read any data from them to see when or where they'd been used, but that wasn't the point. The point was to raise a doubt, to show that someone was thinking things through.

Laura asked me whether there were any potential suspects.

'Take your pick,' I said. 'The disgruntled programmer, Andy Braithwaite. The sacked Operations Director, Gerald Finch.' I went on to list various unhappy consultants, including Eddie Hampshire and Mal O'Donovan. Maybe Tara had had Rory murdered and someone had then paid her back. Maybe Champion, the investors, had taken out a contract on Rory for squandering their money—

'Now you're being silly.'

'Nothing ever surprises me about human beings,' I said. 'Read the papers. Every day, something new and bizarre. I'm not ruling anything out.'

'But you have a theory.'

'As it happens.'

'But you're not going to tell me anything.'

'There's nothing concrete yet, so no.'

I did tell Laura about the visit of Tara's father—the man I still thought of as Major Hoyt. But I didn't think the timing was right to tell her that I'd produced a child by Tara eighteen years before. I still didn't know what to think about this person who was apparently my son. The feelings I had were strange, but not as uncomfortable as I might have expected.

Laura and I arrived at Brands within a couple of minutes of each other. She met me in reception and led me into one of the small rooms and shut the door. This was part of the plan we'd put together. To look as though we were plotting.

After half an hour or so, she went and spoke quietly to Carol, and the pair of them came back with a carrier bag filled with swipe cards. We shut the door again and tipped the cards on the table. They were credit-card size, dark blue, with the name of the company who leased the building written in capitals on one side and nothing but a black magnetic strip on the reverse. Carol had written the names of their owners in felt-pen on each one. They slid and clattered on the table like chips in a casino.

'There are still half a dozen or so to come,' Carol said. 'But I've spoken to everyone and they say they've put them in the post.'

I picked up the cards in handfuls and began to put them back in the carrier bag.

'What are you going to do?' Laura asked me.

'Nothing,' I said. 'Carol, give them back tomorrow. I've got another e-mail for you to send out.'

She looked at me grimly, then pulled a writing pad from the table towards her. I said, 'Tell everyone thanks for responding so quickly. And tell them that I said it's been a great help in the investigation. Make sure you mention my name.'

She looked up. 'How has it helped?' she said. 'You haven't done anything with them.'

'We've thrown out some bait. Let's see if anyone has a big enough mouth to swallow.'

40

ANOTHER EVENING FROST was settling in as I drove through Nantwich towards Laura's house in Tarvin. Approaching car lights appeared in the distance and sped towards me like blue diamonds tearing through dark velvet; the roads shone as though sprinkled with luminescent glitter.

I'd left her in the office and gone home for the afternoon, where I showered and changed. We'd agreed to meet that night. To see where we stood. To talk about what had happened and what we wanted to do about it. And possibly to go to bed again.

I put The Handsome Family into the Cavalier's tape system and hummed along to Brett and Rennie's lugubrious tales of down-home tragedy. With the heating racked up high, the cabin was as warm as the inside of a 20 Tog duvet, and I relaxed into the drive thinking about what had happened between Laura and me the night before, and how it changed everything. I even wondered whether I should tell her about my son. Would it be better or worse in the long run to hide it from her now? Was I being sensible and sensitive by keeping quiet—or was I just a coward? And even if I talked to her about it, what could I say? I knew nothing about this young person who'd casually walked into my life, except his age and his name.

Laura's house was lit like a film set when I approached, which was exactly what I'd told her to do. She had a movement-sensitive security light at the front that she'd ramped up to full-time dazzle, and the two coaching lanterns added their faded yellow light into the mix. She'd also switched on all the upstairs lamps and pulled curtains together, but not far enough closed to shut in the light entirely. The place looked garish all right—but inhabited.

She answered the door already dressed to leave. She wore black trousers and blouse, a long coat with fake fur collar and a Burberry scarf that was more of an accessory than a protection from the cold. She smiled at me brightly. 'You can drive,' she said.

'I know,' I said.

There were no cars behind us as I went through Tarvin, down to the roundabout and on, towards Chester. I'd promised Laura an expensive meal while we considered the next step. Chester was only twenty minutes away and had plenty of ritzy restaurants, plus a McDonalds if they were all booked up and we got desperate.

'Not sure about your taste in music,' Laura said as we began to pick up speed. 'I'd have put you down for a Motown man. Or possibly seventies disco.'

'I'll give you Stevie Wonder, because he was a genius. Apart from that, it's West Coast rock for me. Jackson Browne, The Eagles when they were good and nobody knew them. Neil Young, of course. Randy Newman for the lyrics and attitude. Nowadays it's more alternative stuff. Shall I go on?'

'Would you dare?' She was laughing.

'What about you? What do you listen to?'

'I don't listen to music. Interferes with my thinking. If I want to listen to something I put on the radio and hunt down something that doesn't need me to concentrate.'

We were on the wide approach that sweeps down into Chester and cuts through open country until the very last minute, when it hits the ring-road that circles the city. In my rear-view mirror I saw headlights rapidly approaching, and moved over to let the driver pass.

'I have to have music,' I said. 'Since I was a kid. My dad tried to get us interested in classical, but it didn't work.'

'I can't see you being patient enough for a Bach cantata.'

'You'd be surprised what I'm—Whoa!'

I'd been watching the lights of the car behind slowly whiten the back of the cabin as they grew larger in my rear mirror. The lights had shifted as the car moved out to overtake us. Suddenly we'd touched and the steering wheel leaped from my hands.

'What's going on?' said Laura.

'Hold on!' I said.

I looked across towards the other car, which still hadn't gone past but was racing neck and neck with us. It was large and sleek and seemed to contain a surging power. I could see nothing through its blackened windows.

Ahead, traffic lights were approaching. They showed red but there were no cars waiting. We were on a single carriageway that broadened into a double so that vehicles could filter right. I began to slow but the lights turned green. The other car pulled ahead of me, trying to get its nose in front again. I sped up, jamming my foot to the floor. I felt Laura's hands grab my arm but didn't look at her.

We roared through the lights and down towards Chester, glowing orange ahead of us. There were fields to my left and a full moon overhead lit up a solitary copse of trees in the distance. We were on a single carriage road but the other car seemed fearless. Vehicles that came the other way flashed their headlights and hooted their disapproval as they moved over and screamed past.

The other car was matching my speed, whether I slowed down or sped up. I realised that while I was watching his front wing, I was slowly being edged towards the kerb, as though hypnotised. The kerb was six inches high and was intended to deter people from riding up on to the verge. It would cause a hell of a bump. On the verge itself was a narrow strip of grass running parallel to the road. As I saw this, the overtaking car made one more swerve towards us, this time thumping the side of the Cavalier with such venom that it began to snake.

'Watch out!' I shouted to Laura, as the kerb swung unavoidably towards us. We reared up and bounced over it and on to the strip of grass. Through the windscreen it looked as though the verge had a mind of its own: we weren't heading into it—it was coming to us. From the corner of my eye I saw the other car speed off, its work done.

We rocked heavily over the grass and through tearing shrubs that shrieked as they scraped the side of the car. My hands were welded to the steering wheel but I had no control over direction, which was caught in a grip that I couldn't change. The front wheels leaped into air and lost purchase—I felt the rear end start to slide away. At this point we were still moving fast, and each small shift in direction, up or down, left or right, was magnified and carried through the car in a violent ripple. Laura and I shook back and forth like crash test dummies, held only by the safety-belts and an instinctive desire to ride out the motion.

Now the back of the car was fish-tailing away completely under its own momentum. The view through the windscreen began to rotate us back towards the road we'd just left. I was still holding on to the steering wheel, but for support, not because I had any influence over where we were going. I suddenly realised that the sound I thought was the noise of the car crashing its way out of control was in fact Laura repeating a short swear-word mantra over and over in an increasingly high-pitched tone.

Ahead of us was a group of low wooden buildings. They were on the far side of a wire fence that was held in place by concrete posts at two yard intervals. Just one of those posts would do serious damage and they were heading for us at speed. I wrenched the wheel, trying to slide us away from the post that seemed to have us in mind. But the car refused to turn.

'Hold tight!' I said, and caught a glimpse of Laura's frightened face. I locked my arms to turn into the skid and try to gain some control, and finally the car responded.

But it was too late. We swung violently through forty-five degrees and smashed into the post. The window of Laura's door starred and bulged inwards, then burst into a thousand pieces that fell like confetti into her lap. The car rose and tilted towards me as though it were lifted on a wave, and then it dropped and rolled three more feet before collapsing into a ditch. We bounced one more time and settled.

Then came the silence.

41

UTTER QUIET. I looked across at Laura but she was silent too, leaning back in her seat. I spoke her name—no reply. I put a finger on her neck to check she had a pulse. Then I climbed out of the car and struggled on to the grass verge, which was slick with moisture. I stood for a moment and breathed deeply while cars swept past on the carriageway, unaware of the collision they'd narrowly missed.

No signal on my mobile phone. I tried to wake Laura again but she was out cold. I got my bearings. Towards my left the lights of Chester lit up the sky with an orange glow. To my right, the road headed off into darkness lit only by receding tail lights. I set off towards the city, trudging through the long grass of the verge and stumbling on the series of small hummocks and holes that pocked its surface. Around me I heard the distant noise of a city at night, together with the roar of cars speeding past on their way to celebrations and the occasional honk of a car horn on the ring-road.

After a hundred and fifty yards I came to a Little Chef that was set back from the road and barely visible until you reached it. It was a neon oasis in the frosty night. I walked in, noticing, stupidly, that inside the door there was a wicker basket full of complimentary copies of the Daily Mail. In the main room there were a dozen or so wooden tables, but there were only three people in the whole place to occupy them. They all looked up at me as if I'd entered their private worlds of sorrow. A perky junior with a red cap slid in front of me. 'How many?' she said.

'Can I use your phone? There's been an accident.'

'Oh—okay. It's over there.'

She pointed across the seating area and I mutely followed the direction of her arm. I rang 999 and when it was answered I said I wanted an ambulance and the police and probably the fire service, though there wasn't a fire involved.

'A car tried to run us off the road,' I said. 'It didn't try. It succeeded. I think my partner is hurt. Actually, she is hurt, but I don't know how badly.'

I gave directions, then hung up. When I turned round the young girl with the red cap was looking up at me with the tiniest of furrows on her freckled face.

'Sir?' she said. 'I think you're bleeding.'

She pointed down to the maroon carpet, where a small puddle of bright red was accumulating, dripping from my left hand. She was experienced enough in the world of catering to know that it wasn't ketchup.

Within fifteen minutes an ambulance arrived, followed almost immediately by two police cars. I'd tried to release Laura from her seat-belt but in the end thought it best that professionals do it. A piece of Laura's passenger window had cut my hand when I climbed out of the car, but it was so cold and my adrenaline so high that I hadn't noticed. Laura had been knocked unconscious, had woken up, but then passed out again. At the moment she was conscious but very subdued. She had some scratches on the side of her face, and a lap full of window glass, but I couldn't see what other injuries she might have suffered.

The paramedics scrambled into the car and began talking to Laura in quiet voices. Two policemen approached me.

'Do a breath test on me,' I said. 'I want it on record that I hadn't had anything to drink. We were deliberately pushed off the road by another driver.'

One of the policemen looked ten years older than his companion and he took charge. He breath-tested me and spoke to me for a few minutes, staring into my face and trying to tell whether I was suffering from concussion or under the influence of drugs. I described briefly what had happened.

Other officers had begun to take charge of the queuing road traffic, laying out cones and putting their cars at an angle across the road to direct oncoming vehicles around the incident. One of the para-medics finally managed to undo the safety-belt and forming a human chain they lifted Laura out of the car, head-first. A stretcher was waiting, and after replacing her Burberry scarf with a neck-brace, they began to carry her towards the gaping doors of the ambulance. I went to watch them carry her in.

Laura saw me standing there and smiled. Then she lifted a frail finger and pointed it at me: 'You're fired,' she whispered.

The ambulance doors slammed shut.

42

INSPECTOR HOWARD oozed his usual cultured charm.

'So were they after you or the girl?' he said.

We were standing in a corridor in the Countess of Chester Hospital, three miles north of the city centre. Somewhere along the reporting line, Howard had found out what had happened. Within thirty minutes he came striding through the door, his face a thunderous mix of anger, confusion and, surprisingly, concern.

'I don't know who they wanted,' I said. 'It's my car they hit, but they probably knew she was in it with me. Either I'm the bonus or she is.'

'What did you see of the car? Get a make or any numbers?'

'Not really. Big and powerful. I think it was a BMW like the one I saw at the Brand's house. Overtook me as though I were driving a dodgem and brushed me aside. I'll be surprised if it's even got a mark on it. It was a dark or middling colour but hard to tell. He'd put something on his license plate—it was illegible.'

'One person or two?'

'The windows were tinted.'

Howard stared at me but I wasn't in his vision. We were both so distracted we were barely communicating. He could see this case spiralling out of control while I was worried about Laura. Her left arm had been suspiciously limp as they'd lifted her on to the stretcher.

'Any witnesses come forward?' I asked. 'Someone must have seen it.'

'We're asking but no luck so far. We'd have heard by now if anyone behind you saw it. People driving in the opposite direction would have been past too quickly to see what happened.'

'You've given it some thought, then.'

'This sounds like attempted murder. That's good enough for us to put some effort in.' He hesitated. 'There's something you should know.'

'What?'

He took me by the arm and led me to a row of chairs, where we sat.

'A note was delivered to our Incident Room earlier today.'

I felt my chest begin to thump more quickly. 'What did it say?'

'I can't reveal all the contents. Let's just say it was an ultimatum. We stop looking for Mrs Brand or he kills her.'

'Was there a deadline?'

'He wants us to say something this weekend. Saturday. We're Wednesday now. That gives us effectively two and a bit days.'

I stared at him. 'What are you going to do?'

'We've got to play it very carefully.'

I stood up so quickly my chair fell over. 'For God's sake!'

'Keep your voice down.'

'You've seen what he can do. Put more men on it. Broaden your search pattern.'

'We're not sure the note came from him.'

'You wouldn't be telling me unless you were sure. What did he do—include a finger? An ear?'

He was silent. I knew I was close to the truth. The kidnapper would have had to include some conclusive evidence for his words to have been taken seriously.

'So we've got two days to try and find this murdering bastard,' I said.

'What do you mean by "we"?'

'Just try and keep me out of it, Howard.'

He stood up now. 'I don't think you understand your situation,' he said, his eyes boring into mine. 'Anything you do could make it worse for Mrs Brand. What we do is none of your business. But what you do is definitely ours. So I'm telling you once again to keep out of it.'

'Too late,' I said.

'What do you mean?'

'The killer's already contacted Laura. Told us to back off.'

Howard shook his head. 'And you didn't, did you? I told you at the beginning you'd get in the way. And I wasn't wrong. Everywhere I look your size tens have been there first, muddying the ground and putting people in danger.'

'I have to do what I can.'

'Yes,' he said. 'I'm sure Miss Marshall down there in the Emergency Ward is just full of gratitude for your sterling efforts so far.'

It was a low blow. But he wasn't wrong. Now my revenge fantasy had even more to feed on.

43

I STAYED UNTIL THEY told me Laura was under sedation and comfortable. She was bruised but otherwise OK. I needn't have worried about her arm.

I thought about talking my way into seeing her, but the doctor was stubborn and besides, there was nothing more I could do. After all, I'd done enough.

I walked outside into the cold air that hit me like a slap. A few years ago the city's hospital functions had been transferred from the Chester Royal Infirmary to this more modern building. It was well laid-out with excellent access roads and a sensible plan, but was impersonal and soulless. At that point I knew how it felt. Whenever I'm wronged, I feel a cold, precise logic start to organise my thinking. It begins as a point of concentration between my eyebrows, almost as though I'm staring at something I don't understand. Then the circumstances begin to shuffle themselves in my head like cards being sorted into suits, one after the other. I lose track of what's happening around me and I'm usually rude to people, because all they are at that moment are bearers of information. If I need the information I take it from them any way I can. And I've been told that can be scary.

So I caught a bus into the town centre, then sat on a late train back to Crewe, completely unaware of the journey. I probably looked like a better-dressed version of one of those angry drunks you come across who are inwardly-focused and talking to themselves—until you catch their eye and suddenly you're the enemy. I've no doubt people stayed out of my way.

Although I become logical and focused, I stay angry. And when I get angry I get good at my job. I woke the next morning with my head still working through the thoughts of the night before, as though I hadn't slept at all.

I rang my insurers and after the usual argument invoked the clause that said I could take delivery of a courtesy car. Under pressure they persuaded the hire firm they subcontracted to drop it off before lunch. I rested on the bonnet to sign the copies that guaranteed the rental firm against any further results of my bad driving, and handed over the just-in-case deposit. 'Drive carefully,' the blue-overalled driver muttered as he walked to the van driven by his mate to take them back to their cosy office.

The hire car was a five year old Corsa with the rental company's name and logo painted in large letters down either side. No chance of remaining inconspicuous.

I rang the hospital and was put through to Laura, who was now awake and feeling better. 'The last thing I remember,' she said, 'is getting into the car at my place. Did we talk in the car?'

'We didn't stop. I know every one of your dark secrets.'

'I have to get home. They've put my wrist in plaster because it ached but apart from that I'm fine.'

'I'll pick you up.'

'Should I let you drive me anywhere? After last night?'

'It's not my driving that's the problem.'

'Prove it to your insurers.'

When I arrived at the hospital she was sitting on her bed. Her evening clothes gave her the air of visiting royalty among the dowdy dressing gowns and fluffy slippers of the other patients.

She smiled wanly when she saw me and stood up to peck me on the cheek. There was a faint bruise under her eye and her left wrist was bandaged up to her elbow as a precaution. A cool relief washed through me when I realised how close we'd come to something much more nasty.

'They need the bed,' she said. 'I don't suppose you've brought toothpaste and so forth?'

'No, but I've got some mints.'

'Hand them over. My need is greater than yours.'

We walked carefully out to the Corsa, which Laura eyed with some suspicion. 'I suppose it's only temporary,' she said, sliding into the passenger seat. 'Now you will watch the road this time, won't you?'

As I walked to the driver's side, her eyes followed me around as though I were the one who'd had the more traumatic experience and might collapse any second.

'Do you know what happened last night?' I said as we drove out of the car park.

She closed her eyes for a moment. I didn't know whether she was exhausted or was trying to picture in her mind's eye what had happened the previous night.

'My body remembers the bang as the other car ran into us,' she said. 'I can feel it run up my legs and into my chest. Oh god—' Her eyes flew open. 'That's a horrible thing to remember. I hope I'm not going to be stuck with that. I'll be too scared to do anything.'

'It'll fade away in a couple of weeks.'

'I hope you're right. So who was in that car? Have the police learned anything? Was it kids who'd stolen it, or a drunk, or what?'

I realised that Laura hadn't considered that the crash had been deliberate. She wanted to believe it had been a genuine accident. We were driving out of the hospital now and I could feel her eyes on me, demanding an answer.

'We don't know,' I said. 'The car hasn't been found.' I decided to be honest. 'Laura, I think whoever it was did it on purpose. He hit us twice and was trying to run us into the ditch.'

She looked away uncomfortably and I stared at the road. When I glanced at her moments later there were tears brimming in her eyes. She sensed me looking at her.

'Bastards,' she said. 'First Rory, then Tara. Now us. They're out to get us, aren't they?'

'Who?'

'Whoever's in charge out there, doing this to us and the company. I don't believe in fate, Sam. I don't believe that things happen by accident in the world. It's that old historical inevitability, isn't it? Marx had it right. There are forces out there conspiring against us. Criminals are just doing what they're supposed to do.'

This was something I'd thought about many times, though I'd arrived at a different conclusion to Laura. Dealing with conmen, fraudsters and criminals on a daily basis, you soon construct a philosophy. 'I think crooks are mostly stupid, but cunning,' I said. 'And because they can put one over on people from time to time they get an inflated view of their abilities. They become crooks because they think they're never going to get caught. They think they're just too smart, too far ahead of the game. I hate that. They usually don't get caught, as it happens, but that's down to a thousand reasons, not their own intelligence.'

'The fact that they're stupid isn't much consolation.'

'I don't believe in wickedness and conspiracy. How often does a conspiracy work? They involve plans, and human beings are not cut out for planning. As someone said, if you want to make God laugh, tell him your plans.'

'Does this mean you don't rate people very highly, or just crooks?'

I looked at her. 'There are some people I rate very highly. But villains are stupid and vicious, haven't got the brains to argue or express themselves, so they're violent—basically, they don't care. There's something missing that prevents them understanding what it's like to be someone else.'

She was now clear-headed and was looking at me intently. 'You're on a mission,' she said. 'I didn't see it before, with all that stuff about a professional approach and payment terms and so forth. But you're in this because you want to put things right, aren't you? You really dislike the bad guys.'

'I don't understand them. I don't understand how they can let go of their humanity. They don't take responsibility for what they do—they always blame others. And I suppose I want to punish them for that.'

'Is it your job to punish them?'

'Someone's got to do it.' I paused. 'Listen, Laura. When I was younger I didn't take responsibility for what I did. When Tara and I broke up I blamed her for it. But I was as much to blame as she was. Only I couldn't see it then, because I wouldn't look at the results of my own actions.'

She looked at me with soft eyes. 'Whoever's doing this to us is really getting under your skin. You see him out there gloating and we don't even know who he is.'

'Thanks for reminding me.'

We then drove in silence until I turned into her driveway and into the blazing lights that met us, pouring their intensity into a daylight that swallowed it and rendered it meaningless.

44

I LEFT LAURA'S HOUSE mid-afternoon and headed to Congleton and the police garage to which my car had been towed. My windscreen was filled with heavy clouds that swept moodily overhead, bursting with grey winter rain that, as I watched, broke and swamped the countryside like a bowl of dirty water tipped over by a clumsy hand. My wipers struggled to clear an arc for me to see through. The air in the car turned cold but I liked it and didn't touch the heating dial.

Eventually I reached Congleton, an old town that has slowly been overgrown by creeping housing estates and pedestrianisation. I found the police garage and identified myself to a uniform at the gate. He reluctantly let me in by lifting a striped barrier. Inside the office, the duty officer stared at me while he made a phone call to fetch someone to accompany me. It turned out to be a broad-faced young woman finishing off a sandwich; a muscle in her jaw worked massively as she ate. She wasn't particularly pleased to be interrupted and eyed me suspiciously over each mouthful until she'd finished. Then she lifted a flap in the counter and took me back through the building, along several dim yellow corridors and finally into the garage through its rear entrance.

The large echoing space reeked of ground-in oil and the smell that skin discharges when it's been soaked in grease for years on end. Out on the floor, two young mechanics in white overalls and gloves, their hair tied behind their heads, had my Cavalier up on a ramp and were poking about underneath. The rain pounded on the roof and was already forming small lakes and rivers on the concrete forecourt visible through the huge open doors.

'You won't find any contraband,' I said. 'Unless you think I'm trying to smuggle rust across the county line.'

'Took a bit of a bashing,' one of the mechanics said. 'Hit another car, did you?' He grinned at his mate.

'He hit me,' I said. 'If you look carefully, using all your training, you can spot it by the scrape on this wing.' I pointed up to where the car's maroon paint job had been forcibly overpainted by a dark shade.

The other mechanic let down the ramp and we congregated round the driver side front wing. It was dented and multicoloured, the damage running all down the length of the wing like a particularly vicious piece of vandalism.

On the other side, where the car had hit the post and then tipped into the ditch, the headlight was cracked and the wing and door were both dented. The smashed windscreen had already been taken out. The car was like an outclassed heavyweight that had gone a few rounds with the champion; but it was still proud.

'Will I get it back?' I asked.

The young woman officer raised her voice over the sound of the rain. 'When it's been processed. Could be a few weeks. You want us to catch the bad guy, don't you?'

'I'm not relying on it,' I said. 'Your record so far's not impressive.'

'Don't take it out on me because your car's a wreck. You'll calm down when you get over the accident.'

'I am over the accident. You don't have to patronise me. What happens to the car now?'

She paused. Having finished her sandwich she was now furiously probing her gums with the end of her tongue. I could tell I'd annoyed her but she was still a public servant and I was still Joe Public. 'We go over it, look for any inconsistencies. Eventually we'll contact you and tell you when and where you can pick it up. You might like to contact your insurers.'

Her tone had moved from irritated to bored as a way of handling what she actually felt about me. I wasn't having that. I took a step towards her.

'I know you've done this a hundred times, but a woman could have been killed last night because of whoever was driving that other car. He did it deliberately, and he's probably responsible for another murder and a kidnapping. So do a good job and we might see him getting his telegram from the Queen behind bars. That'll be a result in my book.'

'I didn't mean—'

'I know you didn't. You weren't really thinking at all. You're just doing your job in the same way you've done it for longer than you'd like to admit, and you're bored. I come along and disrupt your routine, and I'm a member of the public, who are not supposed to be here in the first place, so naturally you're upset and pissed off and not thinking very clearly. I know it's sometimes hard to remember who you're doing all this for. You probably think you're doing it for your boss, and his boss, and the division. But you're wrong. You're actually doing it for me. You're upholding the law, but you don't make the law. It probably seems like you do, but you don't.'

By this time I was breathing heavily, and both the mechanics as well as the young woman were staring at me.

It seemed like a good time to leave. I went out of the open garage doors into the rain, and let it wash me down without hindrance until I reached the Corsa and allowed it to swallow me up.

45

THE RAIN HAD STOPPED but the streets of Crewe were shiny and sleek, the Christmas windows glowing with neon cheer against the premature dark. Harassed shoppers stepped from doorway to doorway, avoiding puddles like antelopes picking their way through rocks.

From my office I phoned Brands and got Carol-the-receptionist straight away. She asked about Laura and I told her she was OK.

'So how can I help?' she asked.

'When I spoke to Melissa Ball, she said that Tara had people she could talk to when she wanted to. Who did she mean?'

There was a pause. 'I'm so stupid,' she said. 'I should sit in a corner with a cone on my head. I should have thought of her.'

'Who?'

'Suzi Hampshire—Tara's executive coach.'

'What's one of those?'

She was hesitant. 'I don't really know. Lots of business people are doing it. Especially people in senior positions. Tara used to see her once a month. Either Suzi would come up from London or Tara would go down there. They'd talk for a couple of hours and for two days afterwards Tara would smile and be nice to us. Then it would wear off and we'd be where we were before. Do I sound cynical?'

'Have you got her number?'

She looked it up and told me. I wrote it down then repeated it back to her.

I looked at what I'd written, then said, 'Why does Suzi Hampshire's name sound familiar?'

'Well, she's Eddie Hampshire's wife, if that's what you mean.'

The consultant who was sacked but was still working out his notice.

'That's interesting,' I said.

'It's quite an interesting story. It was when Mr Hampshire was in the SAS. He went through some rough stuff and had to see a counsellor. That was Suzi. That's when he met her.'

That was very interesting.

I called Suzi Hampshire and was about to leave a message on her answerphone when she picked up. I told her who I was and that I was investigating Tara's disappearance.

'Where are you?' she asked. Her voice had the middle-class hard-edged tone of most medical practitioners I'd met, as though everyone had to obey her orders or there'd be hell to pay.

I told her where I was.

'Can you get to Birmingham tomorrow?' she asked. 'I'm meeting a client mid-morning. I'm staying in the hotel—I could see you first thing after breakfast.'

She told me the name of her hotel and I said I'd be there for nine o'clock.

'Hell of a thing,' she said. 'Rory, then Tara. Thank God there are no kids. Kids shouldn't see their parents treated like this. They never get over it.'

'It happens,' I said, and hung up, wondering what I meant.

46

THE NEXT MORNING I drove down to north Birmingham, to one of the suburbs that were built as wealthy Victorian merchants began to distance themselves from the dark heart of their steel foundries and sought the green pastures of what was then open country. The wide roads and spacious architecture of mansion and church had since been overrun by the mini-community of Chinese takeaway, Laundromat and video store, but if you half-shut your eyes you could still see the outlines of the Palladian refuges that the bearded philanthropists had created for themselves and their families.

I turned off a busy high-street thronged with rush-hour traffic and was instantly driving down tree-lined avenues sign-posted for golf courses and country walks. The hotel where I was to meet Suzi Hampshire stood back from the road, up a long driveway hobbled with ramps that tested my patience and the suspension of the Corsa. The hotel stood at the end of the drive like a boxy wedding cake, its cream walls and white paintwork standing in relief against the massive oaks and chestnut trees behind it.

In the lounge, groups of middle-aged men sat together looking at papers or drinking coffee. Businessmen waiting for their morning sessions to begin. The women in the room were mostly in their mid-twenties, were dressed sharply in dark suits with white blouses, and were trying hard to look elegant and business-like. The woman I took to be Suzi Hampshire was alone, sitting in a dark corner and wearing what my mother would have called a powder-blue suit. She looked to be in her late thirties and had the air of no-nonsense efficiency that I associated with go-getting business predators, not the soft-focus warmth I might have expected from a personal coach used to dealing with people in need of help. She radiated hard edges and clean lines, an appearance that was softened only by the sculpted curve of dark hair that was moulded into a tsunami wave falling from one side of her centre parting and coming to a point level with her chin.

I introduced myself and she moved some papers that she'd been reading so that I could sit. She took some gold half-moon glasses from the end of her nose and folded them carefully into their case. She asked if I wanted coffee and I politely refused.

'Well,' she said. 'Tara. I suppose I should choose my words carefully. You will be taking notes, I assume?'

Wearily I took out my notebook and titled a fresh page.

'Has there been any news?' she asked.

I didn't want to mention the deadline that the kidnapper had set. 'Not as far as I know. The police don't keep me up to date with their investigation.'

'All right,' she said. 'Although I was her executive coach I don't suppose that's covered by legal privilege. We had no contract, except an informal one relating to the mechanics of how often we met. I could, of course, refuse to answer your questions and speak only to the police.'

'Have they been in touch?'

'Not yet. I daresay they'll get round to me. What do they do— investigate Rory's murder first, then move on to Tara when they've solved it?'

'The law moves in mysterious ways. I wouldn't like to predict its course.'

She nodded. 'I'll tell them what I'm about to tell you. Tara was a highly confused young woman. She was impetuous but careful, apparently controlled but emotionally volatile.'

'Was a psychological profile part of the service you offered?'

Her face, if possible, turned a little stonier. She said, 'What I say to you is not necessarily what I would have said to her. My role was to offer support and encouragement. I reflected back to Tara what I heard her saying, even though she didn't always say it overtly.'

I took in her own carefully controlled demeanour, hands folded across her lap, legs crossed at the ankle, head angled slightly to one side in an expression of authoritative expertise. I said, 'What exactly does an executive coach do?'

Despite her air of superiority, she wasn't immune to the lure of self-advertisement. She leaned back expansively in the leather chair. 'I help people focus on their real objectives,' she said. 'Usually they have to create a well-formed outcome so they know exactly why they're moving forward. Often people in high-stress jobs lose sight of their real purpose. I can help them articulate what they want out of life and how they're going to get it.'

'So that involves a lot of talking.'

'I'm qualified in this work, Mr Dyke. I didn't walk in off the street.'

'How many clients do you have at the moment?'

'Enough to keep me busy. Is this going somewhere, or are you trying to see how far you can push me?'

'I was married to Tara a long time ago, when she was still called Debbie. I can see you didn't know that. She was a funny, hyperactive girl who wanted a lot out of life and was easily bored. I imagine she enjoyed talking to you and going over all the problems in her life, but she never solved anything by talking about it. Whenever she hit a problem, she did something. As a matter of fact, she usually ran away.'

'Oh my god—'

'What?'

'You're Daniel's father.'

I looked at her but said nothing. She had said something I never expected anyone to say to me. It took a moment to absorb it.

'She never told you,' she said. 'But you know, don't you? It bothered her that she never got in touch, but she didn't know how to. And I think she felt guilty, too.'

'That doesn't make me feel any better.'

'In a strange way, I think having had Daniel and then giving him away toughened her up. Can you understand that? In fact, I would almost say that she felt her emotional life was a little stunted afterwards. When she talked of Daniel, she did it with a sense of loss.'

'Is this relevant?'

'You could make it relevant. Maybe she couldn't feel for people in the same way that she used to. Maybe it coloured the way she behaved towards Rory. It's possible that the relationship she had with you was the last real relationship she had, although I know it didn't end well.'

'That's an understatement,' I said.

Our conversation had shifted on to another level. We both looked away and adjusted our attitudes.

'Don't judge her too harshly,' she said. 'She thought it reflected more on her than it did on you that she ran away. She couldn't deal with the pressure from you or her parents, particularly her father.'

'The Major.'

'Yes.'

'Did she talk about him at all?'

'I'm an executive coach, Mr Dyke, not a psychoanalyst. My work is based on improving the individual's performance at work through an understanding of what their real drives and motives are. I don't touch on the personal.'

'Nevertheless—'

'Of course Tara talked about her family. That's how I know about Daniel. Let's put it this way, family was not something that Tara was good at. Tara did self, not family.'

'She had friends.'

'Indeed. But she needed them to persuade her that she was—shall we say—a normal member of the human race. Friends were supposed to be good for you, so she cultivated them.'

Despite my dislike of this woman, I was beginning to see another aspect of Tara's life and personality. 'What did she say about herself?'

'Tara seems to have acted impetuously but she always said it was because she misjudged situations. Her judgement wasn't much good. If there was a decision to make, she made the wrong one. Then she put on this brave and confident face and brazened it out. It was exactly the same in her business. She said she used intuition and gut-feeling to help her along. In point of fact, she was just sticking a wet finger in the air to see which way the wind was blowing. When she made decisions she didn't have the slightest clue what she was doing. She called it intuition to make herself feel good. Actually it was bad planning, lack of research and no real understanding of business. She wanted to be in business, but she didn't really understand it. She liked winning, and this was just a forum where she could appear to win without actually having to compete.'

'In my experience of business this doesn't make her unusual. Just more honest than most.'

'And then there was Rory.'

'What do you mean?'

'This was a man who invented the word competition. Tara was fascinated by his unwillingness to let anything go. He had to win—at everything. He must have had such low self-esteem.'

'Did you ever meet him?'

She dismissed this. 'No. There were opportunities when Eddie was working there, Christmas parties and suchlike, but living so far away made it difficult to timetable things. And now Eddie's been kicked out—well, shall we say there's little incentive to visit sunny Waverley.'

'I've met Eddie,' I said. 'What does he make of all this?'

'He liked Tara,' she said. 'Really disliked Rory.'

'He gave the impression that he was able to handle Rory but got fed up with having to deal with him on a daily basis.'

'Eddie likes you to think that he's in control. He would hate you to believe that he'd let his real feelings get in the way of dealing with Rory.'

'And did he?'

'What?'

'Let his feelings get in the way.'

Suzi Hampshire folded one hand on top of the other again. She was now speaking very quietly in the gloomy lounge.

'I understand that Rory was difficult to get along with. But Eddie is a big man in all sorts of ways, and he usually gets what he wants. It served him well in the forces. When he doesn't get his way, it hurts. When Rory was making life difficult for him, I know he was very frustrated. He spoke a lot to Tara about it; she told me.'

'It sounds like an incestuous little group. How did you feel about it?'

'You learn to separate out what's important from what's not. I told Eddie to stick to the facts of the matter and not to get angry.'

'Did your advice work?'

'I believe so.'

'But you're not certain.'

'Eddie and I separated a month ago, Mr Dyke. I can't be certain about anything any more.'

'I'm sorry to hear that.'

'You needn't be. Eddie's an exceptional man with a strength of will that you don't come across very often.'

'How did he cope in the Regiment?'

'As I understand it, very well.'

'What made a man like him, with that strength of character, join up in the first place?'

She looked at me with a raised eyebrow. 'When he was four his father abandoned him and his mother. He felt rootless. He told me he needed a strong masculine presence in his life, at least for a short while.'

Who's the Daddy now, I thought. I said, 'That shows a lot of self-awareness.'

She nodded. 'Have you heard the story about the Rolls-Royce?' I shook my head. 'When he was young and in the Army, before he joined the Regiment, he saw a man in his twenties parking a gold Rolls-Royce Camargue outside a house in Twickenham. He had no idea who this man was, but Eddie was struck by the fact that someone so young could have the money or the success to own a car like that. So Eddie decided he was going to have one. He started putting money aside and ten years later, when he hit thirty, he bought his own Rolls-Royce. Not new, of course. He took me to see it once. It's in a lock-up garage in Welwyn Garden City. He takes it out for a spin once a month, if he can.'

'Impressive.'

'That's what I mean by will-power. He sets his mind to something, he gets it.'

She hesitated as if about to say more, but caught herself and looked away.

'What else is there?' I asked quietly.

Now she looked directly at me, and for the first time her face had softened. Her monumental wave of hair showed hints of grey at its roots and I realised she was probably ten years older than I'd first thought. As she was tiring her real age was beginning to show.

'You didn't ask why we'd split up,' she said. 'Very noble of you, though I daresay you were interested, in the current circumstances.'

'I thought you'd tell me if it were any of my business, or if it were relevant.'

She sighed. 'It's relevant. I think Eddie was seeing Tara. Even if he wasn't, he was interested in her. Ever since Rory married her and brought her into the company, Eddie was interested. It got quite embarrassing. He talked about her all the time, made any number of excuses to go up to Waverley and see her.'

'Did she return his interest?'

'I have no idea and quite frankly I don't care. I know that probably sounds odd, but I was married to Eddie, not to her. I was more interested in what he was up to. If it wasn't her it would have been someone else.'

'Things were that bad between you?'

'I guess so. If I think about it. And when things are that bad you tend not to think about it. What's your view?'

'Don't ask me, I'm a beginner in these things. You're the executive coach.'

She smiled wanly. It broke a mood.

I said, 'Do you think Eddie would have had anything to do with Rory's murder or Tara's disappearance?'

'Mr Dyke, Eddie could kill almost anyone with a flick of his eyebrow. Paradoxically, it gives him enormous self-control. If he felt that badly towards someone he'd be more likely to laugh in their faces while making them realise at the same time that he could inflict enormous pain or damage on them. He wouldn't actually have to do it. Besides, as I'm sure you know, he was in London when Rory was murdered.'

'Where is he now?'

'I told you, we separated a month ago.'

'But you're still in business together.'

Her expression didn't change but she knew she was caught in a bluff. Without moving her eyes from my face, she said:

'Somewhere in the Lake District. He's running a team training course. You'll have to phone the client to find out where they are.'

She gave me the name of a well-known oil company and the location of their head office in the UK. 'Or you could ring his mobile,' she added. 'Though he probably won't answer if he's working.'

The hotel lounge was now completely empty except for Suzi Hampshire and myself. Course delegates had gone to their training rooms for the morning sessions, breakfast meetings had ended, visitors had emptied their cafetières and moved on.

'You mentioned that you've separated,' I said. 'Who moved out—you or Eddie?'

'Me. It was my decision. Why?'

I hesitated. 'Do you still have a key?'

For once she looked shocked. 'Do you think I'd give it to you?'

'Mrs Hampshire, one person's been killed and another is missing. I can break and enter, if necessary. But I'd rather go in quietly.'

'You don't even know where the house is.'

'I will when you tell me.'

She let out a short bark that was evidently her version of a laugh. She stared at me for a moment, then reached down for her bag and took out a key ring. She detached a Yale key and handed it to me, giving the address of the house as she did so.

I stood up and thanked her for her time.

'What will you do now?' she asked. Her hard edge had vanished and she seemed older and more vulnerable than the professional sceptic I'd first met.

'It's better that you don't know,' I said.

She nodded, then looked me in the eye with an expression of sincere concern. 'Have you talked to Daniel?' she asked.

'I only found out about him a few days ago. At the moment I don't know what I'd say.'

'I could probably get an address for you.'

'That would be kind.'

She looked at me oddly. 'Do you think so?'

47

THE ADDRESS THAT SUZI had given me was in Hatfield, north of London, about an hour's drive from where I was parked. I got back on the motorway, heading south again, into driving rain. The constant stream of lorries whipped up a dirty grey slush that pounded against the windscreen of the Corsa. I frowned into the road and watched tail-lights intently.

Suzi Hampshire had given me a lot to think about. It was obvious that the relationship between Tara and Eddie was much more serious—at least in his eyes—than anyone had realised. I'd seen that kind of obsession before in middle-aged men. It was more than the usual crisis—the fear that the opportunity for sex or other kinds of happiness was becoming remote—it was a kind of egocentricity, a belief that age had created wonders of technique that younger women would be only too glad to experience, if they had the chance. I'd also seen situations when that belief wasn't matched by the woman's willingness to comply, and a kind of madness had come over the man, making him unable to see things straight. What surfaced then was jealousy, envy and an internal rage that distorted reason like a magnifying glass being passed over a page of type—enlarging conversations and casual remarks that the woman made and warping their meaning.

Had Eddie Hampshire entered this state of mind? Was his relationship with Tara skewed in this way? I still didn't believe that she'd conspired with him to murder Rory and take hold of the business. But at the same time I realised that people changed, and that maybe Tara had been influenced by Eddie's air of confidence. After all, she'd reacted violently against her life with me. Perhaps that was her defining feature—a susceptibility to mood and atmosphere in a relationship. And then a willingness to take drastic action to change it.

She'd altered quite a lot since I knew her. And so had I.

Eddie Hampshire's house was on a new estate of three-storey red-brick buildings evidently aimed at young professionals moving one step up from their starter home. There was a garage built into the front that accounted for most of the ground floor space, though looking around at the other houses, most people seemed to park on the short driveways in front of the garage and probably used the internal space for storage. There was no vehicle on Eddie's drive.

I put the key in the lock and went in. Suzi had told me the house wasn't alarmed, so I shut the door quietly behind me and started to look around. There was a strong smell of citrus in the air—perhaps cleaning products used in the kitchen, which was straight ahead of me. To my left was the side door to the garage—locked. I went into the kitchen. It was one room that ran the width of the house and was split in two by a breakfast bar. There was no washing up on the sink, very little food in the fridge. There was a phone attached to the wall. I dialled 1471 but the last call was from a double-glazing outfit with a special offer. I turned around and went up the first flight of stairs, my ears tuned in to the slightest hint of sound.

Here there was a bathroom done as a fashionable wet-room, all in white with silver accessories. Around the well of the stairs were three bedrooms of roughly equal size. Two of them were furnished as bedrooms, the other was a store room and held half a dozen cardboard boxes fastened down with broad sticky tape of the sort that's dispensed by a gun. The walls of all the rooms were painted plain white, the only decor being abstract prints— splashes of primary colour that had been hurled almost angrily on to the canvas. It was as though the house had been put together by someone of Spartan taste but who concealed an inner passion that had to be released somehow.

The top floor was one large sitting room, a corner of which had been arranged as an office: computer, printer, filing cabinet, two shelves containing management books. The computer sat on what looked to be an antique desk that had drawers either side. The rest of the room was laid out traditionally, with a floral sofa and a couple of armchairs facing a wide-screen television and a modern electric fire that was designed to look like a wood-burning grate. It struck me how conventional Eddie's living arrangements were—but why not? He'd served in the forces and knew how to kill someone easily. That didn't mean he wore camouflage clothing and lived in a tent in the forest.

I turned back to the desk and went through the drawers. It seemed that Eddie filed away his correspondence in a clear plastic folder until he'd dealt with it, at which point he transferred the letters into dated box-files that stood on his shelves. The boxes went back five years. I read a few letters in the plastic folder but there was nothing of interest.

In the bottom right-hand drawer I found a key ring containing half a dozen keys. I put them in my pocket.

I stood and looked around the room. I didn't know what I'd expected to find, but nothing I'd seen so far yelled 'Murderer!' Perhaps I was missing something.

I went to the windows and looked over the front driveway. This was a polite suburban community whose families worked in the IT industry or petro-chemicals or finance, whose mothers took the children to school in the 4x4 and whose fathers spent the weekend playing golf and tinkering with their sound systems. It reminded me of Waverley in its dedication to perpetuating the status quo. It was utterly aspirational and commonplace, and to think that Eddie Hampshire had blown a fuse, murdered Rory and kidnapped Tara was madness.

I felt the keys in my pocket and had a thought. I went downstairs quickly and one by one tried the keys in the garage door. Finally one turned and the door swung open, into darkness. I found a switch inside and turned it on.

The heavy Germanic bulk of a black BMW X5 stood less than a metre from me, its black windows reflecting my own features. I turned and looked down its flank, where a long red streak the same colour as my Cavalier ran down its offside wing and told me all that I needed to know.

48

I RETREATED OUT OF the garage and went back upstairs. I'd remembered something that I'd read a few minutes before. I dug out the plastic folder containing Eddie's current correspondence and burrowed down to the third item. It was a letter written on headed paper from a Mr Charles Samuels, confirming that the property on Meadbank would be let to Edward Hampshire for another year.

I took out my mobile phone and rang Suzi Hampshire. She answered almost immediately.

'Where's Meadbank?' I said.

There was a pause. 'Is that Mr Dyke?' I told her it was. 'Why do you want to know where Meadbank is?'

'Is it the lock-down garage that Eddie rents?'

'Yes.'

'How do I get there?'

'It's in Welwyn. Find the rugby ground and it's just behind. There's a group of half a dozen in a row next to some waste ground. You won't be able to get in without a key.'

'I've got one,' I said.

The rugby club was deserted—not surprisingly for a wet December lunch-time. The ground looked sodden and inhospitable, and this bleakness spread to the houses that backed on to the field of play. I drove around the ground and explored the streets that fed off the main road and finally came across a row of six garages behind an open field. The field was wild and strewn with rubbish and bits of masonry and metal. The garages were single story concrete blocks with up-and-over doors, each painted battleship grey and marked with graffiti and the scars of assaults sustained over the years.

I had a set of keys but no idea which door they fitted, so I worked down the row patiently until I came to one that was guarded by two heavy padlocks. One of the keys worked one of the padlocks, which I undid and pulled out. None of the other keys would go into the second lock. Eddie must have kept the key with him.

I looked back at the Corsa. In my Cavalier I had a kit in the boot that helped a resourceful private detective in all manner of ways. But I hadn't transferred it to the courtesy car, so I had no way of prising off the second padlock.

Angry with myself and beginning to worry that by now people in the houses beyond would be watching, and possibly calling the local police, I started looking around the garages and in the field behind them. After a few minutes trudging through the long grass, I came across a pile of weather-beaten housebricks. I picked one up and hefted it for weight. It felt about right. I took it back to the garage and using both hands began noisily hammering at the second padlock. In a short time the fitting it was attached to peeled away far enough for me to lever it off completely. I turned the handle of the door and slid it upwards. It rose with a horrible graunching noise like the opening of the gates of Hell.

Inside, Eddie Hampshire's pale blue 1973 Rolls-Royce Silver

Shadow gleamed in the dull half-light.

The car had been reversed into the garage, its proud bonnet facing outwards, the Spirit of Ecstasy flying upwards towards nothing but a steel door. One of the keys on the key-ring I'd taken from Eddie Hampshire's office had a Rolls-Royce fob attached to it. With it I opened the driver's door and climbed inside. I sank into the driver's seat and looked at the wood inlaid dashboard and its precision-tooled instruments. The smell of old leather and high-grade machine-engineering was potent, despite the number of years the car must have spent in the damp and forlorn garage. But there was another smell that lay over the expensive aroma of wealth and class generated by the car's component parts—a smell I didn't anticipate and didn't like.

I climbed out and shut the door, then walked to the rear of the car, into the gloom at the back of the garage. I felt a growing tightness in my chest as I inserted the key and lifted the boot-lid— and saw the body of Tara Brand curled up inside, her eyes closed, her fists balled, her lips slightly open as if exhaling a final, unheard, plea.

*

Something broke in my stomach and flooded my mouth with a taste of bile. I stared at her body and felt as though something had come full circle – I'd watched the trajectory of someone's life turn towards me, keep glittering contact for a while, then arc away once more, only to return and end its flight in this dank and squalid place, in a vehicle built less than a mile from where I lived. I was sad for Tara and I was sad for myself. Despite everything, in the end I'd done nothing to change this outcome.

Then from the front of the garage, a voice said, 'Step away from there.'

49

I TURNED AND SAW a silhouette against the open door. The silhouette was short and wide. It took a step towards me and the blurred outline resolved itself into Major Hoyt, Tara's father, still wearing his complicated overcoat but this time carrying in his right hand a Browning High Power Double Action revolver, current model. There was a time when guns were a hobby of mine and I recognised this one easily. More easily because it was pointed towards my chest.

'I said step away,' he repeated, advancing a step. His face was pinched and focused, his hand rock-steady.

I stood back from the boot, barely able to take my eyes from Tara's body. Curled up, she looked younger than her years and incredibly vulnerable. Her hair, auburn and disarranged as ever, fell sideways over her face and shoulders. Had she been dead before Hampshire put her in the boot? Or had she suffocated there? Dying a lonely and terrified death and wondering how she had ever entangled herself with a man like Hampshire in the first place?

I felt a vast reservoir of anger take shape and form inside me.

'What's there?' the Major asked.

I said, 'Sir, it would be better if you kept away.'

'Move back,' he said again. 'I know how to use this, Dyke, and I won't hesitate.'

I stepped further away and watched him edge down the length of the car, turning sideways to manoeuvre himself between the vehicle and the wall of the garage. When he reached the rear of the car, his eyes flicked down into the boot and the hand holding the Browning dropped immediately. A deep exhalation of breath came from him and his legs gave way. I stepped forward and caught him and took the gun from him in one move. He didn't fight me, but immediately stiffened in my grip and raised himself upright.

'Who ... who did this?' he said.

'Don't you know? You've been following me.'

He looked up. 'Of course I've been following you. On and off for the last few days. I don't trust you, Dyke. Ever since Deborah left you I wondered what was the real reason for her sudden departure.'

I couldn't waste my time dealing with the suspicions of a paranoid father, but I was going to need his cooperation.

I explained who Eddie Hampshire was and his relationship to Tara. I told him I thought they'd both been responsible in some way for Rory Brand's death.

He had shaken himself from me and was leaning both his hands against the side of the Rolls-Royce, staring down at the floor and shaking his head. 'Not murder, not Deborah,' he said.

'I don't think she was present.'

'I kept telling her that her choice of men would land her in trouble.' He looked up at me. 'Perhaps I misjudged you,' he said. 'At least you never did her deliberate harm.'

His remark affected me more than I expected. I opened my mouth to speak but my throat was too liquid for any words to emerge. In one way the Major was right—I'd never intended to hurt her—but I'd hurt her nonetheless. Because of my lack of attention, my self-centredness and my unwillingness to understand. And the cost to me now was as high as when she'd left me the first time.

'We must call the police,' Hoyt said. 'We must track down this Hampshire person and get the police on him.'

'I know how to find him,' I said. 'And I'm going after him. But I want you to wait before contacting the police.'

'What do you mean, wait? We should tell them immediately. This is my daughter ...'

He broke and turned away, his head bowed. I reached a hand to his shoulder.

'If we scare him now there's no telling what he might do. I want to confront him and bring him in before he can do any more harm. And I think there's someone else involved.'

'Someone else? Who?'

'I have an idea, but I'm not sure.'

He turned back to me. 'Well for God's sake make sure,' he said.

I left him with his daughter and a plan that we agreed between us, then climbed in my car and headed north. The deadline that Hampshire had set for the weekend had been a feint, a trick. He'd been playing with us and our expectations all along, another element in his desire to show his superiority. Now, with Tara found, it was true that the sense of urgency that I'd felt had vanished.

But I still had a sense of purpose.

50

I DROVE NORTH, avoiding the motorway. Up through Lichfield and Rugeley and on to the A51, the fast country route taking me through Stone and Trentham and Stoke, then sweeping westward towards Crewe.

It was mid-afternoon, after the lunch-time traffic and before the evening build-up of travellers who, like me, were avoiding the M6. The roads were still quiet and easy to drive. But I saw almost none of the scenery, allowing the car to drive itself while I thought through everything I'd heard.

Eddie Hampshire was smitten by Tara. What's more, he couldn't stand Rory. Tara was a keen businesswoman but her judgement was faulty. Maybe her judgement was faulty in more areas than one. Maybe her impetuosity, of which I had first-hand experience, was the trait that got her in trouble. If she and Rory were virtually estranged, as Dominic Michaels had suggested, maybe she and Eddie were planning a coup of their own. But then why would he kill her? Because she was now a threat? Because she refused to return his feelings for her?

I remembered my first trip to her house, when I'd heard them arguing and saw his car vanishing down the drive. What had they been arguing about? Was it a lovers' tiff, or was there something darker taking place, a deeper hurt that only manifested itself completely with Tara's death?

When I got home I called Laura and explained what I'd found.

'My God,' she said. 'Poor woman. What must it have been like for her?'

'I don't know,' I said. 'I can't imagine.'

She heard something in my voice. 'Are you OK?' she asked.

'I'll get over it,' I said.

There was a pause while she thought about this, then she went on, 'I guess it makes sense. He spent a lot of time with Tara. They were always closeted in one of the little rooms, discussing "strategy", or so they said. Well, maybe they were, as far as she was concerned. But maybe he was just taking the opportunity to spend time with the light of his life.'

'You don't sound surprised.'

'My bosses have been murdered and I was run off the road in a car. What actually do you think could surprise me at this moment in time?'

'Point taken. Did you know Hampshire had been in the SAS?'

'Of course—I told you we'd had people who'd been in the forces.'

'Yes, you did.'

'How does that fit in? He never talked about what he did, but presumably he was trained and could kill people. Is that it?'

'Partly,' I said.

I told her what I'd learned about the psychological theory from the book that Mal O'Donovan had given me. I sounded strange even to my own ears as I told her about Berne's theory of Transactional Analysis, and how someone moving into their Critical Parent ego state can bring out the Critical Parent in others. 'Maybe Hampshire is paranoid about this stuff,' I said. 'He took orders in the SAS, and I don't know, maybe he enjoyed it. But maybe he was damned if he was going to take orders from a jumped up egocentric like Rory.'

'Sounds a bit childish.'

'Men are,' I said. 'Don't let us fool you. We can harbour grudges, plot revenge, get our own back.'

'So those messages that were left behind—'

'Think about it—"Who's the daddy now?" He's saying, You're not my parent. I don't do what you tell me to do. And "Where's the little girl?" Perhaps Tara acted like a child with him—needy, temperamental, impulsive, as she could be. God knows I had some of that. I think Hampshire is just playing a game, thinking he's cleverer than the rest of us. Leaving clues that aren't really clues, but showing that he understands this psychology stuff. He knows what he's doing and he doesn't care.'

Laura said nothing for a while. I presumed she was thinking back, remembering the way Hampshire and Tara had been with each other in the office, replaying scenes and incidents and seeing them all through new eyes.

'So what do you do now?' she said. 'Shouldn't you go to the police with all this?'

'You're forgetting he has an alibi. He was in London on the morning Rory was found dead in his office. He couldn't be in two places at one time.'

'Even so, there's plenty for the police to go with, isn't there? Let them check him out. You don't need to be involved any more. You've done your work now.' Her voice had acquired an edge of accusation. 'Sam, I have a feeling you're not listening to me.'

I said nothing.

'You've got some kind of revenge fantasy going on in your head,' she went on. 'But that's not the point. You were hired to investigate the murder and the kidnapping, not to track down and bring the villain to justice, like some kind of Western marshal. You're not Clint Eastwood.'

'This isn't about revenge,' I said.

'Don't fool yourself,' she said. Her usual humour had

vanished.

'Okay,' I said. 'It is about revenge. But not in the way you think. It's not that I want tit for tat. This isn't a schoolyard fight.'

'So what is it?'

'If Hampshire is the murderer, he needs to know it's not acceptable to do what he did. He did it in cold blood. He's taken two people's lives for reasons of his own, but he doesn't seem to have done it out of passion. He's thought about them. And that's what I can't stand. Deliberate cruelty. Malicious intent. And if the police get to him first, he'll enter the system and he'll start feeling self-righteous. They all do. He won't take respons-ibility for his actions.'

'And it's your job to teach him that?'

'I don't have to. But I want to. Tara deserves that, if nothing else.'

Laura's breathing came down the phone line. 'I can't deal with this,' she said. 'I'll talk to you tomorrow.'

'Are you going to be all right?'

'What difference does it make to you?' she said fiercely. 'You're going to play out this little fantasy of yours anyway, aren't you? You don't care what I think.'

'That's not true.'

'Well prove it. Stay home. Tell Howard what you know about Eddie Hampshire then have a cup of tea.'

'I can't do that.'

'Then do what you want,' she said.

The line went dead.

51

I WAS CHANGING MY clothes ten minutes later when my mobile phone rang. I took it from my jacket pocket, expecting it to be Laura with an apology. A familiar booming voice rang in my ear. 'Dyke? Eddie Hampshire here. I gather you've been asking some questions about me. What are you, a tosspot? If you want to know anything you can come out and ask me straight, like a man. You don't have to go sniffing round ex-wives and so forth.'

'You've talked to Suzi.'

'She's still my wife. I can talk to her when I like.'

'But why should I talk to you? People tell me you're a bit of a tosspot.'

He ignored this.

'Come up here and see me. Can't get away at the moment. Paying clients and all that. Got to do the social thing, eat and drink and tell rude stories.' He began to give me complex directions to Mill Gill. I grabbed a pencil and wrote them down. 'Eventually you'll see waterfalls. It's on the maps. I'll see you later tonight, when the dust has settled.'

'I'll be there.'

'Good. You didn't strike me as a tosspot when we met—don't

let me down now.'

With all the phone calls finished, the house seemed emptier than usual. The wintry light and cold snap in each room was a deterrent to good feeling. I put on Uncle Tupelo's Anodyne, played loud, and got my adrenaline pumping while I went upstairs and packed a bag.

When I was packed I switched on my home computer and made some notes. I e-mailed them as an attachment to myself, saved them to a floppy, labelled it, and left it standing upright on the keyboard where it wouldn't be missed. I also made two phone calls, one of them to the hotel that Hampshire had mentioned, and booked a room for the night.

While writing I'd heated up a lasagne in the oven and I ate it standing in the living room, the music banging round the house like a flight of tin trays racketing off the walls and colliding with common-sense.

I didn't have a gun, but I had a sap that I'd taken from a lout in Cromptons Bar in Kirkby. Its unnatural weight moved back and forth as I passed its cool leather between my hands. I lifted a trouser leg and tucked it inside the long socks that I'd put on. I also picked up my Whitby knife with the one inch curved blade. It was small and light in my hand, but comfortable. I wore a black North Face fleece and a thick Berghaus jacket over it with a zip-up neck and corded waist-band. I'd also put on my thickest pair of jeans and a heavy pair of Canadian Columbia boots with a massive tread whose grip I liked. I felt well-protected, though I'd have to turn off the heater in the car or I'd lose twenty pounds before I reached Cumbria.

It was now almost six o'clock and I had a two and a half hour drive ahead of me. I stood in the living room for a moment, staring at the walls. The blue stain where the damp-proof course had ruptured three years ago and leaked ground water into a square foot of wall. The hunting prints that I'd rescued from a charity shop, depicting eighteenth century horses leaping with their legs fore and aft over bramble hedges. The six inches of peeling wallpaper where two edges joined above a radiator and had lost their adhesion. The homely details of an unfulfilled life.

I wondered whether I'd get the chance to fulfil it.

52

I'D ALWAYS LIKED the drive north, pushing through and then leaving behind the messy conurbations of Manchester, Warrington, Bolton and Blackburn, the raw, grey mill towns that had provided the backbone for so much of the country's wealth for so long, before progress and fashion had declared them expendable. In the dark you see nothing of the towns, hiding beyond stretches of greenery and fields and sunk in their own vision of themselves as vital hotspots of sophisticated nightlife.

After Preston the traffic and urban sprawl thinned out, leaving just myself and a few hardy voyagers heading towards the rugged swoop of hill and dale that we couldn't discern against the glare of vehicle headlights, but sensed as a looming companion on either side of the road. Occasionally, when the motorway lights dropped away and left us in comparative darkness, a segment of moon appeared briefly, only to be hidden again by the hulking peaks that smothered us and kept our eyes focused on the trail of red lights leading endlessly north.

An hour and a half into the journey I pulled into Forton Services for petrol and a break from the car's constant vibration. At the speed I was driving, the noise of the small-engined Corsa was setting up home in my head. I didn't want to kick start another migraine. That would be asking for trouble.

I rang Laura from the bizarre circular food hall at Forton that looks like an airport's communication tower. A group of children in the crèche area sat hypnotised by cartoon TV as though they'd never seen it before.

'It's me,' I said. 'I'm on my way to the Lakes.'

'You couldn't wait,' she said.

'He called me. He knows I've been asking questions. He wants to find out what kind of tosspot I am.'

'And what kind are you?'

'The kind that doesn't know how to listen to what other people say. The kind that's too full of his own importance to consider other people's feelings.'

She was silent a moment, accepting the apology. 'Where are you meeting him?'

I told her.

'It's high up there. You don't like heights.'

'There's lots of things I don't like that I live with.'

She said nothing for a while, then, 'Is that music I can hear behind you?'

'I'm taking a sensible break. A sign told me that tiredness could kill.'

Her voice became soft. 'What will you say when you see him?'

'I'll tell him I know everything. That he should give himself up and ask for clemency from the court.'

'Will he listen?'

'No. That's what makes it exciting.'

The radio stations began to crackle as I pushed further into the Lake District's valleys. I put on Neil Young's After the Goldrush and was carried on his thin high voice into the increasingly dark and empty countryside. Tales of spaceships and riverboats seemed alien but somehow fitting in a landscape devoid of features except the occasional lantern burning against a hillside cottage.

At Junction 40 I turned off and took the road towards Kendall and Ambleside. At first it was fast, but eventually we came off the two-lane expressway and hit the dark country roads that twisted and wound towards the lakes. The Neil Young tape finished and I switched off the radio that suddenly squawked at me with some mindless DJ exhorting me to party hard. The silence echoed around the cabin.

Eventually I entered the Langdale valley, moving silently on a pale road between high peaks that rose at either side. There was no other traffic. The clouds had vanished, and suddenly I saw that moonlight was bathing the fields and hills with an ivory-blue tint the colour of bruised skin. After a couple of miles the large red sign of the Unicorn Hotel appeared, at the foot of the ridge I knew to be Dungeon Ghyll. Beyond it rose Mill Gill and the track that kept pace with Dungeon Ghyll Force, the waterfall that tumbled downwards over rock and gully for a couple of hundred feet. I'd had friends in C & E who came up here to walk and climb. I'd seen their triumphant photos: on the peaks; by Stickle Tarn; in the Old Dungeon Ghyll Hotel; getting drunk.

The peaks were high, had crumbled pathways that were unsafe even in daylight, and were shot through with screes, waterfalls and gullies that I didn't know and wouldn't be able to see. Apparently, according to my friends, both Wordsworth and Coleridge had written about this area.

But however poetic the peaks were, whatever beauty they held for the walker who had struggled to scale them, they were no less dangerous at night, in the dark, with a cunning murderer patrolling them like an uncaged bear.

53

TURNING IN BY THE hotel sign, I was now on a private tarmac road that led between tall pines and over humps in the road that were spotlit by small round lamps at either side and painted with diagonal yellow lines. A sign pointed off to stables, and another to the farm. This went on for fifty yards until the pine trees fell away and the glare of the Unicorn Hotel itself came into view. It was an Edwardian mansion that had been converted into a hotel. A semi-circle of driveway passed in front of the entrance and then continued to rejoin the main road further down. A car park stood to the left, and I could see the gleam of executive vehicles shining dully in the moonlight, their massive power just waiting to be unleashed.

The entrance was a blue canopy stretched over half a dozen stone steps that led up to tall wooden doors, one of which was currently open and revealing a welcome glow. An unlit verandah stretched down one side of the building, with rows of neatly chopped firewood like huge cigarettes stacked tidily in front of its glass doors. As far as I could see, every other window in the building was lit, radiating a soft light into the surrounding darkness. I drove past the hotel to the car park and found an empty bay. When I killed the engine and stepped out, the stillness hit me like a blow. I took my bag from the rear seat and walked over crunching gravel to the front entrance and up the stone steps.

From inside I heard the deep-throated conversation and laughter of males in a state of heightened excitement. Pushing open the door it was as though I'd crashed a loud party that was at its height. I was met by a crowd of twenty or so people, mostly male, who were standing in excited conversation on the tiled floor of the lobby. There was a smell of damp and testosterone rising like a primitive cologne from the crowd, as if to entice frailer sexual companions to abandon themselves to some ancient orgiastic rite. They wore parkas and rain gear with hoods and toggles and zips, and one or two carried clipboards holding lists and maps. I spotted three people wielding long torches. It seemed that a night exercise—some kind of group search activity—was in the process of finishing. The noise of self-congratulation boomed and echoed around the panelled lobby as they re-told their tales of bravery out in the Cumbrian wilds.

I fought my way through to the reception desk, where a young woman with a frazzled smile and a dark-blue uniform seemed happy to see me. As I spoke, she tilted her head to one side to demonstrate her keen attention. I told her my name and said that I'd rung earlier. This close to Christmas the management training season was winding down and they'd found me a room despite the large party that jostled and laughed around me. On the walls by the reception desk there were plates awarded by various tourist bodies, illustrating with rosettes and stars the high quality of the hospitality that awaited me.

The receptionist asked me to fill out a card and asked whether I'd like a newspaper or an early morning call. I told her neither.

'Breakfast's between seven-thirty and nine o'clock,' she said, 'and we like the rooms to be emptied by ten. Now can I swipe your credit card, please?'

I mused on the decline of customer service as I handed over

my card. She accepted it with another tilt of her head, and a smile. As she put it through the machine and waited for it to register, she said, 'Oh, Mr Dyke? I have a note for you.'

She leafed through a box and came up with a small yellow envelope, which I took from her and opened immediately. It was from Hampshire:

I trust you've signed in. Ask the receptionist to point you towards Mill Gill. I'm out here till gone midnight, so we can meet and have a proper talk. I'll be the one in the red jacket carrying a torch. You'll find me.

I turned to the receptionist, who was handing me back my credit card. 'When were you given this?'

'I don't know, sir. The girl on the previous shift found it on the counter. Would you like to speak to her?'

I said no, then picked up my bag and made my way through the crowd to the door that led to the stairs.

Once in my room, I kitted myself out. The prospect of Eddie Hampshire waiting for me in the dark, in landscape I didn't know, wasn't promising. I checked the sap that I'd put in my sock and re-seated it, put some coins in each of my pockets to act as knuckle-dusters if necessary, and tied my shoelaces with double bows so they wouldn't trip me up. I did a couple of stretching exercises to warm my muscles, zipped my North Face fleece up to my neck, then left the room. I hadn't even unpacked my bag.

Downstairs, the crowd was thinner because the majority of them had moved into the bar and lounge, which was a kind of glass gazebo with a view over an elaborately paved patio, currently lit up like a stage set. They were flopped on cane chairs as though the bones had been extracted from their bodies. They had barely enough strength to hold their pint glasses. I approached the receptionist and asked her for the quickest way up Mill Gill. She performed her habitual head-tilt and reached for a collection of printed tourist leaflets that were filed in a wire contraption screwed to the side of the reception counter. She placed it before me with a flourish and then pointed to key areas on the line-drawn map on its reverse.

'That's us. You come out of here, through the main door, then turn right and walk past the car park and through this field. There's a gate just here, then you follow the path upwards, but be careful because it's not safe. Are you sure you want to go out this late, sir? There's not much light out there at this time of night.'

An odd expression had come over her face, a mixture of excitement and curiosity. Through the windows to her left we could both see it was pitch black, and now the heat generated by the adventurers who'd occupied the lobby had dissipated, a chill was beginning to settle in the space that the dying log-fire in the corner couldn't do anything to alleviate.

'I'll be fine. I'll be back in an hour. Will I be able to get something to eat?'

'Last orders for the restaurant are nine forty-five, so you should just make it.' Now she frowned, and I thought she was going to give me one more admonishment about going out in the dark. She said, 'I'd try to get back for nine-fifteen, if I were you. Chef's a bit touchy about late-comers.'

But Chef's feelings were the last thing on my mind.

54

OUT OF THE UNICORN I turned right and edged between the cold metallic bodies of the executive vehicles in the car park. At the far end of the field was a gate that I pushed open and went through, stepping immediately onto a gravel and pebble path that crunched and spat underfoot as I headed upwards.

It was shortly after eight, so dark that hedges and tree trunks appeared blue, and the air was cold enough to make my cheeks burn inside five minutes. A muted, visceral throb came from the hotel behind me, but that soon vanished and for a moment I heard nothing except my own feet crackling through bracken and grass that was beginning to freeze.

Then I began to hear the sporadic splatter of Dungeon Ghyll Force, the waterfall that ran down the face of the hillside, dropping vertically in a couple of places and then finding a level amongst rocks and rapids before plunging downwards again.

After a few minutes I reached a small plateau with a view of the waterfall and a wooden bench from which to enjoy it. I stood there, listening to the intricate patterns created by the waterfall, and inhaled the smell of the land, a rich, dark aroma that hit the back of my throat so that I tasted more than smelled it. Despite the accumulating layer of frost, the tenacious odour of soil, tree bark and animal fertilizer punched through to the more primitive parts of my brain, invigorating my senses.

I looked up at the waterfall and to the left, where the pale stone of the cliff face was broken by the dark shadows of trees that huddled together, spreading upwards from the base of the outcrop. Massive rocks, edged silver by moonlight, squatted bulkily at the base of the cliff. They were jagged and brutal and made something in my stomach twist.

Outlined against the sky I could see a figure wearing what I could tell by moonlight was a red jacket, waving a torch in my direction and making slow figures-of-eight with it. I set off upwards again.

The ground was carpeted by small rocks and pebbles. My feet stumbled and slipped despite the outsized grip of the Canadian boots. My breath became shallower as I slowly picked my way upwards. Raising my head, I saw the path continue to wind upwards by the side of the waterfall until it made its way to the top, a hundred feet or more overhead. I pressed on, my breath beginning to rasp in my ears and the sweat gathering in the folds of my clothes.

Another ten minutes and I'd arrived at the top, breathing hard, blood pumping through my chest, my legs aching. The sound of the waterfall was loud and had lost whatever romantic musical quality I'd lent it when I was at the bottom. Turning to my left, towards the cliff face, I could see across the Langdale valley to the hills on the far side, silhouetted and blank against a sky now made bright by the moon.

On the edge of the cliff stood the figure in the red jacket, waiting passively for me to approach. He'd turned off the torch so I saw nothing but the outline of his shape, hunched and surprisingly slim.

It was at that moment of realisation that I felt an arm round my neck and my right hand being grabbed and twisted behind my back. The noise of the waterfall had covered his approach. I heard myself grunt as I was half lifted from my feet and pushed forward, towards the cliff. At the same time, something was being looped around my wrists. When I tried to turn, I suddenly found that my hands were bound together by rope. It had the tension and spongy grip of 10 millimetre climbers' rope; it wouldn't give. As I struggled, the loops wrapped around my wrists were being attached to another rope, like a lead, and this was swiftly pulled tighter. In a moment I'd been tied so that I was turned away from my attacker and helpless to fight back.

I was suddenly pushed forward, then pulled stumbling backwards towards him. The lead was being tested.

'First rule of warfare,' said Hampshire's voice close to my ear, 'never put your back to the enemy.'

I turned my head to look at him, and received a vicious clout on the side of my face. My cheek stung, and fear began to rise in me as I saw the cliff edge coming closer with each step.

55

THE PAIN IN MY head started thrumming in the cheek that Hampshire had hit. Another migraine was about to start up. Great timing. It was as though someone was applying a series of electrodes to my right cheek, then to my temple, then up on to my forehead. The pain modulated from the burn you feel from a slap on the face to the deep, resonant torment of a knife that has punctured flesh and is now twisting and turning, tearing sinew and muscle apart.

I could do nothing. I felt myself going limp from the pain. Hampshire had my arms tied behind me and pulled upwards, so that I began to bend double. I dug in, and started to plant my feet to leap backwards into him, but was immediately pushed forward and mechanically pulled back in the rhythm he'd already established.

'Don't be foolish,' he said. 'I'm good at this. Let's go for a walk.'

He prodded me closer to the edge of the cliff, ten paces ahead. The person wearing the red jacket had vanished. We were alone. The ground was scattered with loose pebbles and was uneven, and I struggled to walk straight. Over the rush of the waterfall I could hear his breathing and smelled his strong deodorant. I had a sense of him looming above me, two or three inches taller and twenty pounds heavier. Despite my own height and strength, I was in trouble. As we came closer to the cliff face, he jerked me to a halt.

'Let's have a look,' he said. His hands moved down over my body, patting for shoulder arms, belt buckles or holsters, leg knives. He found the sap in my sock and pulled it out. He rapped me lightly on the buttocks with it. 'Naughty little tosspot,' he said. 'I'll have that.'

'Eat it,' I said.

He hit me harder on the buttocks.

'Be nice. You'll live longer. Not much, admittedly.'

He pushed me forward again, and I had the sense that he wasn't going to stop. My forehead and right eye throbbed so hard I could barely set one foot in front of the other. I wanted to sink to my knees, but he pushed me on.

'Keep going,' he said. 'Don't get shy after coming all this way.'

'Going to push me yourself?' I said. 'Typical SAS. Keep me in the dark, kill me off, then blame somebody else.'

I got a tug on the rope that nearly pulled me on to my back.

'I thought you'd be a tough old bear,' he said. 'Heard it in your voice, that first conversation. You weren't going to give up. Maybe it's the Yorkshire in you. Had to keep an eye on you then. Throw a scare into you from time to time. Just for fun.'

'Your Beemer's got a nice scrape down the side.'

'Oh well.'

'And I take it that was you who tried to frighten Laura on the phone?'

'Hated doing that, actually,' he said. 'Such a cliché.'

'But you had to cover your tracks.'

'Did my best. People always let you down, don't they? In the end?'

'This is Rory.'

'Not really, but him as well. Major tosspot he turned out to be. Actually I was talking about Tara.'

'So she was in it with you. She wanted Brands and you were happy to help, because Rory fired you.'

We'd come to a halt near the edge. I could see the lights from a village half a mile down the valley. Between here and there was a drop of a hundred feet on to boulders the size of cars. Hampshire took up the slack on my lead and came up close. Casually, he threw three loops of rope over my head, pulling each one tight so that my arms were cinched against my body, immobile, with my hands tied behind me. His icy breath came floating over my shoulder as he pulled the last loop tight and then stood back.

'Great detective work,' he said. 'Completely arsy-versy of course. Did Suzi tell you the Rolls-Royce story? I bet she did. She tells everybody. It's part of my character, Dyke. I've got an obsessive nature. When Brand fired me I was not an happy boy. And I thought bugger it, I don't have to put up with this from a jumped-up tosspot like him. So I started having some fun with him. I'd already started seeing Tara, who liked a little danger, so I roped her in. No pun intended, old man. We worked out there was a mutual benefit. She didn't like what he was doing to a perfectly good business, so we thought we'd have it off him. Couldn't get any investors to play ball, though. Had to come up with another solution.'

'Tara would never murder anyone.'

Hampshire laughed quietly. 'Don't you believe it,' he said. 'That was one tough cookie. I never did get the point of her marrying Brand. Nor you, if it comes to that, not that I know you very well. I think it was a money thing in the end. Women, eh? Just when you think they're different from what you expect, they do something to fit the stereotype.'

'Tosspots.'

'Exactly. Though strictly speaking you can't have a female

tosspot.'

'Do you resent the fact that she was married to me?'

'Good God no.' He seemed genuinely incredulous. 'The past is the past, isn't it?'

'Don't you believe it influences the present?'

'Oh don't go philosophical on me, Dyke. If you must know, like all the best criminals I'm an existentialist. The past is too painful and the future is unknown. The present is all that's worth focusing on.'

'So was she with you that morning?'

'Course not. Let myself in. Rory thought we were going to talk business—thought I had an offer for him. That's why he agreed to the six o'clock meeting, you see. He thought there was something in it for him. Funny thing, Dyke. I hated him and in the end I didn't much like her. But it's weird—I wanted them both to like me. How does that happen?'

'Perhaps they were decent people.'

'I doubt it,' he said. 'Anyway, I got to the office first, let myself in, gave him a telling off, broke his neck.'

'But he knew something was happening. That's why I was there the day before, when you and I met.'

'I was wondering about that. Interesting. Well, you know him—paranoid. Though I suppose it's true Tara and I had spoken to a couple of people. Potential partners. I suppose they'd made one or two inquiries, which he'd heard about. Tara was never careful, was she? I couldn't care less. It was him I couldn't stand really.'

By now I'd opened the small penknife that I'd had in my hand since leaving the hotel. Hampshire had missed it in his search because it was small in my hand. Now he wasn't paying attention. He was comfortable and happy to show off. The rocky ground crunched under his feet as he shifted his weight almost casually. He was distracted by his own sense of importance.

'See that cliff,' he said. 'You're going to enjoy the ride. As we speak, the rope around you is being held on a friction device, a figure of eight kind of thing. Now you can't see me, but I'm looping the slack around a big rock just behind you. What happens is, I push you off and hold on to the rope. The friction device holds you in place for a while. Then I yank the rope, you unwind like a spinning top, the knot on your wrist unties, and you go rolling like a barrel off Dungeon Ghyll and smash like a bastard on the rocks. It's about a hundred feet. And not a mark on you—apart from the broken bones and fractured skull, of course. Oh, and I suppose there'll be some rope burns, but what the hell.'

'I was seen leaving the hotel with a note from you.'

'Not from me, chum.'

'Your clients know you're out here.'

'Don't get desperate, Dyke. Stay cool. They think I'm having a bath before coming down for a drink. Which of course I will, in about half an hour or so. Anyway, you're talking as if I give a damn, which at this point in time I actually don't.'

'Had enough?'

'You could say that. I've seen some things, Dyke. Been all over the world. Done some things as well. I've just got to an age when it doesn't seem worth the candle any more. I thought it might've been fun with Tara, she was a bit of a rush. But when it came down to it, she didn't want to play. Not with me, anyway. I liked her well enough, but I just can't seem to do relationships. Don't know how they work. Just like a man, eh?'

'Is that why you killed her? I said.

'Found her, did you? You can blame yourself for that. When I saw her with you that night, at her place, I thought she might be blabbing. Couldn't take the risk. Bopped you on the head and took her with me.'

'Brave to kill her, weren't you.'

'Oh don't get noble. Didn't really want to do it, but to be honest, I couldn't be in two places at one time. I had to be here, didn't I, with the clients. 'Fraid that was it for the luvverly Tara.'

'You bastard.'

'Even my best friends say so.'

A thought occurred to me. 'Where were you when you phoned Laura? Where were you holding Tara?'

"Listening in, were you? Might have guessed. I was just down the road, in a hotel room. Had her itty-bitty screams on tape. Just played 'em back down the phone line. Then walked down the street and into the office. Shouldn't have bothered, should I? Didn't throw you off.'

I paused in my struggle with the ropes. I had only a limited arc of movement back and forth to cut them, so even though the knife was sharp it was taking some time. Also, because Hampshire was behind me, I had to appear to be struggling with the ropes, not cutting them. I hoped he was too busy with his mechanics to notice what I was doing. My breathing sounded harsh in the dead quiet of the night, and my vision blurred as I looked straight ahead, over the drop, at the lights of the distant village. That familiar sense of falling into nothingness came over me with all its attraction, the letting go, the sense of weightlessness ... the relief.

The moon had risen further, illuminating a clear, bright sky. I felt my blood coursing through me. I was fuelled by adrenaline, my arms and legs pumped up but still so powerless that the blood echoed in my head as it beat from one side of my skull to the other, pounding away like a tide caught in a narrow inlet. The pain in my head was agonizing, but I had to talk, keep him thinking and talking.

'So it's all about your little game,' I said. 'Rory pissed you off by giving you the sack. You didn't like him doing the Critical Parent thing, so you thought you'd get your own back. Showing off with the clues. Tara was a threat because she was being childish. It's all very petty for a big boy like you. Not very adult. Aren't you ashamed?'

'Don't be fucking stupid, old man,' he said. His voice had tightened and I had the feeling he was winding in the rope to brace himself when he pushed me over the edge. 'After what I've done for this country? Waiting for twelve hours face down in African dirt, waiting for a so-called minister—who you know is actually a high-order scumbag—to get out of his chauffeur-driven car so you can plant one between his eyes. Why should I be ashamed of wasting an arse-clinker like Brand? Does nothing good for anyone. Wants everything he can't have. Verbally beats up anyone he can, just because he can think quicker than most. Should get a knighthood, me, for services to industry. Tara, now, she's different.'

'She saw through you. Knew what a vicious thug you were.'

'You've got balls, Dyke, give you that. Now just take a step forward, if you would.'

'Why was Tara different?'

'Let's not get into that now. I told you before, I don't do personal stuff.'

'Now is all I've got.'

'Fair point. Another step, please. OK, thank you. Tara was different because she wouldn't listen to me. Most people listen to me. That's why I'm a good consultant. You know, consultancy's a bit of a con. We sell expertise for extortionate amounts of money, but we haven't got a clue. Every situation's different. Every workplace, every group of people, every social dynamic. So when you're a consultant you soon find out that nothing works. You go in with your usual ideas that you adapt to every situation, but it's all bollocks really. Clients are entertained and amused, and sometimes even learn something. But the only ones who can really change what happens in the workplace are those who hold the purse strings. And they don't come on teamworking courses because by and large they don't like working in teams.'

'She didn't like what Rory was doing with the company,' I said. 'The software division and so forth ...'

'Correct,' he said, more breathless now. 'I tested the damn program and it was crap. But that was one more reason for me to leave. If that was the way we were going, then I was out of there.'

I was distracted by the ropes around my wrist suddenly breaking apart. I held my hands together, holding my breath. 'You've got to move with the times,' I said.

'There's a shepherd tending his flock in a field,' Hampshire said. 'A guy roars up in a big four-by-four and says, "If I can tell you how many sheep you've got, can I have one?" The shepherd says, "Yeah, OK." The man goes into his car and pulls out a satellite dish that he hooks up to a computer screen. After a minute he turns to the shepherd and says, "You've got four hundred and twenty-three sheep." The shepherd stares at him in astonishment. "That's right," he says. The man says, "Can I go get my reward?" and the shepherd says OK. The guy goes into the field, picks up an animal, and walks back to his car. At which point the shepherd says, "If I can tell you what your job is, can I have my animal back?" And the guy says, "All right." The shepherd says, "You're a management consultant, aren't you?" The guy looks at him amazed. "How did you know that?" he gasps. The shepherd says, "You roll up unannounced, use some fancy equipment to tell me something I already know, then prove that you haven't got a clue about my job. Now, can I have my dog back?"'

'Funny.'

'Clients love it. Makes them think they're in on the act. The thing is, it's true.'

'We were talking about Tara.'

'It's clever, this. You're really stretching it out. Much good it'll do you.'

'Does the person who helped you know they're next?'

This time Hampshire didn't reply immediately. I braced myself for a blow on the head, but nothing came. When he spoke his voice was lower and more considered.

'Very good. I was right to take you seriously. No, I doubt that person is thinking very much about what happens next. Forward planning not a strong point. I had to do it all. Good on loyalty and bitterness, though. That's why we worked together so well. For a one-off gig. Okay, up you go.'

I was hoisted suddenly from behind and walked forwards towards the edge of the drop. My head roared with pain. I could see the dark line of the cliff edge coming towards me. My arms were trapped both by his massive arms and by the rope that was still wrapped tightly around me in three loops. I could smell his sweat now, beneath the higher note of the deodorant—rank and oily, like the inside of a mechanic's boot.

'You stink,' I said.

'I love you too,' he said, and dropped me into the void.

56

I FELL FOUR FEET, then the rope caught and I was snapped to a halt. Searing pain shot through my upper arms as they caught the tension on the rope. My forehead bulged as though it would burst, scattering brains and blood on the rocks below. There was nothing beneath my feet. My head bounced off the stony side of the cliff edge. I hung there for several seconds, helpless.

But my arms below the elbow were free. Stretching my neck to look up, I saw the cliff edge only a foot above me, and above that, Hampshire's broad, pale face, white against the dark sky. He was grinning his toothpaste smile, though the strain of holding my weight pulled his mouth down at the edges. He must have been kneeling with his legs apart, the rope tied around the rock that he'd used as a brace looped a couple of times around his upper body. For a moment we were linked together, bound by the blue and yellow umbilical cord that held us both in stasis.

'It's good this, isn't it?' he said tightly. 'Never got the chance to do it when I was in the Regiment. Thought about it, though. Took this opportunity to give it a dry run. All I do now is give one magical heave, and you're all unravelled. It's been a pleasure dealing with such a cooperative client. Thank you and goodnight.'

I struggled with my arms, trying to raise them, waiting for the tension that held me to go slack. The sound of the waterfall hitting the rocks below rose up and surrounded me, and for a moment I forgot the thunderous pain that gripped my forehead and eyes.

Then suddenly he was distracted. He looked back over his shoulder and I heard, faintly, another voice. Hampshire said, 'What the fuck are you still doing here?'

Working my arms up, I sawed with the penknife at the bottom loop of the rope that bound me. Instantly it came away and all of the loops unravelled, releasing me to fall.

But I'd found a toe-hold for my right foot and a grip for my left hand, so when the ropes came free I was already supporting myself, my nose close to the cliff. I smelled the wormy, rich loam of the exposed dirt, breathing it in with rasping breaths. I reached up with the fingers of my right hand and grabbed the cliffside while still holding on to the knife. Looking up, I saw Hampshire's face come back into focus above me. The smile was gone.

'You little wanker,' he smiled, and drew back his fist.

'Grow up,' I said, and jabbed the penknife into the side of his neck. The rage and the pain bursting in my head was funnelled into my arm as the knife broke his skin and dug deep. He looked down at my arm, as if intrigued to find out where it had come from. Then he broadened his smile and pulled my hand, and the blade, from his flesh, twisting my hand till the knife fell from it. Blood pulsed from his neck and splashed on my face. I grabbed the cliff face tighter.

'Nice try,' he said hoarsely. 'You need an anatomy lesson to find the right place. Here, take this.'

He reached down and placed his hand over my face, pushing me away from the cliff. His eyes glittered like diamond chips in the moonlight as he strained against my grip. My back began to arch and the grip of both my hands loosened as he strained to push me off. I kicked my feet deeper into the rockface.

Then there was the sound of a dull thump, and the smile on

his face froze. His eyes continued to stare at me and he bent further down as if to get a better view.

But he kept coming, falling headfirst towards me, all restraint gone, heedless of his destination. I flattened myself to the cliff, my fingers clawing into the stony earth as he dropped like an expert diver intent on breaking the surface with barely a mark. His body flashed past my eyes, riffling with the sound of a sail in wind. The rope that had been looped around him uncoiled and snapped, then fell limply after him. He began to turn and twist in the manner that he'd predicted for my own fall, his arms spreading out and spinning like the blades of a propeller as he gathered speed.

I was glad I didn't hear him hit the ground.

57

THE FINGERS OF MY left hand were still sunk like talons into the stone face of the cliff. My right toes moved in the thick boots and convinced me I had grip.

I pulled my face back from the cliff and shouted, 'Betty! Give me a hand!'

There was a shuffling noise and then Betty's head appeared above me, encased in the red hood of the jacket that Hampshire had made her wear. She stared at me for a long moment, as though contemplating whether to give me her hand or punch me in the face. Our cold breath filled the air between us.

Finally she reached down and gripped my arm. I didn't need the help but I wanted to know her hands were busy until I reached the top. Levering myself between my fingers and the points of my shoes I hauled myself up and collapsed on the grass. The migraine was easing off. I flipped myself over and lay on my back, looking up at the stars and letting the giddiness that I felt ebb away. I knew Betty was watching me. I could feel the tension she created just by being there.

'You knew it was me,' she said at last, her voice cutting through the air. 'Why didn't you stop it earlier?'

I turned to look at her and the world rotated wildly for a moment. I said, 'I wasn't certain it was you. I had to know for sure. Help me up.'

Betty took a step and stood over me. 'He really hated Rory, after he got the sack. He was easy meat for that flighty madam.'

She put out a hand. I raised myself and took it, pulling myself to my feet.

'Tara put him up to it?'

'I don't think so—but they were having a ... a thing. He must have thought she'd stay with him if Rory was out of the picture. When she realised what he'd done, I think she got scared. He told me they had a row. That's why he kidnapped her.'

She carried on talking as we turned away from the cliff. 'He didn't know what to do. He didn't want to kill her but he didn't like the idea of her running around talking to people. Men.' Her face twisted contemptuously. 'You're so stupid. That's all he was, a big stupid thing. Supposed to be the hard man, all that army stuff. But he couldn't deal with a woman with a mind of her own.'

'So why did you get involved?'

'You haven't seen the books. The money Rory took out of the business! God knows where it all went. The company's in trouble because of him. I used to look up to him, thought he worked miracles. I trusted him. But he had this ability to cock things up. He was doing it to his own company. It had all changed for the worse. And he wouldn't stop until it all went down the plug-hole. We would all have lost our jobs, not just me.'

We'd arrived at the stone path that led down towards the hotel.

'So you took a chance with Eddie Hampshire,' I said.

'I got him talking one day. We talked about how you could do it. He was a big-head and liked to show off what he knew, because of his time in the army.'

'He could be quite charming.'

She blushed, her head bowed. 'He didn't really try it on with me. I knew what he was doing.' She looked up defiantly. 'But he was exciting. He said things that made you think. Even though I didn't much care for that woman, I thought they could make it work again.'

'You sent him your swipe card so he could let himself in.'

She stopped, surprised. 'How did you know?'

'The morning of the murder you came in the front door, so you didn't have your swipe card with you. You told me yourself you prefer to use the stairs so there must have been a good reason for you to use the lift. And you let Carol the receptionist use her card to get you into the office. I guessed you might have sent yours to Eddie, who had already handed his back. And I suppose after Eddie killed Rory that morning he left your card in your desk. He probably let himself out the front door, having opened the fire exit to make it look like someone had forced their way in.'

'Yes, he did. I told him not to be so damned clever.'

We started walking again.

'Crooks are never really that clever,' I said. I cleared my throat. 'I thought you were probably feeding him information to protect the pair of you. When he phoned me today I knew you'd probably spoken to him and got him worried. That's why he called me and that's why I'm here.'

'You're saying it's all my fault, this.'

'Then I checked train times—there's a direct train from Waverley at 6.15. Gets in to Euston before nine. His session that morning didn't start till 9.30, so he had time to get a taxi across London.'

'I told him he should watch out for you. I thought you were cleverer than you pretended to be.'

'I wasn't pretending to be anything. I'm just clumsy and dim-witted sometimes.'

'Yes,' she said, 'you are.'

'Why did you come here?'

'Eddie asked me to. He got me to put the note for you on the reception desk. Then he asked me to stand on the edge of that cliff with this jacket and the flashlight. I think he was probably going to kill me, too. So I got in first. I hit him a good one with that rock. It felt good. I suppose I had a lot of pent-up anger inside me. I feel better now. I should have taken up sport or something, shouldn't I? Got rid of all this energy. It was only because I thought too much of Rory, you know. I got so frustrated with him when it started to go wrong. He just wouldn't listen.'

'I know.'

'Will I go to prison for a long time?'

I held out my hand, which she took like a small child hoping to be led somewhere safe.

'Thanks for saving my life,' I said. 'Now let's go talk to some people.'

58

A S WE REACHED the bottom of the slope, we heard police sirens racing towards us. Two cars came hurtling around the corner, their rooftop lights whirling furiously. The cars roared up and juddered to a halt. The passenger door of the front car opened and Inspector Howard got out. He glanced up and down the road and saw me. Sticking his hands in his pockets, he wandered over casually, as though paying a social call.

'Get what you came for?' he said, indicating Betty with a lift of his chin.

'If you go up the path back there,' I said, 'you'll find a man called Eddie Hampshire at the bottom of a cliff. He's the person you're after. You should also take this lady into custody and ask her to explain what happened to Rory.'

'That right?' he said. He looked at me clinically. In the end he shook his head and turned to face the hotel, as if it might do something dramatic.

'You had a call, then,' I said.

He spoke without looking at me. 'Old man Hoyt. Said you were after doing something stupid. No shit, I said. He said you might be in danger. Whoop-te-do, I said. We contacted your lady friend and she filled in the rest. A phone call to Hampshire's ex-wife told us enough to track you down. We are the police, you know. Incidentally—'

'What?'

'We know you found Mrs Brand. We're going to have to talk about that.'

Before I could say anything, a second car door slammed and I turned to see Laura walking in her usual elegant way towards me.

'Well, Beefy,' she said. 'Did you get your man?'

'And woman.' I took a deep breath. 'Laura, I've got something to tell you.'

'It'll keep.'

I thought of Daniel, my son, and how for eighteen years I didn't know that he existed. It seemed that some things needed time before you were ready to deal with them. Third rule of private eye school: know when to shut up.

'OK,' I said.

Cheshire, 2006

ACKNOWLEDGEMENTS

Thanks to Liz for her support over the years, and to Bob Chad for looking at an early draft of the book and making invaluable comments. Also thanks to Phil Donnison for local knowledge and rope skills.

Printed in Poland
by Amazon Fulfillment
Poland Sp. z o.o., Wrocław